Moment of Truth

Whatever Sorcha might have thought of Captain Charles Ashbourne, there was no doubt that he was a skillful and practiced lover. She had not known she could feel like this, so easily shaken to her soul by the feel of a man's mouth on hers.

Even while he was kissing her, his hand found the ribbons of her chemise and loosened them. Some part of her that she didn't know existed gave him back kiss for kiss and made no further objection as first his hand, and then his lips went lower, tantalizing, coaxing a response from her, and everywhere succeeding beyond her wildest imaginings.

Everywhere that Sorcha touched him his skin was like fire. "Oh, yes, my sweet love, my darling. Oh, God you are beautiful, so beautiful," he whispered.

And when the ultimate moment came, she did not weep or beg, but clutched at him and cried out his name.

And in response he replied with a name as well. "Lisette! Oh, God, Lisette," he groaned.

Which, of course, was not her name at all. . . .

SIGNET REGENCY ROMANCE
Coming in September 1995

Emma Lange
Exeter's Daughter

Barbara Hazard
Dangerous Deceits

Gayle Buck
Lady Althea's Bargain

An English Alliance

by
Dawn Lindsey

A SIGNET BOOK

SIGNET
Published by the Penguin Group
Penguin Books USA Inc., 375 Hudson Street,
New York, New York 10014, U.S.A.
Penguin Books Ltd, 27 Wrights Lane,
London W8 5TZ, England
Penguin Books Australia Ltd, Ringwood,
Victoria, Australia
Penguin Books Canada Ltd, 10 Alcorn Avenue,
Toronto, Ontario, Canada M4V 3B2
Penguin Books (N.Z.) Ltd, 182–190 Wairau Road,
Auckland 10, New Zealand

Penguin Books Ltd, Registered Offices:
Harmondsworth, Middlesex, England

First published by Signet, an imprint of Dutton Signet,
a division of Penguin Books USA Inc.

First Printing, August, 1995
10 9 8 7 6 5 4 3 2 1

Chapter 1

"The devil curse all such cowardly spalpeens!" roared Magnus MacKenzie, turning away from the window, his big face full of disgust. As usual when he was moved, he became wholly Scots, despite having left his native country more than thirty years before. "Have they no more pride than to scurry round with their tails tucked between their legs in panic over the mere threat of an attack? I tell you, I've a mind to wash my hands of the lot of them!"

"A sorry sight indeed," agreed his only daughter, quick amusement evident in her eyes. "With the British army rumored to have actually landed within fifty miles of Washington, I am assured that anyone who can beg, borrow, or steal a conveyance or a broken-down mule is in the process of packing up his valuables and fleeing the capital. Really, I fear it will give the British a very low opinion of us."

Magnus looked slightly amused at her remark. "They've that already, lass. But at least I notice ye're not noticeably of a twitter yourself."

"No. But then I suspect you would not hesitate to disown me if I comported myself in such an undignified manner," retorted Sorcha frankly, still with a twinkle in her eyes.

Magnus chuckled. "Aye, that I would, lass. Ye've more sense than the rest of them put together, including the President and that flighty wife of his. But ye needn't worry. I've no brief for the British as ye well ken, lass, but even they are no' so foolish as to tramp fifty miles over enemy territory to take a town that has no strategic importance, capital or no. Nay, it's Baltimore they're after, you may be sure, for it's from there the privateers have come that have harried them so finely—and a grand sight it has been to see the great Royal Navy afraid to put out from port for fear of such stinging gnats."

He was a big, powerful man, with sandy red hair and a restless energy that had brought him as a stowaway at the age of fourteen from his native Highlands to America in time for the Revolutionary War, with nothing in his pockets but a few pounds and an inbred hatred of the British born of generations of Anglo-Scots rivalry. At the moment he was pacing the breakfast room as if it were too small for him, and could not remain long away from the window, where the sight of so much foolish activity could not fail to annoy him.

"As for yon foolish bletherskates," he finished in disgust, "running around like chickens with their heads cut off, I've no sympathy with them. My only consolation is that they're as likely in their panic to run straight into the path of the British army as escape it. You'd think we'd never fought the bloody British before, let alone soundly whipped them."

Sorcha was very much her father's daughter. Her hair was a darker red than his sandy mane, and she was tall for a woman, if slenderly built. She possessed a good measure of Magnus's fiery temper, but hers was slower to stir, and she had inherited enough of the calm nature of her mother, whom she could scarcely remember, to be able to remain serene in the face of her father's quick outbursts and frequent disgust with his fellow man. "Well," she said, thoughtful now, holding her breakfast teacup between both hands, "it goes against the grain with me, but I own there is reason enough for panic, with little or no attempt being made to defend the capital, and our leaders squabbling among themselves like small boys over key military appointments. We may have beaten the British once, when we won our independence, but we've made a poor enough showing this time, I'm sorry to say."

"Aye, lass," Magnus agreed impatiently, "but the British are far from home, and until recently had their hearts in the European war where all the glory is. We've had their second and even third battalions, and as for their officers, that Admiral Cochrane of theirs is a fool, and Cockburn even worse—a dangerous, arrogant, overzealous hothead of the kind the English specialize in. I should know, for we've had our share of them in Scotland over the centuries. He'll do their cause far more damage than any of our privateers could do."

Fairly launched on his favorite topic, he undoubtedly would have treated her to another detailed lecture on the ins and outs of the military situation, had they not been interrupted. For days now they had endured a steady stream of panicked visitors hoping to discover more reliable information from Magnus about the state of affairs than the often contradictory rumors making the rounds. Few, however, had liked his bluntly stated opinion on the subject, and most soon scurried away to seek more palatable advice elsewhere. The Royal British Navy had been marauding up and down the Chesapeake for the past year, virtually blockading it, and had made a series of small forays against scattered hamlets, with nothing to show for their efforts but a few burnt hayricks and "liberated" supplies. Now it seemed as if a large expeditionary force had really been landed, and in light of this new threat few could be brought to accept Magnus's view that Washington was safe.

Now another knock sounded on the door below, and Magnus looked pained. But this time a welcome voice could be heard, and a moment later Mr. Geoffrey Warburton, an old friend of the family, was shown into the breakfast room.

He was a young man of some six-and-twenty, with an open, engaging countenance, who had known Sorcha from the cradle, and was a great favorite of Magnus's as well.

"Ah, so it's you, is it, lad?" said Magnus, going to slap the younger man jovially on the shoulder. "I hope ye're not planning on joining the panicked ribble-rabble down below in such indecent haste to leave the capital?"

Geoff looked amused. "I am leaving Washington, sir, but not in a panic, I hope. Though I had to defend my horse just now from being stolen out from under me at pistol point. Would you believe it, some fool at first tried to buy General from me, and when I wouldn't sell, actually pulled a pistol on me! Give you my word!"

Magnus roared with laughter. "And did ye manage to rescue your steed from this dangerous criminal, lad?"

Geoff grinned. "Luckily I had Cal with me, so the man was eventually . . . er . . . persuaded to give up. But I've been kicking myself ever since for not having had the forethought to send for the rest of my cattle, or buy every broken-down nag I could get my hands on for the past three days. If I had, I could have made my fortune and need no longer rely on disgruntled clients eager to sue their neighbors to make my living. The fool offered me as much as a thousand dollars before he resorted to highway robbery."

Sorcha poured Geoff a cup of coffee and handed it to him. "Which is ten times as much as that short-backed rasher of wind is worth," she teased. "But take care you don't go out to find General stolen while your back is turned. Have you thought of that?"

"Oh, Cal is guarding him for me," said Geoff with his customary easy insouciance. "Besides, you're just jealous. Take care someone don't steal that overfed black you like to peacock about so much."

Sorcha laughed. "Oh, Magnus sent most of our cattle home when the panic first started. I don't know whether it was to protect them from being stolen or as a grand gesture."

"A grand gesture!" agreed Magnus. "Let them see I'm not some frightened virgin quailing at the mere thought of the British."

"Yes, I see you two seem to be the only ones in town not noticeably panicked," commented Geoff, eyeing the leisurely breakfast.

"No. I dare not be, for fear of losing Magnus's respect forever. And I expect he is merely disappointed the troops aren't making for Washington, so he could have the opportunity of killing a few more of the despised English. I have had the greatest difficulty in dissuading him from joining up, despite his age and position."

" 'His age' indeed!" roared Magnus. "There's life in this decrepit old carcass yet. And it's scant respect ye have for your old father, lass."

Geoff grinned, used to such exchanges. "Well, like Magnus, I can't resist the opportunity of killing a few redcoats. General Winder has put out a call for every able-bodied man, and since, unlike Magnus, I've no family or responsibilities to worry about, it seems a shame to miss it. I missed fighting the British in the last great war, don't forget, and this may be my last chance."

"Aye, lad, that's the proper spirit!" approved Magnus. "Not that this precious General Winder of yours is aught but a fool impressed with his own title and starting at every shadow. But whatever the lass says, *I'd* be of far more use out in the field than attending everlasting sessions in the Senate and listening to even more foolish blether than usual!"

Geoff glanced at Sorcha and said pacifically, "I've no doubt you would still give us all a lead, sir! But don't forget we must have some government to depend on. By all accounts most of our top officials are as terrified as the fat merchant who accosted me, and are dashing about only making things worse."

Magnus looked dissatisfied, for he was indeed chafing at the bit at his enforced idleness, and were the British actually to invade Washington, Sorcha knew he would be in the thick of it, whatever she said. She was almost relieved when a fresh interruption occurred.

This time the caller was not so welcome, however. There was a firm, measured tread on the stairs, and Mr. Henry Haskell was shown in. He was a young man of a very different stamp from Geoff, inclined to stockiness, and while not ill-looking, had a precise, deliberate way of speaking and acting that never failed to annoy the quicksilver Magnus. Henry seemed surprised and somewhat displeased to see what he considered his chief rival there before him, but he came forward in his rather ponderous way to shake hands first with Sorcha, then his host, and lastly with Geoff.

"Ah, I see you are here before me, Warburton, and on the same errand, I make no doubt," he remarked in disapproval. "I have naturally come to offer Sorcha my escort since the senator must be busy with affairs of state."

Magnus, who did not like Henry and seldom missed an opportunity to show it, opened his mouth for what was likely to be a blistering retort, but from long practice Sorcha smoothly forestalled him. "Oh, are you leaving Washington, Henry?" she inquired innocently. "This seems very sudden. When last I talked with you two days ago, I was not aware you had any plans to remove from the capital."

Magnus grinned appreciatively, and Henry reddened, but quickly made a recovery. "I hope I am not one to panic at mere rumors, and I am the first to deplore the unreasoned way most people are behaving. Would you believe it? I actually had some fool try to buy my horse from me just now for two thousand dollars."

Geoff and Sorcha exchanged quick grins, but Henry went on, unaware of having said anything to amuse them. "But at the same time, it would be equally foolish to ignore the signs of danger and risk capture or worse, when it might so easily be prevented by a little caution. I must assume Warburton is here on the same errand, though I would venture to point out that your own home, in Annapolis, is directly in the path of the British, while my farm is

situated to the west of the city. And since my sister is luckily
there to act as chaperon, the senator might confidently entrust me
with your safety, my dear."

"You are mistaken, Haskell!" roared Magnus, affronted. "I've
no need to trust my daughter's safety to anyone, I thank ye! As
for being here on the same errand, no such thing. Geoff here is off
to defend his country in its hour of need, I'm thankful to say, not
fleeing like a rat deserting a sinking ship."

"Oh, are we sinking? I thought you were convinced there was
no danger?" murmured Sorcha quizzically to her father. But then
she hastily intervened again before there could be a full-scale
blowup. "Thank you, Henry, but Magnus assures me we are in no
danger. He's convinced Baltimore, not Washington, will be the
target—if indeed it is not merely another feint, like so many we
have endured before. I begin to think the British are no more
eager for a full-scale battle than we are."

"Aye, that at least you may be sure of, lass. Haven't I been
telling you that they've little enough liking for our style of war?
They may have beaten the great Napoleon at last, but Admiral
Cochrane is no Wellington, and they're no' in any hurry to do
aught but harry civilians and burn a few hayricks."

"I am sure I hope you may be right, sir," said Henry stiffly, determinedly ignoring Magnus's insults. "But while I have no doubt
that as a member of the government you must have information
the rest of us are not privy to, I have considered the matter carefully from all sides, and have concluded that it would be inexcus-
ably foolish to risk so much when all danger might be avoided
with a little foresight. I was meaning to return home fairly soon,
anyway. This merely puts forward the date of my departure."

"I only hope that I will be on hand to watch the lot of ye creep
back into town in a few days' time with your tails tucked between
your legs!" roared Magnus in disgust. "Tell me, lad, are ye a man
or a spineless jellyfish? I'd think shame to be so easily routed by
a few panicked rumors."

But Henry's sense of self-importance was proof against even
Magnus's barbs. "You forget, sir, that I have not only myself to
consider," he said calmly. "Were it otherwise, I believe I must
forget all my other responsibilities and answer my country's call,
as Warburton here is doing. But my sister is naturally dependent
upon me, as are the livelihoods of many others as well." Henry
was a wealthy landowner.

Sorcha's eyes, as usual, betrayed her amusement, but she said merely, "I agree that Miss Haskell would be lost without you, Henry. Besides, I must confess I cannot quite picture you dirty and muddy and in the thick of a battle."

Henry looked gratified at this unexpected defense. "Thank you. My sister is not, as you know, a woman of much strength of character—unlike yourself, my dear Sorcha. But then, I am of the opinion that all females must be grateful from time to time to have a man's superior strength to rely upon. I need hardly add, I hope, that were she here, my sister would not hesitate to add her entreaties to mine."

Sorcha knew well that Miss Haskell, a colorless, meek little woman some years Henry's senior, did not like her and would be far from seconding her brother's invitation. But she said merely, "Thank you, Henry, but if the British are indeed making for Washington, I am more determined to remain than ever. It has become quite an ambition with me to see a redcoat for myself. I fear I am inevitably in for a disappointment, for I have heard so many stories all my life from Magnus that my expectations are impossibly high. I fully expect them to have horns and forked tails at the very least."

Magnus grinned. "They may no' have forked tails, but they're devils for all that and don't you forget it, lass."

Henry looked predictably pained, for he disapproved both of such flippancy and of the easy way Sorcha spoke to her father and called him by his first name. Henry was old-fashioned and highly conventional, and the fact that Magnus treated her as an equal and had been known even to take her advice on matters of state, despite her being both his daughter and a female to boot, never failed to shock him. "You will forgive me for finding such levity misplaced at so grave a moment," he said even more stiffly. "Nor do I think you can have any real conception of the danger you are courting. I have no desire to be obliged to alarm any delicate female, but if the senator will but grant me a moment or two of his time alone, I believe that I may convince him that he would be better off sending you away from Washington until all danger is past."

Magnus looked both contemptuous and puzzled, but Sorcha, who understood Henry better, said in amusement, "He means, I collect, that I may be raped or murdered in my bed. But I fear such delicacy is wholly wasted on me, Henry. Don't forget, I grew up on Magnus's tales of the atrocities committed by the

British after Culloden, so there is very little you can say that would shock me. Besides, much as I love Magnus, he does not make my decisions for me. Did you think he did?"

Magnus grinned. "Aye, that's my girl. Besides, if ye had no more sense than to allow yourself to be raped or murdered by the British, lass, I'd have little sympathy with ye."

Geoff changed the subject tactfully. "Do you really think the British will attack Baltimore instead of Washington, sir?"

That successfully got Magnus launched on his favorite topic again. "Aye, lad. And it's to be hoped I'm right, for all the President and that precious Secretary of State of his can find to do in the present crisis is run ta and fra like hens when the fox is in the yard, issuing one order and then another, and succeeding only in throwing everybody into a panic and hampering the militia at every turn. And to add to it, here's Armstrong, despite his grand title as Secretary of War, gone off to sulk because his own man wasna appointed as head of military defense. If I didna hate the British so much, I'd say we deserve to lose!" He was once more striding around, unable to remain still.

"When Magnus becomes enraged, he invariably becomes wholly Scots," put in Sorcha with amusement.

"And why shouldn't I?" he demanded. "Though I'll grant there's reason enough for Armstrong's sulks. The only qualification for the job this General Winder of yours seems to have, lad, lies in his having been a British prisoner up north, which to my mind is scant recommendation!"

"He's scarcely mine, sir," objected Geoff mildly, with little hope of being attended to.

Nor was he. "And what has he found to do in this current emergency? I'll tell ye! He's been riding around the countryside for a month, now, 'studying the lay of the land.' I ask ye! Studying the lay of the land! He'd be far better occupied in throwing up a few defenses in the British way, instead of leaving Washington wide open to the enemy. I tell ye, I've no patience with the lot of them!"

"I know you have not, love," put in Sorcha cheerfully. "But for shame, Magnus, have you no respect for poor General Winder? After all, he looks so very noble and has assured all the ladies that we have nothing to worry about now that he is in charge."

Magnus snort was scornful. "They might as well appoint yourself, lass, or one of my stable lads as head of military defense. In fact, you'd have a sight better notion how to prepare for a possible attack."

"Since it seems I could scarcely have less, that's hardly a compliment," she countered in amusement.

"I am of the strong opinion civilians do as well to leave military matters to the military," said Henry in stiff disapproval, "since we naturally can have little understanding of such matters."

"Oh, I don't know," said Geoff. "There'd be nothing left to talk about in that case. Besides, Magnus has a great deal of military experience, and for my money Sorcha would make an excellent general." He grinned at her. "I well remember the way you marched us up and down when we were children, playing at battle, and fully expected to be obeyed. I always had to play the British, which I never forgave you for, by the way."

He rose. "Which reminds me that I must be off. If you are indeed determined to stay here, Sorcha, I've even more reason to help keep the British out of Washington."

"Aye, take care of yourself, laddie." Magnus gave him another warm buffet on the shoulder. "Ten to one ye'll no' see a redcoat at all, but it's envious I am of ye, and that's a fact."

Sorcha, to Henry's patent disapproval, followed Geoff out to the landing. There she allowed him to take her hands and said with an anxiety she could not quite conceal, "As you heard, Magnus assures me we are in very little danger, but you *will* be careful, won't you?"

"Oh, Lord, yes," he said cheerfully, giving her hands a warm squeeze. "Probably Magnus is right, and we won't get a sniff of a redcoat."

"He usually is," she pointed out philosophically. "All the same, keep in mind that I don't have so many good friends I can afford to lose one."

He made a comical grimace. "That's some consolation— though I could wish for a slightly warmer description of our relationship. If only you had married me when I first asked you, I'd have a passel of children about my knee by now, and could take advantage of Henry's excuse for avoiding any action."

"If I had accepted your first proposal," she retorted, "we would have been a precocious pair indeed, for I believe I was about ten at the time. Besides, I keep telling you you don't really wish to wed me. You need some gentle, adoring wife who will look up to all your pronouncements and think you the most brilliant man alive."

He grinned. "Which you do not! Still, I wonder if you understand me as well as you think you do. After you, I seem to have little liking for meek and mild females with few opinions and still fewer ideas in their heads."

"Which I am not, God knows!" she agreed ruefully. "Still, I suspect I was born to wear the willow. It is my ambition to devote myself to being a political hostess for Magnus, and quickly become a character in my own right, exactly like old Miss Danville."

"Not exactly like. You forget that old Miss Danville has three chins and a wart," Geoff pointed out dryly.

"Nonsense. You underestimate me. With a little effort I have no doubt I can manage to grow three chins, and even a wart," she insisted stubbornly.

He laughed. "I'd give much to see it. Besides, how can you even contemplate remaining an old maid when you might have Henry to guide and direct you, not to mention his manly strength to rely upon?"

She made a face at him. "Oh, Lord. I would make him an even a worse wife than I would you, of course, and what's more, his sister knows it, too. She would be very far from welcoming my visit, I can assure you. But convince him of the truth I cannot, however hard I try. What in the world do you suppose he can find to admire in me? He dislikes what he insists upon calling my "free and easy" ways, blames Magnus for not having brought me up properly, and is convinced I only need his guidance to reform and become a model of propriety, no doubt in the form of his insipid sister. I shouldn't laugh, but I fear I understand him as little as he understands me."

"Well, I have no desire to forward his pretensions, which are as pompous as they are foolish, but I imagine your beautiful face and bewitching green eyes might have something to do with it," Geoff told her lightly.

She gave the quick gurgle of laughter that never failed to bring his grin alive. "Dear me, yes. How could I have overlooked that, I wonder? My beautiful face, as you choose to put it, has to date signally failed to register on most men, and at four-and-twenty I can boast no more than two offers in my life. And one is from my former playmate, who has never broken himself of the habit of imagining himself in love with me, and the other a prosy bore who would make me as bad a husband as I would make him a wife."

"It registers," corrected Geoff dryly. "But most men are terrified of you, as well you know. Much you care about it either."

"I daresay if I kept my mouth closed and learned to simper and seem to admire the opinions of fools whose only claim to authority on any subject is that they are male, I might be very popular!" she retorted with some impatience. "You're right. I would by far remain an old maid."

Geoff burst out laughing. "No, small fear of that, General Sorcha!"

She grinned ruefully. "The truth is, I fear Magnus is stuck with me. Let us not waste any more of our last minutes on absurdities, if you please."

"Yes, ma'am," said Geoff meekly. "*I've* no wish to discuss Haskell at all, as you very well know."

"No." She tried to smile, but it went a little awry. "You must go, and Magnus will murder Henry if I don't get back soon. Promise me you won't get yourself killed, will you?"

His hands tightened on hers. "Yes, ma'am," he said again. "But I fear I'm scarcely the stuff that heroes are made of. And you take care of yourself if it comes to that. I've no desire to invite your disgust like Haskell, but perhaps you should go with him, just to be on the safe side."

"And earn Magnus's everlasting contempt? I'd never manage to live that down. Besides, I'm not afraid of the British."

She hesitated, then mutely lifted her face to him. He kissed her a little roughly, then put her away from him and with a last cheerful word was gone.

She was obliged to wait a moment or two before she could return to the breakfast room with a serene face. There, had she been in a better humor, she would have laughed out loud, for Magnus, bored, had picked up a newspaper and was calmly reading it, while Henry, obviously determined to wait until she returned, even in the face of his host's rudeness, was staring out the window at the confusion that had so exercised Magnus earlier.

He brightened as she returned, however, and said with a jealousy he could not disguise, "Is Warburton gone? I know he is a friend of yours, Sorcha, but I find it rather ridiculous he should be making such a drama of his enlisting. If I had not my sister to consider, I would not hesitate myself to answer my country's call. There is nothing in the least heroic in that."

That roused Sorcha's quick temper, but quarreling with Henry never did any good, and so after a short struggle with herself, she managed to hold her tongue.

"I have attempted to convince your father that whatever he may choose to do as a member of the Senate, it is unwise for you to remain in Washington," Henry went on with a glance of dislike at the still-absorbed Magnus. "But I fear I have had little success."

She could not resist the opportunity. "Really? You surprise me. But despite the temptation of having your manly wisdom to guide me, Henry, I believe I must stay with Magnus. I don't trust him not to enlist the moment my back was turned, and besides, I am determined that if we are to be murdered by the British, we shall at least go together." She spoke with a flippancy she knew would annoy him.

"Aye, that's the spirit, lass," said Magnus looking up in approval from his paper. "Besides, I believe I've no need to trouble Mr. Haskell to protect my own daughter. If things should get bad—which I don't at all anticipate, mind ye—Ham can always take you to safety."

"Yes, while you remain in the thick of it, I have no doubt. No, I thank you! Besides, as I said, I've a curiosity to see a redcoat for myself. They say some of Wellington's crack troops have just arrived from the Continent, now that Bonaparte seems to be defeated at last."

Magnus gave his crack of laughter. "Aye, the *Invincibles*! We'll see about that. But you're right, lass. They've experience and training, which most of the redcoats sent here so far have lacked. But they're too lately arrived, I'm thinking, to mount a major campaign so soon. They've scarcely had a chance to find their land-legs yet. Besides, the British would be fools to launch an attack against Washington. You mark my words, all this needless panic is no' but a tempest in a teacup, lass. The British are doubtless halfway to Baltimore by now."

Henry looked annoyed, but in the face of such intransigence in both father and daughter, was at last obliged to take his leave as well.

Chapter 2

If it was any consolation to Magnus, at least one member of the British forces was in complete agreement with him.

"*Washington?*" repeated Captain Charles Ashbourne incredulously when told of the official military target. "You can't be serious, sir!"

Both Admiral Cochrane, head of the British naval forces in the Atlantic, and his second in command, Admiral Cockburn, were inclined to be offended. "Tut, tut!" said Cochrane a little testily. "I am sure the captain is a very able soldier, but he knows nothing of conditions in America, after all."

Large, grim, and bluff, and exceedingly hardheaded, Cochrane's orders direct from London were to launch a series of short, powerful raids along the Chesapeake, to create a diversion and distract American attention from larger offensives planned in Upper and Lower Canada. Unfortunately, it seemed that he was inclined toward desperate enterprises and determined to give the Americans a lesson. Washington, as both Magnus and Captain Ashbourne well knew, was an inferior military target, since it housed few troops and held little threat to the British. But as the upstart Colonials' capital, it seemed to appeal strongly to both naval men.

But to Captain Ashbourne, of His Majesty's 85th Light Infantry, lately in Spain and arrived in the country less than twenty-four hours before, it seemed a dangerous and foolhardy attempt to take an inferior target merely to salve a few vanities. Wellington himself was far from being a modest man, and certainly had never encouraged even his most senior officers to speak their opinions freely. But then Wellington was a brilliant tactician and would never even have contemplated so foolhardy an exercise merely for the sake of a few public buildings.

"That may be true, sir," Ashbourne said levelly when he could trust himself to speak at all. "But I know my men and what they will do. And setting aside the desirability of such a mission, a third are still suffering from shipboard fever, and none of them are yet in fighting trim. To launch such an attack at this time would be sheer madness."

"Well, upon my word!" bridled Cochrane. "Are we now to take our orders from junior officers, whether or not they have served under Wellington?"

General Ross, the captain's superior officer, tried to make a joke of it. He had accompanied the 4th and 44th Foot and the 85th Light Infantry from Bordeaux and understood far more than the other two what sort of enterprise they were proposing. He was a big, cheerful, decent enough man, reportedly well liked by those under him, and Ashbourne had found him pleasant enough during the months at sea. But unfortunately, as he had already had time to learn, Ross was no Wellington. In addition he was still feeling his way and inclined to be tactful where only forcefulness would have served. "Oh, I was warned when I took Ashbourne on as my ADC that he was a damned fine soldier, but inclined to run the regiment if I would let him," he said cheerfully. "I believe he'd tell Wellington to his face if he thought he was in the wrong of it."

"I would, sir," agreed Ashbourne evenly. "Especially if I thought he was in danger of making so dangerous a mistake."

"Are you saying Wellington's Invincibles cannot do what is required of them?" That was Cockburn in his rather piping voice, a distinct sneer to it. He was more than a little pompous, seemed quick to sense an injury, and from all Ashbourne was able to tell, was that most dangerous of commanders, one convinced he was invariably right and willing to risk his men's lives on the certainty.

The captain's jaw tightened. "No, sir. My men will fight to the last whether or not they are given a reasonable task. But Washington is an inferior target and a more than risky venture, especially given the present condition of the men, sir. Half of them are still recovering from shipboard fever, and what you are suggesting involves a long march over enemy territory, with no compelling military target at the end of it. In my opinion nothing can be served by taking such a risk, even if it should come off."

He might also have said that after a hard three months at sea his troops were hampered not only by the prevalent fever, but by exhaustion and the unaccustomed heat and humidity of a typical mid-Atlantic summer. Even had the men been fully fit, they possessed no cavalry to scout the advance, no wagons to haul supplies, and no field guns. The proposal to tramp fifty miles over unknown terrain to take a questionable target proposed by naval officers with little or no understanding of land tactics was worse than madness. His veteran light troops had mastered every trick of European war and had been trained to rapid raids and hard fighting over difficult ground, but not even Wellington would have asked that of them.

Ross, who understood all of this, was yet uninclined to offend the others. "Well, well, Ash here has a damned fine reputation, but of course you are right, he has not fought against the Americans. Still, there is much in what he says. And the men are still scarcely recovered from the long sea voyage, you know."

"If we were facing Napoleon's finest, all that might matter," said Cockburn offensively. "But I keep telling you these Americans are a very different proposition.

"A raid on Washington would at one blow disorganize the already ineffectual American government and inflict a major blow to their prestige. Besides, I believe Captain Ashbourne forgets that I have operated at will up and down these shores for a year now and met no organized resistance at all. I tell you the very notion of an American army is laughable. They have a long-held prejudice against keeping a standing army, and so rely on local militia for the most part. And even *they* are ill-equipped and even worse trained. When it comes down to a fight, they will not stand. Have I not proved that time and again?"

The captain closed his lips tightly on an even more disrespectful retort. Ross, with a quick glance at him, intervened hurriedly. "Well, well, you must know best of course. But still, I see no disadvantage to delaying a bit until the men are more rested."

But tact did not serve, as the captain had known it would not.

Cockburn was adamant, and his superior inclined to favor the campaign that offered the most chance for personal glory. Ross was easily overruled, and the decision was made to make Washington their major target, with several feints to the north and south to throw the Yankees off the scent. If that succeeded, as Admiral Cockburn had every confidence it would, they would move on Baltimore next and subdue that obstinate port city.

The captain, seeing there was no use saying anything more, turned abruptly on his heel and went out on deck to cool off his temper, without troubling to ask leave of his superior officers.

He was soon joined at the rail by Captain Lucius Ferriby, also of the 85th. It was a cool night, and the stars over the strange American continent shone fiercely, the humid heat having cooled off to an almost pleasant evening. Both looked out over the dark countryside for a few moments in silence, then Captain Ferriby, cocking a knowledgeable eye at his friend's ill-concealed signs of wrath, asked ruefully, "Well, Ash, what's it to be? By the looks of it, nothing to our advantage. Come on, out with it. A forlorn hope?"

Ashbourne gave a harsh bark of laughter. "Nothing so simple, I'm afraid! We are to march overland on Washington, if you please, to be supported, where possible, by gunships on the Patuxent and Potomac rivers."

Ferriby whistled comically. "I . . . see. And you don't call that a forlorn hope! A mere matter of some fifty miles, over an unfamiliar terrain, and in this beastly climate, when the men are half dead already. It did not occur to them, I take it, that half are still weakened from fever, and the rest scarcely up to such a jaunt? And what is to be our target? The public buildings?"

"Both Ross and I pointed out as much, but we were overruled."

"'Pointed out!' I like the delicacy of that term. All I can say is if we are to be under the orders of two men who know nothing of land tactics, we *are* in the suds! And Ross *pointed this out*, you say? We are much obliged to him, it seems."

"Don't!" said Ash bitterly. "It does no good to talk of it. I said as much and far more than I should have, to the point of insubordination, but I was overruled. After all, I have no experience of fighting the Americans, you must remember."

Captain Ferriby was speechless. "They dared—they actually *dared* to say that to your face? One who has served under Wellington himself and was cited for conspicuous bravery?"

"Oh, the Americans are not to be compared to the French," Ashbourne assured him. "According to them they are wholly beneath contempt and will not stand. We have only to march in and the city will be ours without a shot being fired, I gather. But I'm afraid you have not even heard the cream of the jest yet. Each man is to carry three days' rations and sixty cartridges, and Cochrane says we can pick up enough horses to serve as scouts. And since all the guns and ammunition carts will have to be towed by hand, he has kindly offered," he added in a carefully neutral tone, "a contingent of sailors to serve as supply wagons."

Ferriby burst out laughing. "Oh, Lord, I shouldn't laugh, for it's damnable. But I can't help picturing it. They *shall* be a help, unaccustomed as they are to marching! I wonder you were able to keep a straight face throughout these weighty deliberations. It's no wonder you came away."

"I had to, or I would have risked my commission," said Ashbourne ruefully. "I fear I was close enough to it already. Those buffle-headed fools! Well, I was warned the entire American operation had been badly mismanaged, and now I have proof of it for myself. However I blame Ross. He should have been more forceful, but he was clearly bent on offending no one. I can see Old Hookey worried about the sensibilities of a couple of admirals, however stiff-rumped."

"Lord yes! Heigh-ho! What it is to be a soldier," said Ferriby cheerfully. "And to think we might be in Paris now, with nothing to do but flirt with all the prettiest girls. Instead, we have endured three vile months at sea, not to mention the even viler food, and now this."

"What it is to be ADC to a weak officer!" said Ashbourne even more ruefully. "At least you don't have to sit and listen to such nonsense being planned in all seriousness. But I'd best get back before Ross agrees to something even more damnable. I've been gone too long already and came away without leave to boot. But I am beginning to wish I *were* safely back in France again."

"Well, at least I came for a chance of advancement," said Ferriby, grinning. "I've nothing but my officer's pay to look forward to, you know. But I'm damned if I know why you came, Ash. Why did you, by the way?"

Ashbourne shrugged. "Oh, mopping-up operations seemed dead flat, and I'd nothing much to want to go back to England for."

Since this was a delicate subject, Captain Ashbourne's fiancée having married a much richer and older man several years before, while they were at Talavera, Ferriby tactfully changed the subject. "After all, I daresay if you've lived in one ducal mansion, you've lived in them all," he said in amusement. "And life in camp, where you're grateful if you have a roof over your head no doubt has its charms, though I'm damned if I could say what they are at the moment."

Ash abruptly grinned, looking suddenly a great deal younger. "You'd be surprised. I'll take it any day over a sweltering ballroom and the stilted formality obtaining at court. Though I'm at least beginning to be deucedly sorry I volunteered for this particular assignment. Oh, well, I'd best get back. Don't tell the men yet, Lucy. This is news that will have to be carefully delivered to make it at all palatable, or we'll have a mutiny on our hands on top of everything else."

August 21

Even without knowing what the British planned, Magnus found little in the next few days to improve his temper any. Vice President Monroe had taken it upon himself to ride out to reconnoiter the advancing British army, and although in his haste he had forgotten to take a telescope with him, and dared not get any closer than some three miles away, the news he reported back was dismaying. He numbered the British strength at some six thousand men and reported they were advancing inexorably along the Patuxent River, from which they might make a quick raid either upon Washington or Baltimore.

His news was met with renewed waves of panic, and most of the remaining residents of the capital fled, taking what few possessions they could manage and sometimes abandoning in the middle of the road anything that grew too cumbersome. The only ones who did not flee tended to be stubborn, like Magnus, or else merchants who feared looters more than they feared the British, and stayed to protect their property.

This annoyed Magnus enough, but from all he was able to tell, the British advance by land and by sea was largely unopposed. Entire villages seemed to have emptied before them, with apparently no thought given, in the residents' haste to flee, to throwing the least obstacle in the way of the advancing enemy. As Magnus informed Sorcha wrathfully, the roads were everywhere primitive and narrow, and even a few felled trees would have slowed the British up nicely, so that American skirmishers might have harassed their flanks with impunity. Instead, bridges were left undisturbed, food and supplies were there for the taking, and the Americans might as easily have put out welcome mats for the advancing British.

The same was largely true in Washington itself. No one naturally wished to blow up the bridges if the British were making for Baltimore, not Washington; and as for putting up fortifications or redoubts or even simple breastworks, as Magnus was urging, no one in authority seemed to be able to make up his mind where and by whom it should be done. Consequently no one did anything at all.

In the meantime Vice President Monroe, now with the main body of American militia under General Winder, sent hasty word to the President that the public records should be removed from the capital.

Magnus rode out to see for himself what was happening on the morning of the 21st and reported in disgust that the inexperienced and ill-equipped troops were in hopeless confusion, owing to the conflicting orders they were receiving. They were also on half-rations, since the Quartermaster had commandeered most of the supply wagons to rush the government archives to safety instead of provisioning the troops. What was even worse, in Magnus's opinion, though Winder had assembled a respectable force of a thousand (admittedly poorly trained) Maryland militia, to be strengthened by some four hundred regulars, only two hundred flints could be found for their muskets.

Magnus had spoken briefly to Geoff and found him in good spirits, though he reported that many of the men had found themselves sleeping on the hard ground for the first time, and their stomachs were so empty they feared the enemy would be able to find them by the rumbling of their bellies. Reportedly, a few shots had been fired on the British as they entered Nottingham, but again Winder had chosen not to follow it up, even though many of the men, Geoff included, had begged to be allowed to send out some small skirmishing parties. Geoff also reported with a grin that the first night few had gotten much sleep, for on top of the hard beds and the fear of meeting experienced British troops for the first time, in the early hours a sentry had mistaken a stray cow for the British and blazed away at it, waking the entire camp and alarming everyone. They had all been mustered, despite the time, and spent a few anxious hours in full battle array before General Winder had at last decided it was a false alarm and allowed them to return to bed.

Magnus returned more disgusted than ever, and it was clear to Sorcha that he was champing at the bit to be away himself. The Senate continued to meet, but Magnus reported that they could do nothing but bicker among themselves and cast blame for the lack of preparation. Washington lay wide open to the British and was largely deserted, the citizenry having by and large expressed with their feet their shaky confidence in their government's ability to protect them.

Finally, President Madison seemed to come reluctantly to agree with them, for on the morning of the 24th, he and his Cabinet went themselves to confer with Winder. He had received intelligence that the British had themselves broken camp that morning and were clearly marching toward Bladensburg, a small village eight miles to the north of Washington on the main road between it and Baltimore. Tired of the delay, the President himself took over command of the army, and the decision was made to engage the British at Bladensburg if possible, in an attempt to hold them off from either city.

Orders instantly went out for every man who was capable of carrying arms to join in the effort, and the President and Vice President themselves, along with a number of their aides and the Cabinet, set out with General Winder to reinforce the American troops at Bladensburg.

It was all Magnus had been waiting for. He unearthed an ancient claymore that had seen duty at both Culloden and Flodden Field in the hands of his ancestors and prepared to set off, grinning from ear to ear.

Sorcha was resigned and made no attempt to dissuade him. So much skirmishing and marching up and down had been going on that it began to look like neither side meant to do any fighting, but she refused to tie him to her apron strings, even if she could.

Now that he was happy, Magnus would have belatedly bundled her off to safety, but she flatly refused to go. If Dolley Madison, the President's wife, could remain in the White House, undeterred, Sorcha was not about to join the craven exodus. Besides, she knew she was likely to get word faster while remaining in Washington, than she would deep in the country somewhere.

Magnus would at least have left his personal servant, Ham, to escort Sorcha and her maid, Dessy, in case a quick exit from Washington was called for. But Sorcha trusted the sense and unflappability of the grave black man far more than she did her volatile father, and again would not hear of it. She thought she would have ample warning and time to evacuate should the need arise.

"Never mind about me," she said firmly. "Only remember that you are the only father I have, and don't do anything too foolish."

"Aye, lassie, dinna fash yourself." Magnus was cheerful, his earlier impatience and temper wholly forgotten, and becoming more Scots by the moment. "We'll hold them at Bladensburg, dinna ye fear. With luck I'll be home in time for supper tomorrow. And I'll bring ye a Union Jack as a present."

Chapter 3

Captain Ashbourne, once he had his superior alone, had been even more forceful on the subject of the planned campaign, to the point of inviting court-martial for insubordination. Ross did not seem to object to his blunt speaking, but he was equally indecisive. "I don't say it's the campaign I would have chosen, but they are right that they have much more experience fighting the Americans," he said pacifically. "Besides, it won't do to offend them from the outset. Touchy bastards, these limeys."

Progress was every bit as slow as Ashbourne had predicted. The weather was sultry and humid, reminding Ashbourne of the worst encountered in Spain, and the troops were weary but determined. Enough horses, assorted nags, and screws abandoned by the fleeing Americans in their path had been picked up to mount twenty-odd infantrymen, with saddles and bridles improvised from blankets and ropes, to serve as scouts. But all the guns and ammunition carts had to be towed by sweating men, laboring over inferior roads, and by the end of each day's march the men were exhausted. Ashbourne, himself sweating and cursing, thought longingly of Spain, where the most they had to overcome were the French, not bad decisions by incompetent officers.

It was not until the afternoon of the 23rd of August that they broke camp and headed for Bladensburg on the main road between Washington and Baltimore, unaware the Americans had decided to make a stand there.

Sorcha spent that first day after Magnus left trying not to give into anxiety. The day was hot and unnaturally still, for the town was all but deserted, and toward noon, as much for something to do, she put on her hat, and went to call on her father's old friend, Miss Danville, knowing she would have scorned to join the general exodus.

The latter was well over eighty and had been a notable hostess in Washington for more than sixty years. Despite her age and the disturbing events going on around her, Sorcha found her calmly dipping fingers of toast in tea for a light nuncheon, her faithful slave waiting patiently behind her chair.

She greeted Sorcha cheerfully, saying in her cackling old voice, "Ha! So you've not joined the general rabble in this undignified flight. Good girl! Well, come in, come in! Cato, get Miss Mac-Kenzie some tea. On second thought, take this muck away and fetch out the sherry. The good one, mind! We both could use something stronger, I suspect."

When Cato, nearly as old as his mistress and even more imperturbable, had gone on this errand, Miss Danville added shrewdly, looking at Sorcha, "So, Magnus has gone off to fight the British once more, even at his age, eh? Don't look so frightened, girl! If we can't beat the British, we don't deserve to call ourselves a free nation. Bah! When I was a girl, we were fighting Indians like as not, as well as the French and the British. My twin sister was scalped by the Indians, did you know that?" She took almost ghoulish pleasure in the shocking information. "But I lived through it, and I aim to live through a deal more before I'm done. And don't you forget it."

Sorcha smiled more naturally. "I don't, ma'am. You have seen a great deal in your life."

"Eighty-six next spring!" announced Miss Danville triumphantly. "And I can tell you I don't mean to die yet, especially at the hands of the British. Which reminds me. That young man of yours has gone off as well, I hear. When do you plan to put him out of his misery and marry him, missy, that's what I'd like to know."

"I don't know that I do, ma'am," retorted Sorcha coolly, as always restored to cheer by the indomitable old woman. "It seems to me you've led an extremely colorful life, and you've seen no need to lumber yourself with a husband and children."

Miss Danville was pleased, but said merely, "Don't try to butter me up, girl. Besides, what has suited me well enough I've a suspicion won't suit you nearly so well. You don't have that red head of yours for nothing."

"I sometimes wonder, ma'am," admitted Sorcha ruefully. "I am almost four-and-twenty and have never found a man yet I don't despise sooner or later."

"And quite rightly, too! There's few enough who aren't fools. When you find one, snap him up. *I* never did, though. You're the same as your mother, make no doubt. When she fell at last, it was for a penniless immigrant just off the boat with a brogue so broad you could scarcely understand a word he said, and nothing to offer but a passion for life that she had the good sense to recognize immediately. Everyone thought she was crazy, your grandfather included, but I never did. And now Magnus is a United States senator and one of the pillars of the community. Ha! I've always suspected you were just the same, my girl."

Sorcha had opened her mouth to answer in a light vein when they both were startled to stillness by a muffled boom in the distance. Their eyes met, the old and the young, and then Miss Danville said matter-of-factly, "It's begun, then! Don't look so scared, girl. I've lived through too many battles in my time, and women always have the worst of it. Nothing to do but sit and wait and hope for the best."

The bombardment had started in earnest, it seemed, and in the clear, hot air, the sound of the deeper cannon and lighter *tat-tat* that might be muskets could be clearly heard, even at a distance of more than eight miles. Miss Danville seemed unperturbed and sipped at her sherry, when it came, with all the enjoyment of an illicit pleasure, for Sorcha knew her doctor had forbidden her to take anything stronger than a mild claret.

Now the old lady added in amusement, "Which reminds me, I have it on the best of authority that Dolley Madison, whom I've always said was a flibbertygibbet, President's wife or no, fled this morning, taking all the government plate with her, and, even more incongruously, a large and unwieldy portrait of George Washington. I'd have given a good deal to have been there to see it."

Sorcha laughed, as she was meant to, and declined an invitation to come and stay with her hostess until it should be over. "I've got Cato stationed in the hall with a musket, and in a pinch I can still shoot a redcoat or two if I have to," that redoubtable old woman assured her.

That made Sorcha laugh as well, but she said again, "I don't fear the British, ma'am. And Magnus will expect to find me at home. Will you come instead and stay with us? We will make you very comfortable, and Cato may stand guard in our hallway as well as your own."

But Miss Danville was equally determined. "I refuse to be driven out of my own home. As for the British, pooh! They won't get anywhere near Washington. You mark my words."

The slow progress proved costly, as the captain had foreseen. The Americans had had time to entrench themselves in Bladensburg, and though Ashbourne could see at a glance that they were badly deployed, on the heights leading out of the town, it would not be at all easy to dislodge them.

Nor was it. The Yankees, far from seasoned or valiant, and facing some of the most experienced troops in Europe, still resisted as best they could. They broke up the first push through the town, silenced a rocket detachment, and stopped the first rush across the bridge, which they had neglected to destroy, with heavy losses on the British side.

Ashbourne, who had led one of the hard-pressed charges, cursed all incompetence and sent his men on, working stolidly between houses and through gardens, and swarming down to the East Branch of the Potomac in a dozen places. There they were able to splash across, and still under murderous fire, push on up into the orchard south of the bridge, where they at last managed to silence a battery of American guns, but he was angry at such senseless slaughter and furious that his own troops had taken such heavy and unnecessary losses.

Once they were in possession of the town, Ross rested his hard-pressed men again for two hours, and then headed for Washington. Cockburn, who had accompanied them, was in high fettle, and the captain, unable to face such overweening ignorance and folly, took good care to stay out of his way.

It was after dark before they reached the capital at about eight o'clock. Most of the town seemed wholly deserted, and they met with no resistance at all. Ashbourne gave the order to bivouac outside the town, and it was only then he learned the whole of what had been planned.

"*Fire the city?*" he repeated in the blankest disbelief when Ross told him. "When they have offered no resistance? You cannot be serious!"

Ross was slightly apologetic and more than a little uncomfortable. "I know it seems barbaric, but it is in retaliation, you understand. The Yankees fired York early in the war, so they can have no complaints."

"Barbaric! You are generous, sir!" snapped the captain, no longer caring much if he were court-martialed. "I fear you must hold me excused. I have no intention of setting fire to a town that has offered no resistance and is completely under our control. Good God, can you imagine Old Hookey giving such an order? All I can say is that if that is the naval idea of how to conduct a war, it is not mine!"

Still Ross refused to take offense. "Well, well," he said uncomfortably, "I'm not asking you do to it. I don't say it's what I like myself, but it seems to be commonplace over here. I shall conduct the sortie myself, taking no more than three hundred or so men with me, for we don't want any looting or worse."

The captain clenched his jaw and turned away without another word. In his years of long service it was the first time he had been ashamed to wear the uniform of his country.

Toward the late afternoon the sound of the cannon abruptly stopped. Sorcha had found the noise almost unbearable, but quickly discovered the silence was even worse. It seemed probable the battle was over, but it was impossible to guess which side had won, or what might be happening now.

She was strongly tempted to ride out along the road toward Bladensburg, but she had given Magnus her word she would remain in Washington. Instead, she tried not to dwell on what might have happened to Magnus, or Geoff, or any other of the men she knew, who had marched out so optimistically only a few days before.

Around nine, when she had been on pins and needles for far too long, there was unexpectedly a pop of gunfire much nearer at hand, seemingly almost in the next street. She started and ran to the window, but could see nothing. But even as she stood there, an explosion at the other end of town literally rattled the panes of the window she was standing at, and a second later lit up the night sky to the east as if it had been day.

She was shaken, but Magnus had warned her they planned to blow up the armory if the British should threaten Washington. That was scarcely reassuring, but she refused to give in to despair so soon.

Almost immediately there were two lesser explosions, following the first. Sorcha knew they had also planned to destroy both of the bridges crossing the Potomac in case of an attack on the city, and that they had done so seemed to bode no good news.

Still she refused to panic. For a while there were no further alarms, and she could hear nothing in the straining dark. Then, incredibly, a glow of fire flared much nearer, and even as she watched, it seemed to grow and spread rapidly. It seemed much too far away from the river to have been set off by either of the earlier explosions, but for a long time she refused to acknowledge the truth of the evidence before her, unwilling to believe that even the British could be so base.

But it was not long before she had to accept it. "Good God," she said at last in a voice that betrayed far more anger than fear. "Magnus was right, they *are* devils. They've fired the capitol."

From the window of the drawing room on the second floor Sorcha and Dessy both watched wordlessly as the fire grew and spread. What somehow made it worse was that there was no fighting, or even any shouting or alarm. They saw and heard nothing of the British soldiers who must be in the town. They seemed to go about their work with a grim and silent efficiency that was even more chilling than shouting and anger would have been, and the only good thing to be said for them was that they seemed to make no attempt to go door to door, either attacking or looting.

From the direction of the blaze it seemed as if only the public buildings were being targeted, which was scarcely much comfort. In the hot summer weather the largely wood-built city would soon enough catch light, especially if there were any wind at all.

Sorcha's own street remained unnaturally calm and quiet, though they lived at no great distance from the capitol. Nevertheless, she and Dessy began to make preparations to evacuate if the worst came to the worst, Sorcha at least glad to have something concrete to do at last. With Dessy's help she dragged down a feather mattress off one of the upstairs beds, and while Dessy packed a hamper of food and a few necessities, gathered what few valuables she did not wish to part with—either to the British or the flames. With the ludicrous example of the other evacuees before her, she took only a few treasures, including a miniature of her mother and a few jewels inherited from that scarcely remembered lady. More practically, she also took a pair of duelling pistols given to Magnus by the French ambassador.

She moved with unnatural calm, refusing to think of Magnus or Geoff perhaps lying dead or wounded somewhere. Or of Magnus's stories of the atrocities committed by the British soldiers on helpless women and children in Scotland. The sky was growing brighter by the minute, due to the fast-spreading blaze, and despite the heat of the August night it was soon necessary to shut the windows against the smothering smoke.

Dessy, thin and upright, who had been her nurse and had raised Sorcha since her mother's death, also moved deliberately, like Sorcha, scorning to give in to panic. Her own husband, Ham, was with Magnus, but both women refused to give voice to their fears.

There still had been no sound of enemy soldiers in their street or any sign of danger from human sources, but as Sorcha had feared, the fire was already creeping dangerously closer. The night, warm before, was growing decidedly hotter, and it was so light now it would almost have been possible to read a book in the street.

When the roof of the house across the street was ignited by a flying ember, Sorcha was almost glad of the excuse for action at last. She had been tempted all afternoon to go in search of her father, except that she had given Magnus her word that she would remain in Washington, waiting for him. Now that the choice had been taken out of her hands, it was almost with relief that she and Dessy lugged the mattress out to the stables behind the house, now sheltering only one elderly cob since Magnus had sent all the other cattle away, and loaded it into a cart used for moving furniture back and forth between their two homes in Washington and Annapolis. Sorcha herself harnessed the shying chestnut, already disturbed by the smell of smoke, and in a surprisingly short time they were ready to set out.

Even as they left, the house across the way burst into flame, and it was clear their own house would not be long in following suit.

Outside, the smoke was so thick it was hard to breathe. The poor horse was by then white-eyed and trembling, and Sorcha was obliged to wrap her shawl around his head and lead him on foot.

Dessy, upright on the hard wooden seat, had her loaded and cocked pistol across her lap, and had taken refuge in her own shawl, wrapped tightly across her face to keep out the worst of the heat and smoke. Even as they set out, the attic of the house they were leaving caught fire. Clearly there was no going back.

Sorcha herself was coughing and choking by then. She intended to go by her old friend's house and try and make the redoubtable Miss Danville come with them. But the terrified horse, now shying in earnest and threatening in its panic to overturn the cart, was not making it easy for her. Sorcha did what she could to soothe and reassure the poor creature and reflected that it was fortunate that formidable lady lived in the opposite direction from the capitol, where the fire seemed not yet to have penetrated. With any luck they would be away before the flames spread much farther.

She had seen no one as yet, and certainly no British troops. But without warning she was seized from behind, and a rough male voice growled in her ear, "I'll take that horse and the wagon, missy, iffn' ye don't mind. And whatever jewels and money you may have on you! Be quick now, or I'll take even more'n that if ye ain't careful!"

So blinded had Sorcha been by the smoke that she had not seen anyone approaching, but the voice was, incredibly, not English but American. The man had one arm tight around her waist, and the other was pawing at the front of her dress, presumably for jewels, and it was clear he had been drinking.

Absurdly, however, that he was an American made her so furious she almost forgot to be afraid—that and the realization if he took her horse they would be stranded in the burning city, a fate she did not like to contemplate.

Both were ample enough reasons, and she tried to fight him, having no compunctions herself about hurting him. But he was unexpectedly strong, and the reek of the whiskey reached her even over the smell of smoke. His one hand was ripping at her gown, but it was the other arm she was more concerned about at the moment, for it kept her from freeing her pistol. She would not have hesitated to shoot him, but he had lifted her partially off the ground and was constricting her ribs in so fierce a hug that it was difficult to draw breath, even without being half choked from the smoke already.

Still she scratched and clawed, hearing his coarse laugh in her ear, and despite all she could do, feeling the dangerous blackness start to gather before her eyes. There was Dessy to think of as well, and she did not want to speculate on what might happen to them both if she lost consciousness completely. It would be ludicrous indeed if, with British soldiers all around her, she should be raped by a drunken fellow countryman.

For his part he seemed to be enjoying the struggle, his hot breath on her neck, and his invading hand no longer searching strictly for jewels. "Well, well! Feisty little thing, ain't you?" he said and chuckled. "What're you doing still in Washington? Seems you should've gone with the others when ye had the chance."

That seemed increasingly obvious even to Sorcha. The now terrified horse was jibbing at her back, and the man's hot lips were brushing her averted face, his arm tightening still more about her so that she was very near to losing consciousness. "Now, l'il lady, don't act so uppity," he complained. "Besides, you'd rather it was me than some redcoat, wouldn't you? I'll take good care of you, never fear."

The choice seemed a poor one to her, but she could get no breath to answer him, even if she had wanted to. It was a relief to her to remember that Dessy was there, though. Dessy would save her if she could.

At the very thought the man was plucked bodily off her and sent sprawling. Sorcha fell back against the terrified horse, coughing and retching, too overcome even for relief at the moment, and trying to drag the smoke-laden air into her tortured lungs. It did not even occur to her for a few minutes that Dessy, for all her strong will, could scarcely have lifted so strong a man off in such a fashion.

Then she was able to make out a tall figure looming over her in the haze, his own face blackened with smoke as hers must be, and a strong hand clamped the bridle above hers, thankfully controlling the terrified horse with ease. "Are you all right?" he demanded.

"Yes . . . yes." She still could scarcely get her breath back, and her voice did not sound like her own.

"Then," said the grim voice, "perhaps you will tell me what in the sweet name of hell you are still doing here when everyone else in the town has fled? It would have served you right if that man had stolen your horse and cart—or worse! And worse was exactly what it looked like he had in mind."

The voice, in the choking upside down world in which she suddenly seemed to find herself, was incredibly, cultured, upper-class British. And the color of his uniform, even in that lurid light, was unmistakable.

Chapter 4

Sorcha, still overcome with smoke and delayed reaction to fear, nevertheless felt an absurd impulse to laugh, which even she recognized was hysteria. "Oh, God," she gasped. "I can't believe it! Quick! Wh . . . what is your regiment?"

He looked at her as if he thought she were crazy, as no doubt he did. "The Eighty-Fifth," he said even more grimly. "And if you think this is some kind of a jest—"

"No. N-no! It is only that . . . I said I'd an ambition to m-meet one of W-wellington's Invincibles, though I hadn't foreseen it in quite s-such circumstances, I must confess."

Then Dessy was there, alarmed and shaken, and Sorcha was in Dessy's arms. "Chile, chile!" Dessy was saying. "I would've killed him and gladly, but I couldn't get no good aim for fear of hitting you. Are you all right?"

"Yes. Yes," said Sorcha, still coughing and clinging to Dessy's reassuring bulk. "And I couldn't get to my pistol because of the way he was holding me. Thankfully, it doesn't matter . . . th-thanks to the officer here. What happened to the man who attacked me?"

"He run off at the first sign of trouble," answered Dessy with grim satisfaction, "If you ask me, killin' is too good for such the likes of him."

"All this is no doubt touching," remarked the captain grimly, "but you may have noticed it is growing increasingly hot and your late assailant may yet decide to return. Get in! Unfortunately, I cannot leave the horse's head, so you will have to climb up by yourselves. But I'll lead you at least to a quieter part of town."

Neither Dessy nor Sorcha needed any further urging. It seemed to Sorcha the height of irony that it should have been an American who threatened her, and an enemy officer who had rescued her, but they were both still coughing and their eyes streaming, and there was no time for further argument. Still clinging together for comfort as much as support, they gratefully returned to the cart and climbed in.

The captain, with a man's strength, soon had the poor beast calmed enough for them to go on, and led them swiftly to a quieter part of town, where the fire had not yet penetrated and the smoke was considerably less thick and damaging to both eyes and throat. The night sky was still almost as bright as day, and the sounds of the inferno pursued them even there, but it was at least thankfully cooler, and Sorcha no longer felt as if they had penetrated almost to the gates of hell itself.

She had had time to recover from her unpleasant experience, and when her unlikely rescuer at last left the horse and came back to confer with them, she was prepared for it.

He stood looking up at her for a moment, his face streaked with smoke and his expression inscrutable. Then he calmly handed her her shawl, remarking somewhat dryly, "You had best have this back, ma'am. At the moment you would appear to be more in need of it than that wretched animal."

For the first time she remembered that her late assailant, with his reeking breath and horrible groping hands, had torn the neck of her gown, and she looked down almost indifferently. Considerations of vanity, even modesty seemed relatively unimportant at the moment, but she obediently accepted the shawl and wrapped it around her. One shoulder was almost completely bared, and she undoubtedly had far too much skin showing, but she was decently enough covered—just—and at the moment that seemed the least of her worries. But she in turn looked down at her unlikely savior with undeniable curiosity.

In the red light from the fire, and with his face streaked with smoke—which gave Sorcha a fair indication of what her own must look like—it was impossible to tell what he looked like, except that he was tall and obviously strong, from the way he had literally picked up and thrown the man attacking her. He wore the insignia of a captain, and his own eyes were tired and red-rimmed, his uniform almost as black as his face.

He also gave the appearance of a man holding on to his temper only with a considerable effort. Sorcha had no idea why that should be, but the impression was unmistakable. There was a jagged and stained tear in the left arm of his uniform, and he held that arm stiffly, as if it pained him—which might account for at least part of his present temper. But she was still left with the distinct and unflattering impression that she and Dessy were no more to him than a temporary inconvenience. It seemed his present ill humor went far beyond them.

"Now," he said carefully, as if keeping his temper tightly in check, "I do not even intend to ask why, having decided to remain in town against all common sense or reason, you chose this time of all others to go out for a drive, ma'am. But as you have seen for yourself, it is extremely dangerous. The safest thing would be for you to return home immediately and remain there until things have returned to normal."

Sorcha wondered when that would be, with the town burning to the ground around her, but responded with considerable sarcasm, "I would be delighted to do so, Captain, except that you and your men seem to have burned my home out from under me most effectively."

His lips tightened, and his control over his temper seemed to slip a notch. "Very well!" he said at last. "But since the whole da—since the whole city seems to be deserted, there are any number of empty houses you may choose from. All you need do is to barricade yourself inside one of them. I will even station a guard at the door if you are afraid. I can promise you will not be . . . further molested."

"I wonder why that offer fails to reassure me, Captain?" she remarked ironically. "You will forgive me if under the circumstances I have little trust in either your word or your guard. And I have no intention of remaining in town to be burned along with the public buildings."

He seemed to vie with himself, then at last said with obviously fast-fraying patience, "Perhaps you have not yet realized, ma'am, that the town is full of British soldiers—"

"It would be difficult not to, Captain," she pointed out sweetly.

He ignored the interruption. "And if that were not bad enough, the only citizens of your own country you are likely to meet tonight are looters such as the charming specimen you just encountered. Two women out alone and unescorted are just asking for trouble of the sort you have already met once tonight. Especially," he added grimly, flicking another look up at her, "when one of them is young and extremely pretty." Neither his tone nor his glance implied a compliment—quite the reverse.

Sorcha's own temper was none too pleasant by then, and it was a relief to find an enemy to let it out on. "But then, having made the town literally too hot to hold me, it would seem I am left with very little choice, Captain. Even after everything I have always heard about the British army, I own I had not previously guessed that you would stoop so low as to burn a defenseless town that offered no resistance," she said scathingly. "But having done so, I find I do not choose to remain in an enemy-occupied town. None of which, I might add, is in the least your business. I am grateful for the help you have already given us, but your responsibility is at an end. Besides, I would not like to keep you. After all, there are any number of parts of the town that have not yet been put to the torch, and you and your men must still have a great deal of work to do."

His face tightened still more, and his voice when he answered was clipped. "There is nothing I would like better than to wash my hands of you, ma'am. As you correctly point out, saving spoilt and willfully irresponsible beauties is not part of my duties."

That caught her on the raw for some reason. "Spoilt!" she repeated furiously.

"Yes, spoilt! But having chosen to ignore all the warning signs to remain here, in the face of an enemy attack, you are not now going to add to your folly by making a martyr of yourself. I have endured enough already this day, and I draw the line at that."

Even to her, suddenly, it seemed the height of folly to stand quarreling here with a perfect stranger while the city burned around them. She caught herself up on another betraying outburst and after vying with her temper very much in his own manner, at last managed to reply icily, "I have no intention of martyring myself, and I would remind you that whatever I may choose to do is no affair of yours. Nor do I have time to waste in fruitless argument. Pray stand aside, Captain."

He made no move to obey her. "God give me strength!" he exclaimed, apparently appealing to heaven. "And just exactly where is it that you think you are going, ma'am? Perhaps you are not aware that the town is surrounded by British troops, and the countryside itself is full of scared and desperate men who would not hesitate to murder you—or worse—to steal your horse and cart."

This was far from welcome news, for she had hoped only a small contingent of British had been detailed to burn the capital. But she refused to be frightened and said with scorn, "Are you telling me that British soldiers also attack helpless women as well as burn the cities they conquer?"

She thought a muscle jumped in his lean cheek, but he seemed to have gained control of himself again, for he retorted curtly, "I am speaking of American soldiers, ma'am! Your forces suffered a decided defeat this afternoon, and most of them are fled into the surrounding countryside, many of them frightened, wounded, and desperate."

This was even less welcome news, though she had guessed much of it already, of course. "I am not afraid of my own troops," she insisted staunchly.

"If you are not afraid of your own soldiers, then you should be, ma'am!" he said bluntly. "It is clear you have little experience of war." He seemed to strive with himself again, then at last surprised her even more by saying curtly, "Move over! Much as I would like to, I find I cannot abandon you to your just deserts. I have endured more than enough this day without having you on my conscience as well. If you are still determined on so risky and foolhardy an adventure, I will at least see you through our lines. But after that you are on your own. I have neither the time nor the patience to rescue foolish women from the consequences of their own willful folly."

Her temper and her pride both urged her to spurn so grudging an offer. But it was true that his escort must greatly improve their chances of getting through the British lines, a necessity she had not anticipated and certainly did not much relish. And that, she supposed unwillingly, was all that really mattered.

Besides, she had Dessy to think of as well as herself. It seemed to her the whole world had gone mad in the last few hours, but after considering the matter, she had to acknowledge that it would indeed be willful folly not to accept his unexpected help, however grudgingly offered. For all she knew the man who had attacked her might still be lurking in the vicinity, which made her shudder when she remembered those hands fumbling at her bodice and that hot breath on her cheek. And even if he weren't, the captain was right. More looters—or worse—might easily lie out there in the hot dark. Not to mention far less disinterested British soldiers.

Still she could not resist saying mockingly, "Let me get this straight, Captain, for I am finding it somewhat hard to grasp. Having invaded my country and burned my home to the ground, you are now proposing to help me to escape your own troops?"

He did not answer, but instead said abruptly again, as if his patience were long since at an end, "Move over! I have every expectation I shall regret this, but it seems I have little choice."

And without ceremony he climbed up on the narrow seat beside her and took the reins out of her hands.

To Sorcha's annoyance Dessy seemed to take this unexpected intervention far more calmly than she did, for Dessy had already wrapped her shawl once more about her head to keep out the worst of the smoke and made room on the hard bench seat. But Sorcha was less pleased by this cool assumption of authority.

Even more to the point, the seat had never been intended to hold three persons, and she found herself pressed uncomfortably up against the hard length of the captain far more than she relished. She held herself as upright as she could, but it was impossible to miss the fact that he smelled of smoke, which she supposed she must as well, and that at such close quarters she was able to get a much better look at his face.

She thought it strong rather than strictly handsome. His nose was straight and aggressive, his lips well molded, if held tightly together at the moment, in continuing evidence of his present uncertain temper. She had already seen that his eyes were a clear blue, almost startling in that smoke-blackened face. His much hated scarlet coat was also streaked liberally with smoke and other dark stains she suddenly had no wish to identify, and had great patches of sweat under the arms and down the back. He looked, in fact, anything but the immaculate British officer Magnus had described to her so derisively, the sort who sent his men into battle while he remained safely in the rear, a scented handkerchief held to his nose in one hand and a gold snuffbox in the other.

Her first impression, that he was tired and not in the best of tempers, even before their encounter, was merely reinforced at such close quarters. He held the reins in his right hand only, his left arm held stiffly at his side. Now and then, despite all she could do, she was thrown against it, and he grimaced, but made no comment.

They had gone no more than a block, the smoke still strong enough to make her wrap an end of her shawl across her lower face, as Dessy had done, when something at the edge of her vision unexpectedly caught her attention. She sat up straighter, dropping her shawl, and cried abruptly, "Stop! Oh, *stop! Pull up at once!*"

He was startled into obeying her, shifting the reins abruptly to his left hand to free his right, which went instinctively to the pistol at his belt. "Good God, what is it?" he demanded sharply.

But Sorcha had already risen to clamber down from the awkward seat, over Dessy's knees, and didn't bother to answer him.

With a short exclamation of impatience the captain abruptly handed the reins to Dessy and prepared to follow her. What he saw cowering against the wall of a house they had just passed did not seem to inspire in him the same pity as it had Sorcha. A woman with a tiny baby was huddled there, shivering with fright, both of them wrapped in a rough piece of cloth to protect them from the smoke.

The captain swore at this further unwanted complication, but Sorcha was surprised to notice that his face and voice were unexpectedly gentle as he approached the terrified woman. "Who is it?" he demanded curtly. "Do you know her?"

The woman shrank from him in increased terror, hiding her face in her crude shawl and whimpering with fright.

Sorcha said sharply, "Of course I don't know her! Don't come any closer! You will only frighten her more, poor thing. Don't be afraid," she turned to urge the woman. "We won't hurt you, I promise."

The girl—for the face she at last revealed was scarcely more than a child's—was black and almost beyond terror. She clutched an alarmingly tiny baby tightly to her, her eyes rolling with terror, and moaned again with fear.

"Oh, you poor child!" exclaimed Sorcha, pity swamping all other issues for the moment. "Let me help you into the cart. There is room in the back for you and the baby where you may lie down. Here, let me take him, poor little mite. How old is he?"

The girl seemed past answering, but made no resistance when Sorcha gently took the baby from her. She guessed, with pity, that the creature had been left behind, as too weak to travel, when her master and the rest of the household had fled the capital, for the weight of the tiny bundle in her arms was alarmingly slight.

But when she hastily uncovered the bundle, her breath catching with dread, she was greatly relieved to see a wizened little dark face, screwed up as if to cry, staring back at her, and the baby struggled weakly in her arms. She handed it up to Dessy, who immediately took competent charge, crooning to it and rocking it, while Sorcha tried to gently question the mother.

She seemed to continue to regard the captain with abject terror, but revealed at length that she was called Elsie, and the baby Rufus. She was owned by a feed merchant who lived near the capitol and who had resisted abandoning his goods to be looted until the last possible minute. She had been left behind when the others left, since she had just given birth and was still too weak to travel. She had huddled all alone in the house behind the store, terrified of being taken by the redcoats, until the burning had finally forced her out. She had been sure she would be killed, for everyone knew the redcoats would not hesitate to murder innocent women and even infants.

Sorcha's pity increased, and she said in a low voice to the captain, unable to keep her scorn in check, "This is also to be laid at your door, Captain! Help her into the cart, for she is scarcely strong enough to stand on her own, let alone walk."

The captain stood for a moment longer regarding her, his expression again unreadable. Then at last he shrugged and did as he was bid, waiting until Dessy had spread a quilt and some pillows in the back of the cart, and then lifting the black girl bodily onto this makeshift bed.

He waited with obviously increasing impatience while Sorcha fussed over her, making her comfortable and promising that they would not abandon her to the British soldiers. The girl was beyond taking most of it in and seemed to want to cling to Dessy, so at last Sorcha left Dessy to it and allowed the captain to pull her a little apart in the dark street.

"Your apparent belief that we are very little better than barbarians is bad enough, my dear ma'am," he said bitterly. "But you are not seriously proposing to take a woman still weak from childbirth and her newborn baby along with you on this harebrained adventure of yours, are you?"

"What would you have me do?" Sorcha demanded indignantly. "Leave her in the street for your soldiers to find?"

Again he seemed to vie with himself, his lips closed tightly as if he did not trust himself to speak. At last without another word he turned back to the cart. "Get in!" he said, roughly handing her up. "I begin to think I must be as mad as you are."

He took up the reins with unnecessary force and started off again.

Sorcha took perverse pleasure in informing him, "If you jib at the poor horse like that, you will undo all your earlier good work, Captain. You should know better than to take your anger out on animals."

He choked and glared at her, but he did drop his hands. "Yes, ma'am," he said with false meekness. "Is there any other advice or instructions you have to give me? Pray don't hesitate to tell me if there is."

"Yes, now that you mention it," she retorted coolly. "There is an elderly friend of mine that I mean to try and persuade to come with us as well, which is why I brought the mattress in the first place. Turn at the next street corner. Her home is not far from here."

He choked again, and there was a pregnant pause. Then he said resignedly, and in a far more natural voice than any she had yet heard from him, "I don't know what equivalent you may have to Bedlam in this country, ma'am, but I am beginning to think that is clearly where you have escaped from. This half-ill child and her baby are bad enough, but surely not even you can be proposing to take an elderly woman along with you."

"Yes, of course I am," answered Sorcha rather impatiently. "And her elderly servant as well. Turn here."

After a brief hesitation he did so. They were thankfully in a part of town by then where the fire had not yet penetrated, so that it was possible to begin to clear one's aching throat and lungs. Sorcha was doubly thankful, for it meant Miss Danville was likely to still be safe, if no doubt simmering with fury over the perfidy of the British.

But they had not yet reached her elderly friend's house when Sorcha abruptly straightened and exclaimed again, "Oh, stop! Pull up again! Oh, the poor creature!"

"Good God, what is it this time?" demanded the captain by now in the liveliest dread. But he unwillingly did as she bid, if only to keep her from leaping out of the cart while it was still moving.

His expression changed even more ludicrously when he realized that the object of her concern this time was a large mongrel dog, which had obviously fled from the flames and been badly burnt. It was cowering in the gutter by the side of the road and crying pitiably.

"Oh, my God!" said the captain in disgust. "You cannot seriously be suggesting—Take care, you absurd girl!" he broke off to warn her sharply, again thrusting the reins in Dessy's hands. "He may be dangerous!"

But Sorcha was already out of the cart and bending over the pitiful animal. "Of course it is not dangerous," she said scathingly. "And it is not a he but a she," she added, having had time to make an interesting discovery, "for she is very soon to have puppies, poor thing. Oh, she is so badly burnt!"

After a bitter moment the captain thrust her unceremoniously out of the way and himself bent over the cowering creature. He ran his hands over her knowledgeably, remarking dryly, "Not too soon, I trust. That would be all I needed, for by now I have not the least dependence in the world that you would not insist upon setting up a whelping nest here by the side of the road. In fact, nothing is more certain."

Despite his words his hands were gentle, and he seemed to know what he was doing. As with the horse, the poor creature soon stopped shivering with fright and looked up at him in clear gratitude. He saw it and remarked in exasperation, "Don't bother looking at me, you absurd creature, for this is none of my doing. If it had been left to me, I would have driven on without compunction and abandoned you to your fate."

He looked up to see Sorcha watching him, and his expression stiffened. "Get back into the cart, ma'am. I agree—reluctantly!—that you could not possibly have abandoned that poor girl and her baby, however ridiculous the whole enterprise may be. But this is fast entering into the realm of absurdity! In case you do not realize it, you have far more to concern yourself with at the moment than the plight of a stray mongrel bitch, pregnant or not. Besides, there is no room, especially if you are still bent on rescuing an elderly lady and her servant as well."

"Then we shall make room!" said Sorcha stubbornly. "Nor is it any of your concern whom I may choose to take up in my own

vehicle! What is in this portmanteau, Dessy? Just clothes? Then it
shall have to be left behind, I'm afraid. Help me lift her into the
back of the cart, Captain, instead of making useless arguments
which I have no intention of attending to anyway."

After another dangerous pause the captain began unexpectedly
to laugh. "God help me, I am afraid to even speculate what next
you will saddle me with, ma'am. Get out of the way. The
wretched animal is far too heavy for you. I can only pray that we
encounter no further objects of pity on our way through town, for
this is fast turning into a debacle."

Chapter 5

Once he had bestowed the dog, which was black and seemed to be a mongrel mix, into the back of the cart, beside the exhausted Elsie, who made no objection to this new addition, he watched Sorcha see it comfortably disposed, and even sacrifice her much-maligned shawl to make a soft bed. "I thought I had made it clear to you that you are a great deal more in need of your shawl than that wretched animal is," he remarked resignedly. "I know it seems surly of me to mention it, but if you are planning to drive through the British lines looking like that, I should warn you that not even *my* protection is likely to help you, ma'am."

She glared at him and gathered together the torn shoulder of her gown in annoyance. "If you cannot control your men, Captain, you should not turn them loose on a helpless country, to burn and terrorize."

For some reason he seemed a great deal more cheerful, as if he had cast aside his previous bad mood—or perhaps was merely resigned by then to his fate. "It is doubtless a waste of breath to point out that I have done neither," he said, obviously without much hope of being attended to. "And don't think it churlish of me, ma'am, for at this point I am past objecting to anything you may take it in your head to do. But do you propose to put your elderly friend in the back of the cart, along with that child and the stray dog? She *will* enjoy the journey in that case. And I was forgetting her servant as well. How thoughtless of me."

Sorcha ignored his sarcasm and started to climb back up onto the seat. "Good God, do you think she will object to that? She fought the Indians when she was a child, not to mention the British in the last war. You will find, Captain, if you have not already, that American women are far from being the ornamental and helpless creatures you are used to."

"So I am beginning to understand, ma'am." He handed her up with exaggerated ceremony, as he did so taking another look at her and adding resignedly, "Here, you had better have this."

"This" turned out to be his own uniform jacket, which he stripped off and put around her shoulders, despite her protest. It smelt of gunpowder and tobacco, and as a symbol of British tyranny around the world, she should doubtless have rejected it out of hand. But in light of her torn gown she was glad enough of its cover, and since despite the conflagration, the night had begun to grow chilly the farther they got away from the center of town, was grateful for its warmth as well.

She looked curiously at the blood-stained slit in his left shirt-sleeve, around which she could see a hastily tied bandage, heavily stained and not very clean. But she made no comment and neither did he.

He followed her direction to Miss Danville's house on the outskirts of town, merely remarking as he drove, "You are a remarkable woman, ma'am."

"Why?" she countered. "Because I choose not to abandon my friends to the brutalities of the British?"

"I knew we would soon be back to that. But no. Or at least only in part. How old are you anyway?" he asked curiously.

"Four-and-twenty—next month."

"It is perfectly clear to me you will not live to see your next birthday. But then I am surprised to learn you have lived so long."

She ignored that frivolity. "How old are you?"

"One-and-thirty—though at this moment I feel a hundred. Out of curiosity—and I suspect I will regret this, too—where do you intend to go if you do succeed in making it out of Washington?"

She hesitated, then shrugged. "My father was at . . . Bladensburg. I mean to find him if I can."

"Good God! I'm sorry I asked. My dear girl, you do realize it is a full eight miles there, and far more dangers may await you on the road than a mere enemy army?"

She scornfully ignored that as well. She had made up her mind as soon as it was clear they would have to evacuate from Washington. Magnus might still be there, and though if he were still alive and unhurt—and she would not allow herself to think otherwise—he would certainly try to return to Washington to find her, it might be difficult with the British in possession of the town. Always presuming, of course, that any of it still stood by morning, which was by no means certain.

All in all, it seemed to her better to find Magnus instead. And if, after her recent experience, the thought of the long drive through the dark was at least a little daunting, it seemed preferable to cowering in some strange house, waiting for it to catch fire, too, or for enemy soldiers to break in. The captain's earlier offer of a guard struck her very much like detailing a fox to guard the henhouse.

When she remained silent, he sighed. "The only thing that surprises me is that you consented to allow your father to go off to war without you. From what I have seen of you so far, my dear ma'am, I wonder you did not take up a musket and insist upon marching off with him." He seemed to consider the matter for a moment and added in amusement, "In which case the results of today's battle might have been very different."

She glanced at him. "You were there?" When he nodded, she asked unwillingly, "What happened? Will you tell me?"

He glanced at her rigid face in the dark, and his own softened slightly. "As you must have gathered by now, we carried the day. The American forces were ill-trained and overmatched, but they were not without courage. They launched at least one suicidal attack, which caused more losses than were necessary. You have nothing to be ashamed of."

She lifted her chin. "I'm not in the least ashamed," she said staunchly. But she was oddly grateful to him all the same. After a moment she added even more unwillingly, "You were wounded?"

He glanced indifferently down at his arm. "It is nothing. A sabre cut is all."

"Did you serve in Spain under Wellington?"

"I did—and most devoutly wish I were back there!" he said surprisingly. "Napoleon's troops seem simple by comparison. Which way do I turn here?"

She told him, but for once the captain seemed to be in luck, for when they reached her elderly friend's house, it was dark, and no light showed, even at the upper windows. Sorcha was puzzled, for she did not think even so redoubtable a lady could simply have gone to bed in the face of a British attack.

But the captain said cheerfully, "No one is here. It seems clear she at least has had the good sense to leave already. I can only thank heaven for even such small mercies."

Sorcha was less certain and insisted upon going to knock on the door. He helped her down resignedly, merely commenting mockingly, "If your elderly friend should happen to be at home after all, don't hesitate to accept an invitation to take tea with her, while she packs up all her household belongings and half of her plate. My time is wholly at your disposal, ma'am."

Sorcha ignored his sarcasm, but he insisted upon going to the door with her, though she warned him that he might find himself shot by the ever vigilant Cato. "At this point nothing would surprise me, ma'am," he retorted and forcefully pulled the bell.

But no shot sounded, and no one came to the door, even though he rang again, and even plied the door knocker with considerable force.

After a few minutes Sorcha was obliged to turn away, hoping worriedly that Miss Danville had been convinced by the devoted Cato to leave already, and was not lying inside unconscious from smoke inhalation or worse. But there seemed very little smoke in that part of town, and all the curtains were tightly drawn, so that she could not even peer in at any of the windows. Short of breaking into the house, she did not see how she could get in to check for herself.

"I can only assume she has already gone to safety," she said unwillingly, not sounding convinced.

"As I said, heaven be thanked for small mercies, ma'am," he said. But then he took a look at her and added, somewhat to her surprise, "Still, despite the ever vigilant Cato, I think I had best endeavor to make sure. After all, the crime of breaking and entering seems almost natural to me after a mere half hour spent in your company."

He disappeared around the corner of the house and was gone for some minutes. No shot sounded, but he was gone long enough that she had begun to grow nervous. Then without warning he startled her very much by reappearing suddenly, as if conjured up

out of the shadows. "No, the house really is empty," he said in relief. "I encountered no elderly ladies nor black servants with shot-
guns. Does that satisfy you?"

"Yes. And . . . thank you," she added grudgingly.

He gave her a surprisingly charming smile and helped her back
into the cart.

They soon reached the outskirts of town, where it seemed the
entire British army must be camped, for Sorcha had never seen
such a seemingly endless sea of makeshift tents, their campfires
showing almost as far as the eye could see. It looked a peaceful
enough scene, but Sorcha suddenly shivered and was glad of her
formidable escort. Bravado or no, she would not have liked to
have driven through that camp of enemy soldiers on her own.

As it was, they were stopped almost at once, just outside the
town, by a rough-voiced sergeant who barred their way at musket
point. Then, with a distinct sense of shock, he seemed to recognize the driver of so curiously laden a cart and smartly saluted.

"Beg pardon, sir!" he said stiffly in broadest Cockney. "Din't
recanize you for a moment, sir!"

"It's quite all right, Sergeant. I don't recognize myself," said
the captain "Is the road clear to Bladensburg?"

The sergeant scratched his nose. "Not to say clear, sir," he answered doubtfully. "We saw no need to secure it, if that's what
you mean, for it's likely the Yanks are still running."

The captain glanced at Sorcha's set face and drove on.

They encountered a good many curious stares as they drove
through the camp, but with the captain driving no one dared to as-
sault them. Sorcha looked straight ahead, still bridling from that
last remark, and very aware she was surrounded by her enemy,
who had harassed and frightened the countryside for more than a
year now, and had that very day committed an inexcusable act of
retaliation against a defenseless town.

But at last they were through. There, too, they were challenged;
only this time the captain got down, and Sorcha accepted the reins
from him, telling herself firmly that she would be glad to see the
last of him. Nor was she in the least afraid to go on by herself;
that went without saying.

But instead of taking his leave of her, as she had fully expected
him to do, the captain engaged in a low-voiced conversation with
the sentry there, a corporal this time, who had saluted him re-

spectfully and seemed even more surprised at his unlikely companions.

She could hear little of what was said, and though there was a certain gulf in the pit of her stomach, she tried to convince herself it was merely because neither she nor Dessy had been in any mood for dinner that night—or lunch either, if the truth be told.

At last the captain came back and stood looking up at her for a moment. She began to take off his coat to return it to him, but he said shortly, "No, keep it! I don't want a mutiny on my hands on top of all else. Corporal Wilkins tells me there are sorties of American soldiers all along the road between here and Bladensburg," he told her bluntly. "Your chances of getting through are almost nonexistent."

She lifted her chin stubbornly. "Nevertheless, I will still take my chances, thank you."

He sighed, as if it was no more than he had expected her to say. "Let me be even blunter, ma'am. The chances of your father being in the town are slight, for we are still in possession of it." He did not bother to add what she could all too easily infer on her own. If her father were still there, he was either dead, severely wounded, or a prisoner. And the British were not known for their kindly treatment of prisoners.

"None of this changes my mind, Captain." After a short struggle with herself she said with reluctance, "I would be grateful if you would add to your kindness by writing me a note of safe passage so that your men will admit me when I get there."

"I would and gladly," he answered impatiently. "But that will hardly protect you from your own soldiers, ma'am! I hesitate to remind you, but it was one of your own countrymen who was attacking you when I first came on the scene. Nor are soldiers the world over known for their gentle manners."

"If you are trying to frighten me, you will not succeed," she said coldly. "Besides, you have left me with little choice, remember."

"Stop saying that!" he protested irritably. "I neither ordered nor had anything to do with the burning of the town. But you might with perfect safety return to your elderly friend's house, or any one of the vacant ones in the town. What you are proposing is madness."

"Yes, with one of your stout guards. I have not forgotten," she countered scornfully. "You will forgive me if I place little belief in your guard—or your word, Captain! Whatever you say, I am still determined to find my father."

"I only wish he were here now, and the responsibility for your safety were in his hands, not mine!" he retorted. "I have yet to decide, ma'am, whether you are remarkably brave, or merely remarkably foolish! Tell me, what is your name?"

It was so unexpected she could only frown suspiciously down at him. With a start she realized that he looked very different from the stern, disapproving soldier she had first encountered. There was quick humor in his face, as well as a certain rueful resignation, and his eyes smiled up at her with surprising warmth. "My name?" she repeated, oddly reluctant to give it for some reason. "Why? What has that to the purpose?"

"Nothing whatsoever. But still I would like to know it. What is it?" he persisted.

She raised her brows, but could think of no reason not to tell him. "It is MacKenzie. Sorcha MacKenzie."

"You are Scots?" he asked quickly. "With that hair I suppose I should have guessed. Moreover it explains a good deal. The Scots regiments were among the bravest of our troops in the Peninsula—and the most hardheaded! Well, Miss Sorcha MacKenzie," he said with wry humor, "it seems I am indeed as mad as you. And that we are stuck with each other for a while longer, at least. For I cannot continue to live with my conscience if I left you to fall into the hands of either the American or the British army, much as I might like to. And you may take my word for it, that is exactly what would happen. You are too tempting a morsel, for all your stubborn independence, and I shudder to think what might happen to you. I will escort you at least as far as Bladensburg. And God help me, for I have a feeling I am going to need it."

She opened her mouth to argue, but to her immense surprise Dessy forestalled her, saying with quiet dignity, "Thank you, Captain. We will be glad of your escort. Now hesh up, chile, and thank the captain. My name is Dessy, by the way, and I am much obliged to you, sir. My husband, too, is with the senator, and I am anxious to see that he is all right."

Sorcha closed her mouth in bemusement and said no more. Dessy rarely asserted herself, especially in front of strangers. When she did, both Sorcha and Magnus usually admitted defeat at once, for no one could be more stubborn or more determined. Besides, she felt suddenly ashamed, for in her concern for Magnus, she had forgotten Dessy's own worry for Ham.

The captain blinked, as if astonished by such sudden docility on Sorcha's part, and then unexpectedly grinned. "You are welcome, ma'am. And I am glad to see that there is someone Miss MacKenzie will listen to."

He then took the reins again from a bemused Sorcha and climbed back into the cart, saying casually to the sentry, "If General Ross should happen to inquire where I am, Corporal, inform him I have escorted a lady to find her father in Bladensburg. I don't know quite when I will be back."

"S-sir?" stuttered the corporal, clearly shaken. "I mean, yes, sir! As you say, sir!"

Ignoring his obvious astonishment, the captain calmly drove on.

In many ways it was a journey even stranger than the one they had already accomplished. The fire of the city could be seen as a red glow behind them, but once away from it the road was dark enough. Now and then Sorcha caught a furtive movement in the dark at the side of the road and wondered if it were some wounded American soldier. But they encountered few stragglers on the road, and those the captain dealt with summarily, obliging Sorcha to own that she was glad enough of his escort, despite her dislike of his high-handed manners.

Once a drunken backwoodsman melted out of the shadows to demand a ride, claiming to be tired and half-dead. When the captain curtly refused, pointing out that the cart was clearly full, the man abruptly became ugly.

For answer the captain coolly drew his pistol and faced him down. "There is no room as you can see," he said again. "You have had your marching orders. Not get moving!"

The backwoodsman tried appealing to Sorcha instead. "I bin walking fer hours, ma'am," he whined. "Iff'n you'd throw that darkie out, there'd be room. Or thet mongrel! Ain't a man worth more to you'n a mongrel or a darkie?"

Sorcha's own ready sympathy instantly dried up, and she was glad when the captain ignored him and drove on, though she had to resist the urge to look fearfully over her shoulder for another half mile or more.

But in the face of the captain's obvious impatience, she found herself trying to excuse him. "I daresay he is very tired. He must be one of the militia pressed into recent duty," she said defensively.

The captain glanced at her. "If so, the only reason he has for being tired is from running so far and so fast when he found himself under fire."

Sorcha was instantly indignant at the implied slur. "What did you expect against such seasoned troops?" she demanded furiously. "Two-thirds of our so-called soldiers were working their farms a week ago."

He sighed, as if regretting his words. "I'm sorry. I certainly meant no contempt. Your troops were hastily raised, ill trained, and even more poorly equipped. Against seasoned troops, as you say, they stood not a chance. Even so, some of your sharpshooters were among the most determined and accurate fire I've ever experienced. They were also damn fools, holding on long past the point of reason, but I have seldom held that against any troops."

For comfort it was but gloomy cheer, but she was both surprised and grateful to him for his words, little though she might wish him to guess it.

The backwoodsman was by no means the last they encountered to have consoled himself with liquor. One, little more than a boy, in begging a ride broke down and wept, claiming he had not rested nor eaten since the day before, and that he was wounded as well.

He certainly had a bloodstained bandage tied round his arm, and left to herself, Sorcha might have given in to his importunities. But the captain said coldly, "If you are seriously wounded, there are doubtless any number of houses along this road where you may claim aid. And you may always return to Bladensburg, where you can get medical help."

The boy suddenly straightened and spat in the dust at his feet. "From the redcoats?" he sneered. "Ye're a goddamned limey bastard yerself, if you ask me! I should shoot you where you stand."

"I wouldn't advise it," said the captain and drove on without a backward glance.

Sorcha couldn't help shivering a little and had to make herself sit as boldly upright as the captain beside her.

But no shot sounded, as she had half feared, and after she felt the danger had been left behind, she could not resist asking stiffly, "How did you know he would not shoot you in the back?"

"If he'd had the nerve to shoot me, he would have done it from the beginning, without stopping us and asking for a ride," he answered coolly. "There was little danger."

She began to develop a grudging new respect for her escort. She did not like to admit that she herself had gone through a few bad moments, and that even now her heart was beating a little rapidly.

Elsie and her baby had both long since fallen into an exhausted sleep. Even the dog had curled herself up tightly against the black girl for warmth and comfort, no doubt, and though clearly in a good deal of pain, seemed to have constituted herself in some part their guardian, for she had growled weakly each time they had halted, and only curled up again, with a whine, when all danger seemed past.

Dessy seldom spoke her mind except when members of what she considered her family were the only ones present to hear her, but it seemed clear that for some reason she had awarded this enemy captain her respect, for she said now, repressively, "The captain's right. You don' want to regard them, Miz Sorcha."

Sorcha was astonished, but again remained silent. She was relieved when they at last reached Bladensburg without further incident. It had been an extremely long and wearing day, and an even longer night, and she dreaded to discover what lay at the end of it. Not that she had any intention, of course, of admitting as much to the captain. Or that she was beginning to regard with considerable dismay the time when their formidable escort, enemy though he may be, at last abandoned them to their own resources.

She had full confidence in her own courage and ingenuity, of course. That went without saying. Magnus had never allowed her sex to serve as an excuse for weakness or lack of resolution and had always expected her to take care of herself. He was more inclined to box her ears for missishness than to want to wrap her up in cotton wool.

Besides, with any luck she soon would find Magnus, and Ham, or even Geoff. What she was to do if she did not was something she had not yet allowed herself to think about.

Chapter 6

As they approached the town, they were again challenged, but the captain answered briskly, "I am Captain Ashbourne, of the Eighty-fifth! Is Captain Ferriby still in charge here?"

The sentry came out to examine them more closely from the shadows. "Gor-blimey!" he exclaimed. "It is you, sir!" He, too, peered doubtfully at the wagon and its unlikely occupants, but said merely after a moment, "Aye, Captain Ferriby's still in charge, though I don't doubt he's asleep, sir."

"Then we'll wake him!" said the captain with ruthless cheerfulness. The further they had come from Washington the more his mood had improved, for some reason. In fact, he was hardly recognizable as the same man who had so grimly and reluctantly taken on their charge. "Nothing stirring, Sergeant?"

"Nossir, bar a spot of confusion when a pig was found hidden in a cellar, and a bunch o' the boys mistook it for a Yank, sir!" He grinned, stocky and tough-looking. "But the enemy was dispatched without further ado and was put to good use, sir, for I had a bit of it for me own supper. Come to think of it, it's the best meal I've had since we left France, sir!"

The captain laughed. "I'm glad to hear it. Carry on, Sergeant."

The latter saluted and told them cheerfully where Captain Ferriby was quartered in the village, again cautioning them that likely they'd find him asleep. Sorcha had developed enough knowledge about her escort by then not to doubt that he would rouse that unfortunate officer out of his bed without the least compunction, but luckily they found the captain in question standing outside his hastily commandeered quarters, smoking a cigar.

The sight of his fellow officer in such company also seemed to astonish him. "Ash!" he exclaimed. "By all that's holy! What brings you here?" He, too, took in the mixed nature of the passengers in the cart and began to laugh. "Good God!" he added. "I might have known. What the devil are you up to now?"

"Escort duty!" said Captain Ashbourne dryly. "Miss MacKenzie here is looking for her father."

"Is she? I mean . . . beg your pardon, ma'am! How do you do?" faltered the captain, peering curiously up at her in the dark. He added with a puzzled frown, "Are they all looking for wounded relations?"

"Not all of them. Unfortunately Miss MacKenzie has insisted upon rescuing every stray human or animal who crosses her path. This is her maid, by the way, whose husband is also missing. The child in her arms, and the poor creature in the cart, as well as the dog, are all objects of Miss MacKenzie's pity."

Captain Ferriby grinned, seeming much more human suddenly. He was a cheerful young man, subtly less decided in manner than his friend and much more approachable. "Oh! I see! How did she drag you in . . . I mean, where did you encounter her, Ash?"

"Your first conclusion was the correct one. You don't seriously suppose any of this was my doing, do you?" demanded Captain Ashbourne. "I stumbled across her while she was fighting off an extremely drunken American, who at the very least intended to commandeer her cart, and at the most, would not have been in the least unwilling to add Miss MacKenzie to his haul," said the captain, not mincing matters. "The mother and child and the wounded dog came afterward. In fact it is only due to the unexpected kindness of fate that we did not add an eighty-year-old woman and her butler to our menagerie, for someone else had already rescued them, I thank God."

Captain Ferriby was still grinning. "I see," he repeated again. "Well done, ma'am."

"Captain . . . Ashbourne exaggerates," said Sorcha coldly. "But I am indeed anxious to find my father, that much at least is true.

Do I understand you to have some wounded prisoners here, Captain?"

Captain Ferriby rolled an inquiring eye toward his friend, as if seeking assistance. "Oh . . . ah, yes, ma'am, but I must warn you it is not a pretty sight. Best let me make inquiries first."

"Oh, what does that matter?" she exclaimed impatiently. "Pray take me there at once."

Captain Ferriby still looked doubtful, but after detailing a man at Captain Ashbourne's request, to bring Elsie and her baby in and to find them something to eat, and shaking his head over the dog, before sending another astonished soldier to find some ointment for its burns, he led Sorcha across the town, followed by Captain Ashbourne and Dessy.

He said apologetically again as they went, "I am afraid you will find conditions pretty primitive, ma'am, but I promise you we have done all we can. And of course, once we leave, the Ya . . . I mean the Americans will be free to come in and take over their care."

"Thank you, Captain." Sorcha could scarcely hear what he said for the sudden pounding of her own heart. Before she had been wholly preoccupied with getting there, but now she found herself faced with the possibility of finding Magnus seriously wounded, or perhaps dying. That fact even overshadowed the continuing irony of finding herself in the company of enemy officers, who were going out of their way to serve her and behaved very much as if they had met in an ordinary social situation. One moment they were burning her home, the next escorting her with solicitation across an uneven ground, and warning her with real concern that she might not like the sights she was about to see. She thought she would never understand men.

Captain Ferriby was saying now, as if in an effort to distract her thoughts, "Well, we have been in the country scarcely a week, so I suppose I shouldn't have been surprised Ash is already up to his old tricks again."

That at least caught Sorcha's attention. "His . . . old tricks?" she repeated somewhat blankly.

"Lord, yes. He was famous in the regiment for his absurd rescues. Always had some lame . . . er . . . ." he trailed off in some embarrassment, remembering to whom he was speaking.

"Some lame duck in tow?" she finished his sentence for him. "You need not spare my feelings, Captain."

He grinned. "Sorry and all that. But it's true enough—though I must say you are the most decorative he's ever rescued to date. There was a whole family of Portuguese who had been dispossessed by the war, I remember. There were six or seven of them at least, and he dam . . . er . . . devilishly near supported the lot of them for a year or more. And that at a time when our own pay was in such arrears that we were all going about in rags. Sad case, really, and I don't mean to say that we weren't all sympathetic. But only Ash bothered to do anything about it. Bullied us into finding a house for them, and donating enough of our own meager stores to set them up in it. Never anyone like Ash to get others to do what they don't wish and end up thinking it was their own idea all the time."

Sorcha was more than astonished, for the story ill-accorded with Magnus's tales of the depraved British. "You're making that up," she accused, remembering Captain Ashbourne's resistance to her own earlier rescues.

Captain Ferriby grinned down at her. "Word of honor! Though mind you, that was one of his more reputable charities. There was also the time he adopted an orphaned goatherd. Even that didn't turn out so badly, come to think of it, for at least the regiment always had milk. But I don't know if you've ever been downwind of a herd of goats, ma'am? If so, you'll know what I mean. Despite the milk we were all deuced relieved when Diego—that was the boy's name—found his brother and went to live with him. And then there was the time he more or less adopted a whole village in Spain."

"I am sure Miss MacKenzie has no interest in my past crimes," remarked Captain Ashbourne from behind them.

In truth, Sorcha was not sorry he had put an end to the stories, for she was not sure she liked being reminded of the humanity of her enemy. It was strange enough to be here in the British camp, having to suffer their unexpected kindness without that being thrown in. Especially when she remembered again with a pang that less than twelve hours ago a battle had been fought in this very town where each army had tried to kill as many of the other as possible.

She shivered at the reminder and pulled the captain's coat, which she absentmindedly still wore, more closely around her. And when they reached the area where the prisoners were held, there was no time for anything but the horror and pity she was feeling.

Captain Ferriby explained somewhat apologetically that there was no room to house the prisoners indoors, but fortunately it was a warm night, so it was no real hardship. But she was scarcely listening. Even in the dark and from a distance the groans and smells were bad enough. But when the captain reluctantly held up his lantern so that she could begin her search, the sights she encountered very nearly overcame her resolve from the start. Men lay everywhere, some of them on makeshift beds, the others lying on the ground. Their plights brought swift tears to Sorcha's eyes, and soon made her thankful that she had had very little to eat that day, for fear she would have humiliated herself completely.

Everywhere she looked was some new horror, for she could not have imagined the reality of the aftermath of war. There were men with shattered limbs and gaunt gray faces, or ghastly wounds, and though some called out at sight of her, begging for water or laudanum, many more were too ill and apathetic to even turn their eyes away from the light of the lantern. She knew from the recruiting that too many of the volunteers had been young boys, excited and proud at answering their country's call, or older men like Magnus, and far too many of both seemed to be here. Boys too young to shave, let alone suffer so much for their country, and men far older than Magnus, grizzled and stoical.

She had to dash back the foolish tears, almost forgetting Magnus in the sheer volume of horror she had found. Her first instinct was to help them, but she had no skill at nursing and didn't even know where to start. She was not even aware that Captain Ashbourne had come quietly and taken her arm in a firm grasp until he said quietly, "It seems worse than it is. Our own doctors have seen to them, and all that can be done for them is being done, I promise you."

She shuddered and made no answer. Each time Captain Ferriby illuminated another gray face with his lantern, she feared to look, in dread that it would be someone she recognized. Magnus, Ham, Geoff, even someone else she knew personally might all be here, and she was limp with relief each time the face of a stranger looked dully back at her. And yet each must have a wife, mother, sweetheart, as anxious as she to know what had become of him.

Sorcha blindly reached for and gripped Dessy's hand, knowing she must be feeling much the same, for she was almost battered into insensitivity by the sheer volume of the suffering. Slowly they went on down the interminable rows, silent and pale with horror. She could have kicked herself for not having thought to bring bandages and medical supplies with her, or at the very least food and water. But when she said as much, Captain Ferriby said quickly, "It looks bad, I know, ma'am, but they really are being looked after. As Ash said, our own doctors have seen to them, once they had finished with our own chaps. I warned you it would be best for you not to come here. Bound to upset a delicately nurtured female like yourself."

"Upset!" she repeated incredulously and was ashamed that her voice broke. "*Upset?*" She thought that anyone with a conscience must be upset by the sights she had seen, whichever the side the suffering belonged to. Magnus had always told her the truth of war, not glossing over its brutalities, but he had never prepared her for anything like this. She no longer understood how he could have gone off so cheerfully to fight, knowing that this was the inevitable aftermath—how anyone could. For the first time in her life Sorcha seriously doubted her own courage.

"Yes, heaven forbid that a delicately nurtured female, as you say, should be upset by such unpleasant sights," she managed bitterly. "Oh, why did we not think to organize hospitals and gather medical supplies, Dessy! At the very least it would have been something to do, not just sitting around in such dreadful suspense waiting for news."

Even Captain Ferriby found nothing to say to that, so they went on. Captain Ashbourne's grip had tightened on Sorcha's arm, so that he was half supporting her, though she was barely conscious of the fact. At each place where she mutely shook her head, his face grew a little grimmer, and when they had traversed the pitifully wide area and had not found any face she recognized, he said briskly, "I said you wouldn't find him. With any luck he is halfway to Virginia by now. Come on, let's get out of here."

She allowed herself to be led away, too swamped by relief to think of anything else for the moment. Her hand still clung to Dessy's, whose ordeal must have been at least as great as her own, and outside the dreadful makeshift hospital they halted briefly, both too overcome even for tears, which might have brought a certain measure of relief.

But when Captain Ferriby asked quietly over their heads, "What now, Ash?" she realized with a sense of shock that she herself had never allowed herself to think that far ahead. Her one stubborn goal had been to prove to herself that Magnus was not lying dead or dying; and she had not gotten to the point of thinking what she would do afterward.

Of course she had not looked at the bodies that must be gathered somewhere, or perhaps already hastily buried. But even she shrank from that ordeal, for she was not at all sure, in her present state, that she could endure it.

"Good God, you fool! Shut up!" said Captain Ashbourne with surprising violence, also speaking over her head. "Can't you see she . . . they . . . have endured about enough? How long has it been since either of you has eaten?" he demanded of Dessy, plainly not trusting Sorcha to answer with the truth.

Dessy weakly shook her head, probably like Sorcha unable to remember by then. Sorcha's own stomach threatened to rebel at the very thought of food, but she had sense enough to know she was going to need her strength. So, she weakly allowed herself to be shepherded back to Captain Ferriby's quarters, beyond making plans for the moment.

There they were given privacy to wash and freshen up, and Sorcha took in her appearance, too spent for any thoughts of vanity. The captain had been generous to call her tempting, however, for with her face smudged with smoke, and her hair whipped into a dark red tangle about her smoke-streaked face, she doubted many would find her attractive at the moment. She was beyond caring, but wearily washed her face and hands and allowed Dessy to do what she could to smooth out the worst of the tangles. Her hair had always been her bane, wild and thick and too blatant in color, refusing to adapt itself to the demure styles so much in vogue at the moment and now she was content merely to have it bundled out of her way.

The torn neck of her gown she could do little with, either, but Dessy managed to pin it up for her, so that she was at least fit to be seen. The captain's coat she determinedly folded and put aside to return to him, though it cost her an unexpected pang, for despite the heat of the night she felt cold and shivery for some reason.

When they returned to the main room, it was Captain Ashbourne who bullied and stood over them both until they had managed to choke down some dry bread and cheese and a bowl of hot soup of some kind, more sustaining than it was tasty and surprisingly full of onions. He also made each of them drink a glass of wine, which Captain Ferriby admitted cheerfully had been appropriated from the cellars of the house they stood in, owned it seemed by the mayor of the town. Sorcha remembered the story of the pig and could only be grateful they had not been offered any of the purloined pork, for she was quite sure she could not have gotten that down.

At last Captain Ashbourne said in a tone she suspected he used to bark orders to his men, "It is clear neither your father, nor your husband, ma'am, is here, as I told you from the start. Now we must think what is to be done with you. And no," he added harshly as Sorcha started to speak, "you are not going to remain to nurse your countrymen. I know you too well, my dear Miss MacKenzie, but I would be most surprised to learn either of you has any nursing experience, and they will be claimed quickly enough, I promise you, once we evacuate the town. It is equally clear you cannot return to Washington. But surely you must possess friends or acquaintances in the area? Someone you could go to until your father can rejoin you?"

Sorcha thought dully of Henry, no doubt safely asleep in his own bed at the moment. It did not help to be obliged to acknowledge that he had been right and she wrong. If she had accepted his invitation in the first place, she would have been spared all that she had gone through that day and night, which he would no doubt be pleased to point out to her.

But it seemed the hot soup had been helpful after all, for at least a little of her spirit was returning. Experience was always useful, as Magnus was fond of pointing out, and even for all its alarms and horrors, she was not sure she would have traded the night's various adventures to sit and make polite and meaningless conversation with Henry's colorless sister and to try to pretend she was not on pins and needles for news of Magnus. She had been angered, alarmed, terrified and horror-stricken, in roughly that order, and little of which she had enjoyed at the time. But the alternative was to accept Henry's view of the world—and no doubt Captain Ashbourne's as well—that females were to be sheltered from the more harsh realities of life and made to sit at home sewing while history took place all about them.

She stiffened, thinking that she would be damned if she would meekly go to Henry's now, to endure his lectures and his smug I-told-you-sos. In fact her first goal must still be to try and find

Magnus. He might guess she had gone to Henry's and look there for her, especially when he learned of the fate of Washington. But far more likely—

She lifted her head, knowing suddenly exactly what she meant to do. Magnus must still be alive—she would not let herself believe otherwise. And she knew where Magnus would expect to find her. It was the first place he would go, to lick his own wounds in private, for she had to belatedly acknowledge a fact she had known but until now had refused to admit. If the British had won this battle, the progress of the war might be very different from now on, and Magnus was likely to be taking it hard. With his typical confidence and energy, he had thought he only had to appear on the battlefield to overcome months of mismanagement and delay, and almost comical misdirection by those in power.

Yes, his mood would be very bitter, and he would be almost frantic to find her as well. And in those circumstances she knew he would go home, to Annapolis. The Washington house had never been home to either of them, merely a place they had bought when Magnus had been elected to the Senate; and though she had been furious at the house's wanton destruction, she had shed no particular tears over its burning.

But suddenly, like Magnus, she wanted to be home with all her heart, and was impatient at the thought of the time it would take her to get there. She would go to Annapolis, and not even the many miles that lay before her, or the obstacles she might yet encounter, could alter the instinctive leap of her heart at the thought of being home. She would be safe there, and Magnus would be waiting, and she could begin to forget the horrors she had seen that day.

Unfortunately, she would have nothing but her own wits and courage to rely upon, this time, for she would no longer have the captain's formidable if resented protection. But she stubbornly refused to admit that Henry was right after all, and in the first test of her strength and courage she would forget all her much-vaunted principles and look for a man to rely on. After all in the early days of her country, women had struggled right along with their men, fighting Indians and disease and starvation as Miss Danville had done. In comparison to that, a journey of some fifty miles over country that might or might not be occupied by enemy forces seemed a mere bagatelle.

Chapter 7

But when she calmly announced as much, Captain Ferriby looked astounded, and Captain Ashbourne even more thunderstruck. Nor did he hesitate to issue a flat veto. "Don't be ridiculous, ma'am!" he snapped, returning to some of his earlier impatience. "It is completely out of the question. I have abetted you this far, but what you are proposing is lunacy. Aside from the fact that you would be more or less heading in the direction of a contingent of our own troops, the countryside must be crawling right now with wounded or desperate men of the stamp I would have thought you had already seen far too many of tonight."

"I thank you for your opinion, Captain," said Sorcha lifting her chin in a way that Magnus, at least, would have recognized as a sign of distinct danger. "And . . . grateful though I must be for your earlier escort, do you imagine that gives you any right—*any* right!—to dictate to me?"

Both captains exerted themselves to the utmost to dissuade her, Captain Ashbourne, at least, in increasingly graphic terms, but Sorcha was scarcely attending. The notion of Annapolis as a safe haven had taken a firm hold in her mind, and besides, even more important, she knew instinctively it was the place Magnus would go to look for her. Besides, the alternative, to drive through the countryside aimlessly searching for him was too daunting a prospect even for her. To make for home, she knew stubbornly, was the only sensible conclusion.

Captain Ferriby, far less dictatorial than his friend, at last said helplessly, "I can see you are determined, ma'am. But is it wise?"

"No, it is extremely foolish, as I have just been at pains to point out to her," answered Captain Ashbourne harshly. "But my experience of Miss MacKenzie to date shows me that reason does not figure largely in her actions. How goes it to the rear, Lucy? Any action?"

Captain Ferriby seemed grateful for so neutral a topic. "Not much. Word is there was some skirmishing a day or so ago on the Potomac south of the capital. But the Yanks . . . er . . . the Americans scuttled their own boats, and I understand most of them were engaged here. So far as I know it's quiet enough—though that doesn't mean it's safe for Miss MacKenzie to drive through," he added hastily, clearly afraid of undermining his own argument. "Seriously, ma'am, Ash is right, you know," he added to her. "We've a sortie or two out ourselves, but we are likely to be the least of your problems. Word is the Yanks . . . I mean the Americans . . . Well, I'm afraid there's no way to wrap this up in clean linen, ma'am. Your army was wholly disorganized after the engagement today, and I understand many of them fled and are hiding out both to the east and west of here. What I mean to say is, not a situation for a young and gently bred woman like yourself—especially with no male escort. In fact, you'd do better to remain here in lieu of any better solution. I'll turn this house over for your use, and you can be comfortable enough. If you are still determined to reach Annapolis, you may travel under our escort in a few days' time."

She wondered why they persisted in believing themselves a haven for her. "Thank you for your offer, Captain," said Sorcha sardonically. "But to travel in the tail of the . . . British Army is an honor I fear I must decline. Nor can I afford to wait a few days upon your convenience. My father will be as anxious to find me as I am to find him."

"Save your breath, Lucy," said his friend. "Miss MacKenzie is as stubborn as she is foolish and is clearly bent upon making a martyr of herself!"

"I am nothing of the kind!" she retorted, irritated. "Besides, as I have already pointed out on more than one occasion, it is none of your affair what I may choose to do. I am not a Spanish goatherd, a dispossessed Portuguese family, nor any other of your lame ducks. In fact, I recommend you wash your hands of me as you have been longing to do from the outset. After all, in light of all that has happened in the last few days, the fate of a few Americans can scarcely matter to you."

Captain Ashbourne closed his lips even more tightly on a retort. He, too, had cleaned up and looked surprisingly presentable. His hair in the lantern light and out from under his shako was revealed to be a light brown with a tendency to curl that the temperature and the day's exertions had done little to discourage. His eyes were the clear blue she had already noted, and his face was seen to be firm but humorous—though at the moment he looked anything but amused—with a stubborn mouth and an assertive nose, both of which accurately reflected his inclination to have his own way. His complexion was brown, no doubt from so many years spent out in the open in hot climes, and all in all, if Sorcha had met him under different circumstances, she was obliged to own she would probably have liked him.

As it was, kind though he had been, she could not manage to forget that he was her enemy. They might find their actions that day all in a day's work, but she could not.

When Captain Ashbourne, his face grim, made no answer, his friend Ferriby looked between them in some interest and said with the no doubt admirable intention of relieving some of the tension, "Which reminds me. I've been meaning to ask you, Ash. What the devil's been going on in Washington? Looks like the entire city's on fire from here. Did you meet with resistance?"

"I can answer that," said Sorcha contemptuously. "No, you met with no resistance. Most of the residents had long since fled. But even so, your soldiers systematically put as much of the city to the torch as they could manage. My own home was burned from beneath me, which is the reason I am now forced to remove to Annapolis."

Ferriby's amiable face revealed astonishment, and he looked quickly to his friend as if for corroboration. "It's true enough," said Ashbourne curtly. "Ross and three hundred handpicked men set fire to the public buildings."

Captain Ferriby surprised Sorcha even more by exclaiming hotly, "You can't be serious! I heard something of the sort was in the wind, but I wouldn't believe it. Well, I never thought I'd be ashamed to wear this uniform, but I am tonight! Why didn't you stop Ross, Ash, especially seeing as you're his ADC?"

"*Acting* ADC. It is becoming a more and more important distinction. And I argued with him to the point of insubordination, I promise you." He sounded unexpectedly bitter. "Unfortunately, he is wholly under Cockburn's thumb at the moment. It was done in retaliation for the burning of York, if you please. And you are right to be ashamed of your uniform tonight."

"I should think so! It's—dash it! It's unheard of!" Captain Ferriby's pleasant face was full of anger.

"It is damnable!" said Captain Ashbourne, not mincing matters. "Why do you think I am escorting Miss MacKenzie? Without, I might add, my superior's leave or even his knowledge. If this is the way the American war is to be conducted, I shall indeed regret my decision to volunteer for duty here instead of going home."

"And you say Ross agreed to this?" Ferriby seemed not to be able to get over it. "Well, I was beginning to lose all respect for him after his earlier vacillations, but this is the outside of enough. He served under Wellington, too! Catch Old Hookey laying waste to a city that had offered up no resistance! If nothing else, he knew very well that we were likely to need their goodwill in the future. And besides, damme if it don't go against all the rules of war! I beg your pardon, ma'am, but it's no wonder you are upset. I shall begin to regret I came as well if this is how it's going to be. And as if that weren't bad enough, to think of the Invincibles taking orders from the navy is enough to make a fellow want to sell out immediately and go home to raise pigs!"

Sorcha was looking between them in growing doubt and astonishment. "Let me understand this," she interrupted, frowning. "Are you trying to convince me that you don't *approve* of his having burned the city?" she demanded skeptically.

Captain Ferriby was inclined to be indignant. "There ain't no *trying* about it. Of course we do not! We never behaved in so shabby a fashion in the Peninsula, and, begging your pardon, ma'am, we'd far better reason there, for your troops are no match for us. Damme, it's poor enough sport as it is, without this. Half your soldiers ran before the first shot was fired this afternoon, and the rest had not the least notion of military tactics. It's almost like shooting fish in a barrel. I've little enough taste for it already, without adding this disgrace to our record!"

Sorcha looked searchingly at Captain Ashbourne, trying to read his expression. His face looked grim, his eyes were bloodshot, and he needed a shave. He looked, in addition, tired, dispirited, and bitterly proud and angry. If he did feel as he seemed, it explained much that had earlier puzzled her. His stiffness and anger when he had first come upon them, a mood that only gradually lightened as they put the burning city behind them. Even his insistence upon helping them had obviously been an effort to make up for his shame at what his troops were doing. And if all that were true, it seemed her ideas were being turned upside down that night.

"Do you feel the same?" she asked him searchingly and read the answer on his face. "Then why didn't you say so, instead of sitting there like a . . . like a cold fish and looking so grim—and, I might add, letting me blame you for something you had no control over?" she added with justifiable resentment.

It was again Ferriby who answered. "It's little wonder he was looking grim, ma'am. I would have done the same. You must know that Ash here tried to talk them out of the whole misguided campaign in the first place. Washington was no military target and held no strategic importance to us, as Ash pointed out to them from the start."

"Good Lord, then Magnus was right!" she exclaimed involuntarily. "He said from the first Baltimore would be your target, not Washington."

Captain Ferriby nodded. "I don't know who Magnus may be, but he was right, ma'am. The whole was designed to teach you Yankees a lesson. But if you ask me, it's one we're likely to regret in the long run."

"Extremely likely," said Ash with impatience. "But talking pays no toll. Can Miss MacKenzie get through if she is still so set on this madness? Are the roads clear at least?"

"Oh, they're clear enough," answered Ferriby. "But that's a different thing from saying she can get through. You're not seriously thinking of allowing her to make the attempt, are you?" he demanded incredulously.

The realization that they disapproved of the British action in burning the town almost as much as she did had shaken Sorcha and gone much to soften her toward her present companions. But she stiffened again at the suggestion it was up to them to allow her to do anything.

But before she could say so, Captain Ashbourne again managed to confound her by beginning to laugh helplessly. "I may be mad, but I am not yet that mad. I am going with her, of course. Between our soldiers and hers, and whatever objects of pity she may meet on the road and decide to rescue, it should make for an interesting journey, at least. In fact, I am beginning to think I wouldn't miss it for the world."

Captain Ferriby seemed unsurprised by the news but Sorcha stared suspiciously, wondering if he was indeed mad. She was not averse to his continuing escort—in fact, she had been acknowledging for some time that she would sorely miss it. But they were still enemies, and surely he had his own duties to attend to. "If you are indeed ADC to General Ross, won't you be missed?" she demanded skeptically.

Captain Ashbourne's grin widened, making him suddenly look much younger and approachable. "Why else do you think I am coming with you, you absurd little fool?" he asked. "In case you haven't guessed by now, I am somewhat . . . displeased with my commanding officer at the moment. I have every hope that my continued absence may pay him back at least in part for the inadvisability of ignoring my advice. If he is so fond of naval company, let him endure it for a while in unalloyed pleasure."

Captain Ferriby was grinning reluctantly, too. "No use protesting, ma'am," he told her. "Once Ash has made his mind up to something, there's never any talking him out of it. Devilish stubborn, you know. In fact, Ross is greatly to be pitied, though he don't know it yet. *I* wouldn't be in his shoes for anything you could name.

Even so, Sorcha felt obliged to try and talk him out of it, though with indifferent results. He would only say that he refused to have her fate on his conscience, and besides, she had best be grateful for his decision, for without his escort she was not stirring a step.

That of course put up her back again, but she finally gave in, secretly more relieved than she cared to reveal to be overborne. Captain Ashbourne might be many things, most of them infuriating, but he was a more than reassuringly formidable escort.

Captain Ferriby also seemed resigned, though he urged them at least to spend what remained of the night in comfort. But Sorcha was increasingly anxious to have the journey over, and for once Captain Ashbourne seemed to agree with her. No doubt he thought, as she did, that even with his escort, traveling at night was likely to be safer than the daytime, for they were less likely to encounter roving bands of either army.

So it was that their ill-assorted party was soon loaded up again. Captain Ashbourne did balk a little when he discovered she meant to take Elsie and the baby with her, and even the dog. He argued with some force that the girl might be returned to her home by a military escort when she was more fit to travel; and the dog could easily remain in the town, where it was likely to be adopted when the Americans returned.

But Sorcha pointed out just as stubbornly that Elsie's master's home lay almost directly on their way, and she would be terrified if left among British soldiers, which was undoubtedly true. As for the dog, now that the worst of her wounds had been treated and she had eaten an excellent meal of scraps, so the shy private who had been detailed to look after her reported, there was no reason why she could not travel on with them. Besides, from the looks of her she was to have her puppies any day and caught in the confusion between two armies, was unlikely to find much sympathy for her plight.

Captain Ashbourne seemed to have given up protesting, for he merely shook his head and admitted defeat. He did suggest, however, that Dessy should get into the back with the girl. Sorcha, after a quick look at her exhausted face, made no objection, for she was struck with sudden doubt and guilt. Dessy was no longer as young as she once was. Perhaps it had been a mistake to drag her along on such a journey. -

It was too late for repining, however, and Sorcha knew Dessy well enough to know she would have refused to permit Sorcha to stir a foot without her. Dessy, however, agreed to the captain's suggestion with a meekness that either was a sure sign she was indeed at the end of her strength—or else had accepted the captain's authority without reservations, a piece of perfidy Sorcha had not believed her capable of.

Sorcha commandeered more blankets from the obliging Captain Ferriby, hoping that both the girl and Dessy, not to mention the baby, would sleep most of the journey if wrapped up warmly enough. The dog was lifted onto the front seat beside Sorcha by the grinning young private, and they were finally ready.

Captain Ferriby gave them a rueful salute, and Captain Ashbourne gave another of his disconcerting laughs. "If I'm not back within two days, Lucy," he said in amusement, "you'll know I'm either dead or have been embroiled in another of Miss MacKenzie's absurd rescues. In either case, give me up for lost, for it will undoubtedly amount to the same thing."

"And if Ross court-martials you?" inquired his friend resignedly.

"He shall be doing me a favor. Don't let him burn this village down about your ears if you can help it. Once would seem to be enough, even for him. See you in a few days."

As they drove on through the sleeping village, Sorcha inquired curiously, "Will you be court-martialed?"

"God knows. It needn't trouble you, ma'am. It doesn't me."

He baffled her, for she still didn't know what to make of him. He was going out of his way—and risking a considerable amount it seemed—to do them a service, and yet she had no notion why. His excuse that he wished to punish his superior officer rang hollow, and though in any other man she might have suspected him of gallantry, the captain's only references to her appearance had been slighting ones. His friend had been far more appreciative, in fact. For the most part her present escort treated her as if she were no more than a slightly annoying, and not very bright child.

That was scarcely flattering, of course, but preferable to his becoming suddenly amatory, or trying to force his unwanted advances on her. Though, as to that, she acknowledged in amusement, it would be fairly puzzling were he to do so, with such an ill-assorted collection of chaperons. Then she remembered what she had looked like when she had first arrived in his borrowed coat, her face black with smoke and her gown torn, and was even more amused. The wonder was that even Captain Ferriby had looked at her in admiration.

She was cold and suddenly immensely weary and snuggled gratefully into the coat that he had insisted upon her taking again. There had been some sleepy murmuring from the back for a while, but now came nothing but the sounds of quiet breathing, indicating that all were asleep. The poor dog had crept closer to Sorcha on the seat and laid its head gratefully on her knee, before closing its own eyes wearily as well. It soon gave every sign of sleeping off the worst of the day's effects, not to mention the large meal it had just consumed.

Sorcha absently stroked its rough head, trying not to think of the horrors she had seen in the village or imagining Magnus in the same state. Despite all his energy and bravado, he was no longer young. What chance had he stood when even those boys had been so horribly wounded?

For the first time she squarely faced the fact that he might indeed be dead, and she gave an involuntary shiver, not knowing how she could face life without Magnus.

As if reading her thoughts, Captain Ashbourne said surprisingly, "Stop imagining horrors. Your father is fine and probably searching for you at this very moment. That you did not find him among the wounded is proof of that."

It was a mark of the depth of her exhaustion and fear that Sorcha betrayed the worst of her present nightmares. "I should have looked among the . . . bodies," she said with anguish. "What if he is lying there, even now, and I don't know it?"

His hand came quickly to cover one of her cold ones. "Don't think like that," he said roughly. "It was not even a very bloody battle. I'm sorry if you don't like it, but the truth is most of the Yankees fled before there could be many fatalities."

She didn't like it and only afterward wondered if he had said it merely to prop up her flagging spirits, knowing she would react angrily. "Magnus would never have fled!" she cried indignantly. Then as she realized the truth of what she said, added in a whisper, "Oh, God. That's why I am so afraid. You don't know how much he hates the British. He would never have run away. Never."

"The wiliest soldiers—and the Scots are those, God knows— know when to run away to fight another day," he told her calmly. "Your forces were hopelessly outnumbered and unprepared, and it would only be common sense to minimize your losses and prepare for the next time. Didn't you tell me your father had fought in the late Rebel . . . er, the Revolution? Well, there you are then. I understand that was one of your chief advantages in that war. In the middle of an engagement our own troops would suddenly find the enemy had simply melted away, with no sign of where they'd gotten and no trace of them. Then they'd pop up again at the most inconvenient moment. My own light troops are trained in much the same way, so I know what I'm talking about."

She made herself smile tiredly, knowing he meant to be kind. But at the moment her private horrors were too great for easy comfort. Her conviction that Magnus would return to the Annapolis house, at least once he learned of the fate of the one in Washington, had been strong and instinctive. But it was impossible to keep the sights and sounds she had seen that night at bay, or to convince herself that Magnus was any more invincible than those poor wretches.

"You don't understand," she said helplessly. "Ham is even older than Magnus. And then there is Geoff—so many others I know. The President, Mr. Monroe, even General Winder, ridiculous though he may have been. They all went off with such high hopes." Despite everything she could do, her voice broke.

He quickly glanced at her again, but said merely, "I'm afraid those are the realities of war. Ham is Dessy's husband?"

"Yes. Short for Hamlet." She answered absently, still trying to keep the dreadful pictures at bay.

But there was unexpected amusement in his voice as the captain said, "Let me guess—and Dessy is short for what? Desdemona?"

"Yes. Magnus was . . . is . . . fond of Shakespeare. Oh, God!" She bit her lip over her own betraying slip.

Again he unexpectedly put his warm hand over her cold ones. "Don't," he said gently. "I know you don't believe me now, but I've lost enough friends to know that it's no good anticipating grief. He will get to you if he can. And if he can't—well, I've seen enough of *you* by now to know that you will cope with it. He would be the last one to want you to tear yourself apart and lose your nerve at this late date."

She might bridle at the implied slur and move her hand after a moment, unwilling to appear weak before him. But even so, she was strangely comforted.

After a moment she said reluctantly, "You are an enigma, Captain Ashbourne."

He glanced down at her briefly in the warm dark. "How so, Miss MacKenzie?"

"I can't make you out," she admitted. "You are my enemy, and yet you have gone out of your way to help me. It might be different if I had been—"

"In the least grateful?" he finished for her in amusement. "Not to mention having saddled me with this ridiculous menage. We may be enemies, Miss MacKenzie, as you never seem to tire of pointing out, but you have a skewed notion of war, I suspect. I am at war with your government not private citizens like you. And don't bother throwing the last twenty-four hours up to me as you are no doubt longing to do."

"What a convenient cavil, Captain," she said bitterly. "And yet it is not the government who suffers and dies on battlefields, but innocent citizens like those I just saw. And it was not the government who will suffer from having their homes burnt out from under them and their livelihoods destroyed by your government's actions tonight."

He sighed. "I said private citizens, Miss MacKenzie. Soldiers must take their chances. And I am far from approving of what my own government did tonight. But it seems to me you are not much better. Are you seriously proposing to restore that poor child there to her master?"

That at least succeeded in rousing Sorcha from her present gloomy thoughts. "Of course I am," she said indignantly. "Not only it is illegal to do anything else, what would you have me do with her?"

"You surprise me," he remarked somewhat dryly. "I had not realized you would allow a little thing like the law to stand in your way. Besides, it has pleased you to be righteously indignant at our conduct this evening. As it happens, I am far from disagreeing with you. But allow me to point out in my country's defense that at least we outlawed slavery a number of years ago." He glanced over his shoulder toward the back of the cart, where the now-sleeping Dessy lay. "I find your possession of slaves slightly inconsistent with all your talk of freedom and liberty."

She sat up angrily. "Be quiet!" she hissed. "Do you want Dessy to hear you? She is no more a slave than you are. In fact, she is the closest thing I have to a mother, and I won't have her insulted by the likes of you. My father freed her long before I was born, and Ham as well, for he, too, finds slavery inconsistent with freedom and liberty. But as for that poor child back there and her baby, not only would I be breaking the law to spirit her away— which troubles me very little, I must admit! But I would be doing her no service, believe me. She knows no other life, and indeed, would in all likelihood not know how to go on if she were forced to shift for herself, particularly with a new baby. I am taking her to her home, and you may believe me that she regards it as such."

"The very fact that they abandoned her in the face of an invading army hardly argues that, Miss MacKenzie," he pointed out stubbornly.

She was even more indignant. "Elsie told Dessy how that happened. The cook had been left behind to look after her, but she fled in panic when the fighting started. Elsie was too weak to go

and so was left to shift for herself. When the fire started, she had
no choice but to drag herself out of bed and flee. Besides, if we
are casting blame, don't forget it was your country who set up the
slave trade in the first place, and made a great deal of money out
of it, I might add!"

She could see his flashing grin in the dark. "I knew I would regret starting this. I certainly refuse to discuss politics with you at
this hour, you ridiculous girl. But I also knew that nothing was
likely to jerk you out of such uncharacteristic despondency as
arousing your quick temper. You don't have red hair for nothing.
Now try and get some sleep. It has been an extremely long and
exhausting day, and likely to be an even longer night."

She rejected this advice with scorn. However high-handed he
might be, and however much he might be convinced he understood her, she had no intention of leaving him with the whole burden of their responsibility. Just because he was a man, he clearly
thought himself in charge, and that was a misperception she
would take delight in disproving as quickly as possible.

Still, he continued to confuse her. In fact, it was growing increasingly more difficult to remember sometimes that he was one
of the despised English that she had heard so much about all her
life. It was true that he was extremely annoying, and if he thought
her stubborn and used to getting her own way she returned the
compliment, for she had seldom met a man, apart from Magnus,
who was more intractable. Where Magnus stormed and blustered,
the captain was deceptively quiet and persuasive, but it had not
escaped her notice that he ended up prevailing through sheer per-
sistence more often than not.

But it was impossible to deny any longer that if they had met
under any other circumstances, she would have found herself
oddly drawn to him. In fact, he was very much like Magnus in
many ways. He was not as colorful and mercurial, and on the surface no two men could have been more different. But she was belatedly coming to recognize in the captain a certain recklessness,
zest for life, and a certain way of quietly appreciating the inevitable folly of others, that Magnus possessed in abundance. So
did she, perhaps, to a lesser extent. In fact, the captain and she
were more alike under the skin than she wanted to acknowledge,
enemies or no.

Even so, she did not mean to relinquish all responsibility for their safe passage. She was still very much in charge of her own fate, and she did not mean to let him forget it for one moment.

Still, despite this very praiseworthy resolve, it had been an extremely long and exhausting day as he said. She found it increasingly difficult to keep her eyes open and twice jerked herself awake just in the nick of time. She shook her head to clear it and sat up straighter on the hard seat, reflecting that it was indeed a mark of her emotional as well as physical tiredness that she was in any danger of falling asleep at all, for the wagon had not been built for comfort.

However that might be, the third time her eyes closed proved to be fatal. Her head drooped and found a convenient resting place; and this time she did not jerk herself awake in time.

She woke with a start some time later to two unpleasant realizations. The first was that her head was resting comfortably against the Captain's broad shoulder, to her intense embarrassment, with his arm warmly about her. And the second was that it was beginning to rain.

Chapter 8

Sorcha sat up with a jerk, her cheeks hot. "Good God! Why did you not wake me? How long have I been asleep?" she demanded guiltily. She had lost all sense of time, but it seemed to her that even with the gathering clouds the sky was not so dark. It must be near to morning.

He grinned down at her, looking very different from the grim-faced officer she had first met. If he had needed a shave before, he quite definitely did now, and he had removed his hot shako to allow the light rain to dampen his hair. "Not more than an hour," he told her cheerfully. "As for why I didn't wake you, you needed the rest. Besides, I find it distinctly safer when you're asleep, since you can scarcely be getting into any mischief for the moment. I was afraid the rain would disturb you, but since it has, take a look behind you. At least it is good for something."

She glanced back quickly, frowning and still half stupid with sleep. For a moment she didn't understand what he meant; then she saw that the glow in the distance that was the burning city, which had been a grim reminder most of the night, making an artificial sunrise where no sunrise should have been, was gone. In its place was only an unnatural darkness, as if the pall of smoke still hung suspended. The rain, which seemed to have started to the west, had clearly been providential in dousing what fire remained in the city.

She blinked again as she remembered the incredible happenings of the night, and would almost have believed she had dreamt them if it weren't for the presence of an enemy officer beside her, and her renewed clutch of fear for Magnus's safety.

More, with the coming light she became unwillingly conscious, as she had not been before, of how she must look—and that she was still huddled warmly into the captain's coat while he was getting decidedly wet.

The rain was still no more than a light drizzle, but she looked quickly behind to the occupants of the cart, and realized thankfully that they were warmly huddled in the blankets and were likely to be dry enough, unless the rain grew much heavier. The captain was another matter, however, and she said stiffly, "You are getting soaked. Take your coat back, please. I should have given it to you long ago."

He glanced down at her with a strange amusement in his eyes. "I think you had better keep it," he remarked. "It is no doubt safer for both of us."

But she was already stubbornly half out of it, refusing to still wear it. "No, I insist. You are wounded as well, a fact I somehow had forgotten. I should not have let you drive all this way. Let me take the reins, and you try and get a little sleep."

"My dear gir . . . My dear Miss MacKenzie," he corrected himself quickly with a grin, "it is the veriest scratch, I assure you. But I will confess that I have been sitting here wondering how in the devil I let myself be talked into this."

"You were not in the least talked into it!" she retorted indignantly, roused to her usual quick wrath. "As I remember, you insisted upon coming and threatened to lock me up if I would not agree to it."

"Well, at least in that case I had some sense remaining, for I couldn't in all conscience have let you embark on such a harebrained scheme on your own. I have also been wondering," he added in amusement, "if all American women are like you, though my mind somewhat boggles at the possibility, I must confess."

She ignored that. "No, of course they are not," she answered somewhat impatiently. "Any more than I suspect all English women are alike. Though from what I have heard, we are all at least a great deal more independent than British women seem to be."

"So it would seem," he agreed lightly. "In fact, I have been trying to imagine any of the women I know setting out on such an absurd adventure, and I confess I can't. Is it the newness of the country that is the difference, do you think?"

"Yes, I suppose so. Though even we are by no means as independent as we used to be. Miss Danville—the elderly lady whose house we stopped at—assures me that when she was a girl, women were considered every bit as strong as their men, and had to be. They fought Indians and toiled in the fields, and endured all the hardships and more that their menfolk did."

"It must have been an extraordinary life," he remarked in amusement, watching her face. "You sound as if you are sorry you missed it."

"I am. Both Magnus and Miss Danville say that much of the challenge and most of the fun have gone out of things now that we are getting so civilized and settled."

"Well, I wouldn't worry too much. It seems your own recent adventures could hardly be described as tame."

She shrugged and looked at him, unwillingly acknowledging another bond between them. "And what of you?" she inquired dryly. "You must have little liking for the safe, overcivilized world you came from, or you wouldn't be a soldier."

He laughed. "You are quite right. We are both misfits in a way, I suppose. I can't quite see you, for instance, looking at home in a ballroom, flirting with a fan and making polite conversation."

She grimaced. "No, I am not at home in a ballroom. I never learned to simper and murmur inanities and pretend that the man I am talking to, however much of a fool he may be, is uttering the most profound and brilliant of remarks."

He burst out laughing. "You didn't need to tell me that. I can see the drawbacks to being a female are clearly greater than I had realized. And what do your American men make of you, Miss Sorcha MacKenzie. Do they appreciate your outspoken independence?"

"No. I suspect they are at heart as conventional as you British. Magnus sometimes despairs of me, for my outspoken independence, as you call it, is inconvenient for him at times. But to give him his due, he has never tried to force me into a mold I dislike, or put the least restrictions on my actions."

"That also seems obvious, though I could wish, for my own

sake, that he had put a few more restrictions on your actions. Why do you call your father Magnus by the way?"

She shrugged indifferently. "I don't know. I always have. My mother died when I was small, and I can scarcely even remember her. It was always only the two of us. And Dessy and Ham, of course. Dessy complains that he let me grow up wild and should have made me learn to conform, but I am grateful to him. I would have loathed a childhood spent sewing samplers and playing on the pianoforte as other little girls my age were obliged to do. In fact, about the only thing Magnus ever punished me for was not disobedience or even outright sins, but for what he called missishness. He used to box my ears if ever I squealed or showed fear, and never let me use my sex as an excuse."

"He sounds . . . a most unusual father, but I suppose that explains a lot," he remarked thoughtfully. "What did you do instead of sewing samplers?"

Again she shrugged. "Largely whatever I wished. Geoff and I—my childhood friend—used to roam all over, limited only by Magnus's fiat that we were not to wander away from town, and I had to be home in time for supper. We used to get up at dawn to go out with the crabbing boats, or hang around the docks, hoping some ship fresh from an exotic port would come in. I doubt I ever returned home without my dress torn and my stockings around my ankles and my face filthy, but it merely amused Magnus, and Dessy was resigned by then." She looked at him sideways and added with deliberate malice, "We used to play at revolution when I was quite small. I always made Geoff play the bloody British."

It was his turn to grimace, but he laughed too. "I wonder why that doesn't surprise me. It has been clear from the outset that most Americans regard us as little better than the devil incarnate. It would be useless, I suppose, to assure you that most of us are quite human, and the Spanish and even the French used to be amazed that we actually paid for what we took and did our best not to lay waste to the country we passed through."

"It would," she agreed scathingly. "Magnus's father fought at Culloden. He himself well remembers the way you 'refrained' from laying waste to the Scots countryside, and I don't recall him ever mentioning any payment for what you took. Besides, I have just had my own demonstration of British so-called notions of *honor*, don't forget."

"Lord, why did I ever start this? All that was long before I was born—and your father as well, I suspect. And I approve of much of our dealings with Scotland no more than I approve of the burning of Washington."

"And yet you are a British officer," she pointed out even more scathingly.

"Yes, I am. You are a loyal American, and yet you told me you disapproved of your country's policy on slavery. One can love a country and not approve of everything that is done in its name. I thought that was the essence of democracy."

She discovered she was too tired for such arguments. "It is not the same at all. You are merely trying to confuse me," she said irritably.

He grinned. "What, don't tell me the stubborn and independent Miss MacKenzie is at last silenced? Is your father really a senator, by the way?"

"Yes. And I am not in the least silenced. I just don't wish to talk any more."

His grin grew, but he was obligingly quiet for a pace. Sorcha quickly discovered, however, that that was worse, for it gave her too much time to think.

In the end it was she who stirred and asked with rising if unwilling curiosity about his own life, "Have you always been a soldier?"

"Since I came down from Oxford, yes. I am a second son, you see, and so had my own fortune to seek. For which, I might add, I have always been very grateful."

She was about to treat him to a diatribe on the evils of the aristocratic system and particularly the custom of primogeniture, which left all to the son who, by a mere trick of fate, happened to be born first, and nothing to later siblings, who must fend for themselves. Then, after another look at his face, she prudently changed her mind.

He seemed to understand and be amused by her obvious inner struggle. But all he said was, "If you are really four-and-twenty—which I question, for you look absurdly young at this moment—why have you never married? In spite of your independence and awkwardness in a ballroom, I can't believe all American men are blind."

She was amused at that, despite herself. "You should be able to answer that yourself, Captain. You have not found your time with me exactly . . . restful, admit it."

He laughed aloud at that. "No. Restful is not the word I would choose to describe you, Miss MacKenzie. Infuriating, ridiculously stubborn, annoyingly independent, and willfully naive are words that come more readily to mind, I will admit."

She took offense to only one of those. "I am not naive!" she objected indignantly.

His shoulders shook again with laughter, but he repeated firmly, "Willfully naive, I believe the term was. You may be very far from a simpering and helplessly dependent female, my dear Miss MacKenzie, but you know far less of the world than you think you do—despite your unusual upbringing. But even though I am the first to admit you would be anything but a conventional wife, and a man would have to be brave indeed to try to take you on, you do possess one or two assets, you know. I won't believe you don't boast a number of determined suitors."

It was her turn to be amused. "Well, you're wrong, for I have exactly two. But I am most curious to know what these 'assets' you mention may be. You see, I am not used to your paying me compliments, Captain, however backhanded they may be."

He glanced down at her for a brief moment. "On the contrary, I have never denied that you are a most remarkable woman, Miss MacKenzie. Most of your virtues turn out to be defects as well, as it happens," he added in amusement. "But perhaps that is more common than we generally admit. You are remarkably brave, for one thing—though sometimes to an absurdly foolish degree. You are obviously intelligent as well—though unfortunately you do not always bother to use the brains you possess. All in all, and even taking your more annoying qualities into consideration, I will admit you are a surprisingly good companion."

But she could not resist breaking in at that. "Good God! This must be the smooth British flattery I have heard so much about. Or do you expect me to believe that you have found me a particularly good companion? If so, you have concealed the fact very well I must point out."

"You are mistaken," he returned calmly. "In fact, I shudder to think what this journey would have been like had I been saddled with any of your more missish peers—or most of the women of my acquaintance, for that matter. Don't misunderstand me. I am very far from approving of your father's methods in raising his only daughter. In fact, I have been comforting myself for some miles in imagining what I would like to say to him if he should turn out to be in Annapolis as you believe. But I will say one thing for him—and you. You are distinctly unlike any female I have ever met in my life, and that is decidedly a compliment."

She was taken somewhat off guard and covered it with one of her rallying speeches. "If a decidedly double-edged one as well, I notice!"

He smiled. "Then I will give you another," he said lightly. "However annoying you may sometimes be, you underestimate yourself most shockingly. In fact, I have never known a female less aware of her beauty—and don't bother denying that you are beautiful, for it is a waste of breath. You are not conventionally beautiful, I will admit, but I am not in the least blind, I assure you."

"Yes, and particularly after having seen me at my very best!" she countered scathingly. "But then why should I be surprised at receiving such a grand compliment? Perhaps I should cultivate a blackened face and torn gown whenever I wish to make an impression on anyone."

His mouth quirked slightly. "I suspect I am seeing you at your best, Miss MacKenzie—and a side of you that few are permitted to see. I count myself among the fortunate ones. But I take it you don't approve of grand compliments?"

"Of course I don't. Do you?"

"No, I don't suppose I do," he agreed appreciatively. "Which of your two suitors is given to grand compliments, I wonder?"

She was rather startled, but after a moment admitted in some amusement, "Henry. He clearly imagines that they please me, but nothing could be further from the truth."

"He sounds a fool. I at least hope your other suitor understands you better?"

She had no notion how they had gotten off on such a ridiculous topic, but her mouth curved involuntarily at the thought of Geoff, though with a pang she realized that she had no idea whether he were safe or not either. But she admitted softly after a moment, "No, Geoff is not into paying grand compliments. He and I grew up together, and he knows me very well indeed. It was he who usually had to play a British soldier in our games," she added mockingly.

He laughed. "Poor devil! He has my sympathy. Was he at Bladensburg as well?"

When she nodded reluctantly, he made no other comment, except to say dryly, "I gather he is the favorite in the marriage stakes?—though I take leave to doubt he is the husband for you if you have had the upper hand since you were children."

But she was no longer listening. Her attention had been distracted by the poor dog, whose head was still on her knee, and who was growing miserably wetter and wetter. Now the poor thing had begun to whine and tremble, and at first she feared its burns must be bothering it again. Then a second look informed her of the true state of affairs, and she could not resist saying in amusement, "I fear your trials are just beginning, Captain. For unless I am very much mistaken, this poor animal is about to give birth."

He stiffened. *"What did you say?"* he cried incredulously.

"I said, we are about to have puppies. And unless you wish to have them right here, I would suggest you pull over."

"You can't be serious!"

"Very serious. It seems that not even war deters Mother Nature. Let us hope that it is the poor creature's time, despite all her traumas, and not that she has gone into premature labor, for the puppies may not survive if so."

He glanced at her, amused despite himself. "You will forgive me for not being particularly alarmed by the prospect. You ridiculous girl, it was bad enough when you insisted upon bringing her along. Now you no doubt expect me to play accoucheur to a litter of newborn puppies, and then bring them along as well."

"Certainly," she said crisply. "We can't just leave them to die, poor things."

He sighed and obediently began to pull to the side of the road. "I take back everything I said before, Miss MacKenzie," he murmured ruefully. "I begin to think I wouldn't have missed this adventure for the world."

Chapter 9

The captain pulled off the road to the protection of some trees and lifted the obviously straining animal down and deposited it in a nest Sorcha made for it. Then, having been told that he was very much in the way, he grinned and retired to a convenient stump under the trees out of the rain.

The remaining occupants of the cart had awakened, and Dessy, ever practical, took in the situation at a glance. She then occupied herself by shaking out the quilt that had been protecting them from the rain, and proceeded to pull out a hamper of food. Even Elsie had roused slightly and sat up in the cart, cradling her baby and talking shyly with Dessy.

To Ashbourne Elsie seemed incredibly tiny, and her scrap of a baby scarcely made a bump among the layers it was wrapped in. But the infant would seem to have taken a surprisingly lusty grip on life, despite the circumstances of its birth, for it possessed a powerful set of lungs and had used them frequently during the journey.

The cry was always quickly answered by murmurs between Dessy and the girl and soon replaced by the sounds of contented grunts and suckling. Women never failed to amaze him, the captain thought. At one moment they could be paralyzed by panic, and the next calm and practical, as now, dealing with the ongoing realities of life as if that were all that mattered. And no doubt it was.

Sorcha's unembarrassed acceptance of such facts of life also amused and amazed him, for in his world, young unmarried ladies never so much as acknowledged that they knew such things existed, never mind spoke of them. Even married women did so only in euphemisms and in whispers. Now here was this remarkable girl not only displaying absolutely no embarrassment over the situation, but calmly proposing to play midwife to a mongrel bitch, as if that were all she had to worry about.

He shook his head and grinned again, not sorry to sit and stretch for a while. It had been a long twenty-four hours, to say the least, and he had had scarcely any sleep in the past forty-eight. The sooner he got Miss MacKenzie and her menagerie to safety, the better it would be, of course, but he supposed an hour's delay would make little difference.

Sorcha, of course, was at the moment wholly engrossed in petting and soothing the ridiculous animal and appeared blithely ignorant of the true dangers of their situation, caught between two armies and vulnerable to both. But Captain Ashbourne was all too grimly aware of them. Even assuming he could get her to safety in Annapolis, which was by no means certain, there was still the return journey to be made, and mopping-up operations afterward, once he was back with the regiment. Of the three that last was the least appealing, for he was finding it increasingly difficult to cope with a duty he was heartily sick of already.

Unfortunately, that was the reality, and this absurd adventure merely an amusing distraction. With luck he would deliver Miss MacKenzie to her father, and that would be the end of it. Certainly he was extremely unlikely ever to see or hear of her again.

For some reason that thought was not nearly so welcome as it would have been only a few short hours ago. He frowned over it, knowing the dangers of getting too involved with her, entertaining as she might be. Stubborn, courageous little fool! Any man would indeed be a fool to take her on permanently.

A yawn nearly cracked his jaw. God, he was tired—tired in a way that even the hardest-fought battle in the Peninsula had never left him, bone-weary and disgusted, with a bitter taste left in his mouth that he did not care for. If this was what soldiering had become, he would be left with no choice. Even selling out and returning home would be far preferable, though he had resisted those thoughts earlier.

Home. He thought of it as of an alien world, hardly familiar any longer. Spain and Portugal seemed far more like home to him now, and even this raw and half-civilized country was more real and immediate. He thought of the stiff formality and snobbery he had left behind, and it seemed to have nothing to do with him.

He thought of his brother, Gerry, acceded to the title now, and growing more like their father every year. Well-meaning, unimaginative, finding safety in tradition and fulfillment in ceremony and sameness, they had never seen eye to eye. Gerry was married to a woman who would have fainted dead away at the mere mention of some of the things Miss MacKenzie had seen and done this night. Charles could not begin to imagine Helen coping with war and fear and horror, let alone the whelping of a very ordinary stray dog.

Perhaps he was doing Helen a disservice, but he doubted it. In her world—Captain Ashbourne's own, he supposed, for he had been born into it as well—the mere fact of a title made one superior, and wealth and privilege were taken for granted. Women, as Miss MacKenzie had said, were largely decorative and to be protected even from the mere mention of the seamier side of life. They flirted and shopped, exchanged the latest gossip, left the running of their homes and the raising of their children to an army of servants, and sulked if their husbands did not pay them enough attention, or their lovers left them for another.

He blinked and yawned again, his exhaustion and the extraordinary past twenty-four hours having somehow sharpened his vision, as if he were seeing his old life clearly for the first time. The women he had known were children, spoilt and aimless, and it seemed to him that the men in their lives deliberately kept them so.

His eyes, as if of their own accord, shifted again to Sorcha, who was calmly kneeling in the mud and wet, her striking red curls damp about her face and her attention all on the creature she was helping. She was ignoring their danger and whatever news may lay at the end of her journey to soothe and pet an unlovely animal his own mother or Helen, or any of the other women he knew, would have shrunk from in horrified disgust. She was indeed stubborn, opinionated, annoyingly independent, and determined to have her own way at any cost. On the other hand, he had never known a woman could be so recklessly brave, or refuse to give in to fear or doubt, or admit that there was anything she could not do once she set her mind to it.

He thought of Lisette, and for once the memory did not bring its usual flicker of pain. He supposed he was simply too tired for bitterness or anger or the numbing sense of loss he had carried around with him for too long. He could still conjure up her face without any trouble, of course: infinitely beautiful and desirable, alight with that indefinable charm she possessed, sure of herself and her power over him, laughing and teasing or pouting by turns.

He had fallen in love with her in the first moment of setting eyes on her, as most men did, and when he had become engaged to her within a fortnight, he had thought himself the luckiest man on earth.

She had begged him, with tears in her eyes, to marry her before he returned to the front, or to sell out completely. But he had been full of his duty and no doubt maudlin nobility, he acknowledged with a grimace, and had feared that if he swept her off her feet, exactly what did happen in fact would occur and she would ever after blame him for it.

It had been small comfort at the time to discover he had been right. It had taken her less than six months to tire of her fidelity to a man tiresomely unavailable to squire her to the balls and parties her soul craved, and no doubt his brief letters, scratched forth when he could snatch a stolen moment, had been a poor enough exchange. In the end she had married another man, far richer than Charles had ever been, and with a title to boot. That he was easily old enough to be her father and had grown daughters her own age had apparently not weighed with either of them.

She had written to tell him of it with her usual insouciance, pushing most of the blame off onto him. She had never been any good at waiting, he knew that. More, she had begged him to marry her at once and not to go back to his tiresome war. If he had done as she'd begged, they would have been deliriously happy, but however much she might love him—and she assured him that had not changed—he could not expect her to wait until he tired of his chivalric games, or was killed or horribly maimed.

It had sounded so much like her that he could almost have heard her say it; and along with the aching sense of loss, and considerable bitterness, had been the awareness that in an odd way she was right. Perhaps he should have married her when he had

had the opportunity. It had been madness to expect one so beautiful and vital to wait patiently for her absent lover, eschewing the gaiety and admiration she could not live without and all for the sake of his own selfishness. One did not blame the butterfly for flitting from flower to flower, after all.

For the longest time he could not bear to think of her in the arms of another man—especially an old satyr, who had bought her with promises of jewels and expensive titles. But in time the pain had lessened, of course, and he had been left with a certain cynicism and the conviction he would never find that same sort of headlong, dizzying love again.

Now for the first time, in this quiet spot in an alien and hostile country, it occurred to him that perhaps he had had a lucky escape. The thought was a new and startling one, but he wondered if that were not what Lisette, with her acute sense of self-preservation had sensed all along. He had loved her, true, almost to the point of madness. But even so, even in that first heady intoxication, when he thought he could not live without her, he had not given in to her demands to marry at once, and to hell with the consequences.

Now he wondered why he had not. To save her from herself, of course, and all that noble muck. That was what he had told himself. But perhaps the truth was that if she could not live without admiration and gaiety, he had known instinctively that the world she lived in was not for him. The endless breakfasts, reviews, loo parties, promenades in the park, and visits that made up her life, seeing the same people over and over again, hearing the same gossip, doing the same things. The balls in the Season, sometime as many as two or three a night, where one danced too much, drank and flirted too much, and tumbled into bed only with the dawn, to rise late and heavy-headed the next morning to do it all again. The easy flirtations, the casual infidelities, the meaninglessness of such a life might be amusing for a fortnight, but he would soon have grown fatally bored.

It was, after all, exactly what he had joined up to escape. Now he wondered if they had not married for the simple reason that each was too selfish to give up the preferred way of life.

But then, he supposed, even during their brief engagement the signs had all been there. There had been tears and storms from the first, followed by tender reconciliations. Lisette had threatened to break the engagement, marry someone else, do something drastic, for like a child she had never learned to live with waiting for what she wanted, or being thwarted in any way. And like the insufferable young prig he had obviously been, he had talked of honor and duty, when perhaps all it really melted down to was that he had been enjoying himself too much to give it up, even for her.

That had been two years ago. And though the first freshness of the wound had scaled over, of course, he had carried it always as a faint ache. He had thought it was the reason that when the war in Europe had ended and he had had the chance to go home, he had gladly volunteered instead for the American campaign, still not able to face seeing her happily married to her aging roué. But now he wondered, extraordinarily, if it had simply been because he was still not ready to give up his fun. He was no longer even sure he had ever really loved her at all. Or had he merely been dazzled by her beauty and the stroke to his vanity of winning her in the teeth of all opposition? And perhaps she had merely been dazzled by his uniform as well.

He almost laughed out loud, for he had put Lisette on a pedestal and adored her, but if the truth be acknowledged, this young American, with her prickly ways and proud courage, aroused a quiet admiration in him that Lisette had never done, no matter how beautiful and fascinating she might have been.

He absently lit one of his cigarillos and sat enjoying it, watching Sorcha at her labors and surprised at how peaceful he felt at this moment in this quiet and most unlikely of spots. He tried to compare her to Lisette, with the latter's husky laugh and her beautiful, kissable mouth and the grace of her quicksilver movements, but it was impossible. Lisette, for all her beauty, was a hothouse rose, delicate and fragile and fragrant, and not quite real. Sorcha was . . . he tried to think of a uniquely American flower, but could not.

The comparison was ridiculous anyway. It would be difficult to find two women more opposite in every way. Lisette was fair and tiny, always dressed expensively in the very latest fashion, petted and surrounded by admirers wherever she went, and very aware of her power over men. Then there was stubborn, opinionated, headstrong Miss Sorcha MacKenzie, with her hair in an untidy tangle about her head, her dress torn, her skirts muddied and streaked with smoke and even bloodstained where she had knelt in the makeshift hospital, and seemingly wholly unaware of any of it. It was impossible to imagine her in a ballroom, as he had said, or flirting with a fan. Obstinate, willful, annoyingly pigheaded, refusing to listen to reason or bow to her own limitations, or give in to even overwhelming odds, there could be no comparison between the two. It would be a relief when he could wash his hands of a responsibility he should never have undertaken in the first place, and turn her over to her father, who had a good deal to answer for in his rearing of his only daughter.

He grinned, again wishing he might have just five minutes alone with that remarkable gentleman. The worst of it was she did not seem even to realize that her actions from first to last had been outrageous. She had unconscionably dragged him in as well, not to mention that poor maid of hers, and that terrified child with a child of her own and even that wretched dog. None of them had the least conception of what they were letting themselves in for. Of course now that he came to consider it, he supposed their fate if she had not interfered might have been questionable. But that still did not excuse her.

But then, she had not strictly dragged him in, as at least he conceded in reluctant amusement. His eyes rested on her again with unconscious appreciation. She was wet and bedraggled, still in his coat, which was much too large for her—her eyes too big for her face, her torn dress hastily pinned up, her hair escaping in drying tendrils about her too-white face. He supposed, still assessing her dispassionately, that she was striking, but not really conventionally beautiful at all. Next to Lisette, for instance, she must appear blowsy and perhaps even vulgar. Her coloring was too blatant, for one thing, and her remarkable green-flecked eyes too straightforward and unyielding, her mouth and chin decidedly unfeminine in their determination.

And yet there was character in her face and unconscious grace in her movements, and not even Lisette had possessed such glorious white skin. He would like to see her in green velvet, or old gold, with emeralds around her throat.

Then he was startled at the unseemly direction his thoughts were wending and deliberately dragged his eyes away. They were enemies, as she never tired of pointing out to him. And besides, his future was uncertain enough at the moment without throwing any more complications in the way. He would be lucky to get her safely to her home, and he still had to deal with all the difficulties of a war he was fast coming to regret. Nothing was more certain than that he would never see her again.

The rain had begun to come down in earnest, but under the

trees they were more or less protected. Avoiding decidedly un-
fruitful and foolish thoughts of Miss Sorcha MacKenzie, he lazily
watched Dessy unpack her lunch, and Elsie unembarrassedly
suckle her baby. But his eyes strayed to Sorcha again, liking the
way she concentrated her full attention on what she was doing.
She was oblivious of his scrutiny, and he thought that it was perhaps that unfeminine quality of forgetting herself that most appealed to him.

He yawned and closed his eyes, feeling them burn from lack of
sleep, and allowed himself to drift for a few moments. He did not
believe he had been asleep, but he woke with a start, his senses
instantly alert, to discover Dessy was quietly approaching him
with a plate of food in her hand.

He blinked, rubbed his tired, unshaven face, and accepted it,
thinking by the desultory progress of the birthing process that he
could not have been asleep for too many minutes. Sorcha was still
on her knees, encouraging the dog, as if she had not endured such
horrors only a few hours ago, and the fate of a few mongrel puppies were the most important thing in the world to her at that moment.

Dessy followed the direction of his gaze and remarked calmly,
"You a married man, Captain?"

He was surprised, for she had said very little on the journey so
far. She was surprisingly self-possessed, with no discernible air of
subservience, though she seldom put herself forward. She spoke
with a soft cadence, more educated than any other of the few
slaves he had so far come into contact with, and he wondered
what went on behind that impassive dark face of hers. But he said
merely, "Me? Good Lord, no."

She nodded, as if confirmed in some private thought, but made
no comment. He straightened and stretched, then asked resignedly, "Does that ridiculous girl really propose to carry a
bunch of newborn pups along with us? Don't bother to answer. It
would be useless, I suppose, for me to try to suggest that the kind-
est thing would be to drown the wretched creatures and be done
with it?"

Dessy merely looked amused and again made no answer. She
had no need to, for as he had said, the question had been merely
rhetorical. He began to eat, surprised to discover how hungry he
was, and that the food was unexpectedly good. There was cold
ham, chicken, and some spicy cold dish he did not recognize, and

he reflected that at least they would not starve, whatever else
might befall them.

He was about to say as much to Dessy, when he caught a sound
he knew well. He did not need the pricked ears of the chestnut to
know that there was a party of riders approaching, and not too far
distant.

He glanced again at the whelping which seemed to be progressing at a snail's pace and cursed under his breath. It didn't much
matter which side might be approaching, British or American, for
it would perhaps be best to avoid them altogether. If they were
British, she would be safe enough, though no doubt uncomfortable; but he himself did not particularly relish the awkward
explanations that would be necessary. And if they were American—which he was afraid was more likely—things could be even
more awkward, if not downright dangerous. She seemed not to
have any fear of her country's hastily assembled militia, but he
was far from being so sanguine. Besides, his own position might
be more than a bit risky. All in all, he came to the conclusion it
would be best to avoid the whole problem altogether, if it were
possible.

It might not be possible. He had no desire to alarm the others
unnecessarily, but had developed a considerable appreciation for
Dessy's calm good sense, and so said quietly, "Go and tell Elsie
that it is time to go. Cover yourselves with the quilts, as before,
and remain lying down. I will warn your mistress."

Blessedly Dessy did not argue. The captain thought her one in
a million and wished that her charge were likely to prove so bid-
dable.

Chapter 10

He walked calmly to Sorcha's side and said quietly, "We have company. We may have to leave rather quickly."

She looked up sharply from where she knelt beside the puppies, but showed no panic. "Who is it?"

"I can't tell whether it's your army or mine, but I own I would just as soon not find out."

In the end she behaved better than he had expected. After hesitating, she rose and said matter-of-factly, "Lift the mother back into the cart. I'll bring the puppies." There were three of them by then, blind and mewling, and she tumbled them gently into her much-maligned shawl, and lifted them, remarking calmly, "Poor things. What a start to life. It may be crowded, but I think they had best all go in the back."

The captain was relieved to have gotten over that hurdle so easily, but there was still an even more serious one to be negotiated. "I think you should all get in the back," he said firmly. "Keep low, and whatever happens, don't raise your heads. I have already instructed Dessy to keep the blankets over you. With any luck they may pass us by, for we are more or less hidden from the road, and our chances of outrunning them are almost nonexistent. But it is as well to be prepared for any contingency."

He did not add that his own blood was running cold with the

thought of what might happen, or that he had absolutely no faith at all in the discipline of her so-called militia.

But he might have known he would not have it all his own way. Sorcha said with equal firmness and far more stubbornness, "I am coming up on the seat with you. Don't stand there arguing! We don't have a minute to waste, and besides, there is no room in the back, and you may yet need me. I can shoot as well as a man, and you will have your hands full driving."

Having deposited her load of puppies beside their weary mother, she promptly climbed up on the high seat and took her place, not waiting for an answer.

The captain sighed, knowing that short of removing her physically—which he was strongly tempted to do, for he was not in the least accustomed to having his orders countermanded—he could see no way of dislodging her. And she was right—there was no time for an argument. He climbed up beside her, taking the reins and saying grimly, "If you were in my regiment, Miss MacKenzie, I would soon break you of your habit of ignoring orders. It would be better for all of us if your father had done so long since."

"But then I am not in your regiment," she retorted. "How long before they reach us?"

But he was frowning and made no immediate answer, for listening intently, it seemed to him the sounds had halted and were coming no nearer. "They seem to have stopped!" he said briefly. "I am going to go back and take a look! Keep quiet, all of you. As for you," he added to Sorcha, "if anything happens, don't wait for me. For once do exactly as you're told, and drive like the very devil. Don't stop for anything! Do you understand?"

She gave him a wide-eyed look, but made him no answer, though she did accept the reins from him. He thought resignedly that she would do exactly as she pleased, as ever, and he could only hope her sense of self-preservation would prompt her to be sensible for once. It did not seem very likely.

There was a considerable wood surrounding them at that point, stretching on either side of the primitive road, and he made his way carefully through it, as silent and invisible as any backwoods trapper. He was obliged to go back a good half mile before he discovered any signs of the troop of half a dozen or so that he had only heard before.

He discovered there were five of them, some in bedraggled

American uniforms, some in the homespun that melted so well
into its surroundings and made the wearer almost invisible even at
close range. They seemed, he was relieved to see, to have followed his own example, and in light of the steady downpour that
was now falling, taken refuge in the wood on the opposite side of
the road.

One of them sat sentry duty, stolidly enduring the rain that no
doubt trickled down between the trees and found its way under
his collar. But the others had wrapped themselves in coarse blankets and seemed to be trying to get some sleep. Already to all intents and purposes they appeared dead to the world.

He grimaced, some at least of the uncustomary dread he was
feeling lightening a little, and turned to make his way back as
silently as he had come.

He must have startled Sorcha, for she jumped and gasped when
he appeared out of nowhere to climb into the wagon and take the
reins back from her.

"Well?" she demanded almost belligerently.

"There are five of them—Americans," he confirmed. "They
have stopped to escape the rain and to rest." He looked at her and
added with careful neutrality, "You could, given your blind faith
in your fellow countrymen, simply drive back and ask them for
protection. They might very well agree to escort you to Annapolis."

Her clear green eyes did not give away her thoughts, and she
merely asked after a moment, "And you?"

He was amused. "You needn't concern yourself with me, my
dear Miss MacKenzie. I daresay I can get back easily enough.
Well? What's it to be?"

She hesitated, then abruptly lowered her eyes, as if to hide
them from him. At length she said stiffly, "Let's go on. If you do
not wish my fate on your conscience, I refuse to have yours on
mine. Besides . . . " She hesitated again, then added as if unwillingly, "You have proven your point, Captain. I am not quite as
naive as you seem to think me."

He was relieved, but took care not to show it. "Very well. I
think, under the circumstances, we will have to risk it and drive
on. The rain is decidedly heavier now and with any luck may
drown out our noise. If not"—he grinned abruptly and added with
mockery—"if you can actually shoot that pistol of yours, Miss

MacKenzie, and did not bring it along merely for show, you may soon get your chance to prove it."

Then he saw without much surprise that she already had it in her lap. Dessy said with unexpected determination from the back of the cart, "I have the other one, and I can shoot, too, Captain."

He grinned over his shoulder in approval at her. "By now I confess I would be surprised at anything different, ma'am. Stay down, all of you, and keep as quiet as possible."

He did not return immediately to the road, preferring to drive through the trees for as long as possible, where the mat of dead leaves at least muffled their passage slightly and they were more or less hidden from the road. Of necessity he drove slowly, for at times the way was scarcely broad enough for the wagon, and the tired horse, though it had gotten a brief rest, might need all its reserve of stamina, and soon.

Everyone was tensely silent, including Sorcha beside him. She sat bolt upright, and he was tempted to make her get down on the floorboards where she would at least be out of danger of any stray shot. But in the end he abandoned the notion as being not worth the inevitable argument. Among the trees they were protected from the worst of the rain as well, but he knew it would not be long before he was obliged to rejoin the road, for the trees were getting thicker and the way more and more difficult.

In fact, they had gone no more than five hundred yards or so when he could go no farther. He pulled out carefully onto the road, and Dessy, in the back, reported gratefully that there was no sign of any pursuit. The rain had indeed grown heavier, and visibility was limited, a fact that might also work in their favor, the captain hoped.

He had almost begun to relax, thinking that there must indeed exist a benign providence to protect the foolish, when the baby behind him, interrupted in the middle of breakfast, or perhaps merely sensitive to the extraordinary tension around him, let out a thin wail.

Dessy must have quickly stifled its cries in folds of the blanket, but the captain, cursing, feared the damage had already been done. There was as yet no sounds of pursuit, but the captain, abandoning caution, shouted, "Get your heads down and keep them down! All of you. We'll have to make a run for it."

And God help us, he thought grimly. Seasoned campaigner though he was, his blood ran cold with a fear that had little to do with his own personal safety. But he was never one to panic in an emergency, and his hands on the reins were as steady as ever. He was again tempted to push Sorcha down to the floorboards at his feet, but doubted she would stay there, so he concentrated instead on getting as much speed as possible out of the poor tired beast between the shafts.

The rest may indeed have helped, or perhaps like the baby it caught some of the tension, for it roused itself to a tired trot, and then obligingly lengthened its stride still more, until they were galloping down the road at a fair clip—which doubtless did the occupants on the hard boards behind little good.

For a moment or two longer he actually thought their luck would hold and they would get safely away. Then Dessy reported breathlessly that a solider on horseback was following them, though seemingly not at top speed. It looked more as if he were uncertain and had ridden out to satisfy his curiosity than out of any real sense of danger, though he had sped up at sight of them.

The captain knew the very nature of their headlong flight was likely to rouse his suspicions, but felt uninclined to stop and try to make explanations. "Just keep your heads down," he shouted, abandoning all hope of quiet. "You too, Sorcha! Don't fire unless it becomes absolutely necessary, either of you. And then don't hesitate, but shoot to kill."

Without warning and without apology he abruptly pushed her down onto the floorboards at his feet. Neither of them seemed to notice his use of her first name, but somewhat to his surprise she remained down, but only, he was amused to see, because it enabled her to see better behind them. "I'm not going to kill my own men," she insisted scornfully, seemingly breathless but unafraid. "You just drive, Captain. I'll take care of the rest."

He almost laughed, though it was scarcely a laughing matter. "Never mind such heroics, you little fool! Just keep them down in back. Don't you know that if it comes to an exchange of shots we are all in the suds?"

There was a strange glow in her green eyes, and her cheeks had taken on some color. "Of course I know it. But I am not beaten yet, if you are. Give me your pistol. It will save reloading so often."

He did laugh then, startled into helpless and highly inappropriate mirth. But after a moment he obediently handed over his own pistol. She was right that he would need to concentrate on his driving, and at that point he would put nothing beyond her. "You are a woman in a million," he told her. "But whatever happens—and God alone knows what that shall be, for I certainly don't—don't waste your time worrying about me. If something should happen—God's teeth!"

She had no need to ask what was the matter, for the lone soldier who was trailing them had apparently made up his mind and had loosed off a shot after them. The captain could almost feel the bullet whiz past his cheek and felt decidedly vulnerable up on the high seat with his back all too invitingly broad a target. But at least the shot had served one purpose, he realized a moment later in some amusement. It had succeeded in making the chestnut bolt, tired though it was.

He made no attempt to control it, allowing the cart to bump and jolt at speed over the uneven road. He had been in many a tight corner in his day, and if this was a tad different, and the outcome far more serious than the mere preservation of his own hide, he was, as ever, cool and collected in an emergency, refusing to allow himself to think of that. They were in some danger of being overturned, but that seemed a minor enough risk under the circumstances, and even if they all broke their necks, he thought such a fate preferable to some he could name.

Sorcha, too, had remained amazingly calm, kneeling on the floorboards to face backward, her pistol aimed and held as steadily as she could manage. The rain had plastered her dark red curls to her forehead, and she was very wet, but she seemed to disregard that minor discomfort as well, although she now and then brushed her eyes as if to clear them.

Dessy reported from the depths of the mattress in back that the soldier had reloaded and was gaining on them.

"Shall I fire?" asked Sorcha with a coolness to match his own. "It might serve to discourage him."

The captain could no longer help it. He had always had an acute appreciation for the absurd, and despite everything he quietly gave himself up to enjoyment of the present situation. "Go ahead. It seems we have little to lose," he acknowledged. He himself would have had no compunction in killing the man, but he was not surprised when she took careful aim over his head, merely trying to frighten him. The captain thought in appreciation that the poor devil would be frightened indeed if he knew who it was that was shooting at him, but Sorcha at least, he was interested to see, did not even jump at the sound of the explosion.

There was, however, a scream from Elsie in the back, and the baby began to cry again in earnest. But the remarkable girl beside him showed neither fear nor panic. She calmly took up his pistol, handing the first back to Dessy for reloading, then took aim again and fired.

Dessy reported in triumph that the soldier had slowed, seeming to lose some of his enthusiasm for the chase.

The road they were bumping over was increasingly rough, and both Elsie and her baby were wailing by now in terror. Even so, the captain, glancing over his shoulder, almost began to believe that they might actually make it, for the pursuit was definitely slowing.

Despite himself he glanced again at the determined face beside him, now very wet. He could no more picture Lisette crouching there firing to frighten off a pursuing soldier than he could picture her flying. Of the two, he was bound to own he much preferred his present companion, he acknowledged with a grin, for a case of hysterics at this juncture he could well do without. The young black girl was quite bad enough, clinging to the jolting carriage and whimpering with fear.

Whether or not the soldier's enthusiasm was fading for the chase, Dessy suddenly reported, uncertainly, that he was swinging off the road into the trees on the opposite side. She seemed to think that meant he had abandoned the chase, but the captain, his untimely amusement abruptly vanquished, feared otherwise.

Sorcha, with a glance at his grim face, seemed to guess the truth as well, for she said quickly, "Perhaps we should find some cover and stop. With three of us, we should easily be able to hold him off."

The last thing the captain wanted was a standoff—especially with four others nearby and unlikely to sleep through the exchange of gunfire. Besides, it was doubtful if he could have halted the runaway chestnut by that point even if he had wanted to.

His eyes felt gritty from lack of sleep, and the sabre cut in his arm was beginning to throb, and it would have helped to have the full use of both arms. He smiled down into the strained face beside him and said cheerfully, "Don't lose heart on me now, sweetheart. You're doing splendidly. And Dessy, too."

Sorcha looked startled, and he found himself absurdly wanting to smooth away the frown between her brows and kiss the telltale tremble in her lips that she so quickly bit to stop him guessing that she was in any way afraid.

Good God. He dragged his thoughts away with an effort, wondering where on earth that had come from. He had best keep his mind on the present or they were indeed lost.

Still, it would be too bad if she threw herself away on either of her two suitors. She clearly needed someone able to put his foot down and stop her wilder notions, but still able to appreciate her courage and spirit. Life with her would frequently be infuriating, but never dull, he thought with a faint grin.

He could handle her, he suspected, but of course he had given up on the idea of marriage. Everyone knew his heart had been broken and was no longer his to give away. It wouldn't be fair to marry anyone, especially someone like Sorcha, under those terms.

And yet it was growing increasingly hard for him to remember that his heart was broken. Even the thought of Lisette did not bring its usual pang or the certainty that there could never be another serious love for him. He wondered again if he were over her at long last, but the conviction of his being ruined for any other woman was too strong to easily let go of. Of course he still loved Lisette; that went without saying.

He realized belatedly that there had been silence for some time now, no more shots being fired from either side. He glanced at Sorcha's face and again smiled reassuringly down at her with a confidence he was far from feeling. With luck their pursuer had indeed given up and returned to his companions.

But the captain didn't believe it.

He was not much surprised when Dessy gave a muffled scream and reported in a shaken voice that she could glimpse their pursuer through the trees, where he had apparently, as the captain suspected, gone for cover. Far from giving up the chase, he was gaining on them, able to maneuver through the trees far more easily than the cart had done.

Sorcha, apparently abandoning her qualms, was trying to get a bead on him, but the trees hampered her aim. She squeezed off one shot, looking white and determined, but Dessy reported in disappointment that the bullet had harmlessly struck a tree, for she had seen the splinters it kicked up.

Sorcha took the pistol Dessy handed her and coolly took aim again. But before she could fire, a second shot resounded. The captain, still sitting vulnerably upright on the high bench seat, felt a searing impact above his left ear. For all too brief a moment he saw colors and lights he had never imagined possible. Before the blackness stamped down to replace them, he had time to think with despair not of his own death, for which as a soldier he had long been prepared, but of what would become of the wagon load he had just so abjectly failed to protect. And though it was Sorcha's face he saw, his guilt was for all of them.

Then his head seemed to explode with fire and pain, and he knew no more.

Chapter 11

The first thing Sorcha noticed was the captain slumped over, falling heavily sideways on the hard wooden seat. She looked up in alarm and saw his face covered in blood. His eyes were closed.

For a moment horror nearly overcame her, for she thought he was dead. Then of a sudden she was filled with such rage that she did not even hesitate. It no longer mattered that he was her enemy and the man following them her fellow countryman. She sighted along her pistol and shot the pursuer without compunction. He was by then close enough that she could see his grin of triumph in his unshaven face, and the subsequent surprise as he was thrown back, and then out of the saddle.

Sorcha had already forgotten him by the time he hit the ground. Dead or not, the captain was in immediate danger of pitching out of the wagon, and she grabbed him desperately, holding whatever gave her purchase, his belt, his sleeve, his leg. She was in an awkward position, but at last managed to slide up to sit beside him in the swaying, bucking seat, putting her arms tightly around his lifeless form. The reins were luckily still wound around his hand, so she was able to grab them, but for the moment that was the least of her concerns. She clung desperately to him, realizing that he was bigger than she had thought, and heavier. Above all there was no time to worry about her own safety, now that she was perched up beside him so conspicuously.

Dessy's voice came to her, raised over the sound of their headlong flight. "Is he dead?" she asked fearfully.

"I . . . I fear so. I don't know." Sorcha's own voice was more desperate than she wanted. "Oh, Dessy! Is anyone still coming after us?"

Dessy took a moment to look. "No, I think you shot him clean out of the saddle, chile." There was nothing in Dessy's voice but relief. "Jus' hang on, chile, and we'll be safe."

Sorcha almost laughed at that, for driving headlong over an inferior road behind a bolting horse, hanging on for dear life to a man who might already be dead, did not strike her as particularly safe. But then never in the direst disaster had Dessy failed to remain calm and optimistic, even after a life spent with Magnus and the storms he brewed wherever he went. "Yes, all right," she managed. "But I don't think . . . I can hold him much longer."

"Now don't you give up. You know you can always do what you has to," pronounced Dessy quietly as she always did.

Sorcha almost laughed again, though there was nothing in the least funny about their present predicament. The captain was a dead weight and growing increasingly heavy, and she could see nothing but blood, even on her own face and hands. He had shown not one flicker of consciousness ever since he had been hit, and she feared indeed that he was dead.

Guilt and horror almost swamped her at the thought, but as Dessy said, there was no time for that. She sat more upright, and as if in answer to a prayer, suddenly saw a turnoff just ahead. From what she could tell, it was an even rougher road, little more than a cart track, veering off to the right of the main road. But she did not hesitate. She jerked the reins over hard with all her strength, hoping the panicked horse would take the command, and that they would not all be upended in such a steep turn.

The frightened chestnut by now had great patches of sweat on its sides, but blessedly it veered and took the almost right angle turn at a dangerous pace, slipping and nearly coming to grief on the mud and grass, and righting itself only by a miracle. And that seemed to be the end of its flight. No one was shooting at them anymore, and the near fall had sufficiently frightened it that he began to slow almost immediately, too tired to maintain such headlong panic.

Sorcha let him go on for another half mile, for safety, but his stride had become uneven, and in a remarkably short period he had come to a complete stop without her urging, his head droop-ing and sides heaving, clearly too tired to put one foot in front of the other.

Sorcha released her stranglehold on the captain's body and straightened her cramped limbs thankfully. After having been bounced and jolted for so long, the lack of motion was a relief, and she dared not wonder how Elsie and the baby had fared through it all. Or even the newborn puppies. She had somehow forgotten about them completely in more pressing worries, and she almost laughed again at the memory of the poor things, bounced around and helpless, and perhaps wondering indeed about the world they had just entered.

But there was no time to think of that. At least the baby set up a wail at that moment, reassuring her, and the puppies, too, now that things were still, could be heard mewling piteously.

Then Dessy was there to help her with her burden, and between them they lowered the captain's inert form onto the wet grass at their feet. It was still raining, and Sorcha was soaked by then, as was the captain, but she scarcely noticed any longer. Now that they had stopped, however, she found she was shaking so badly she could scarcely stand, and though she was ashamed of herself, it was Dessy who cleaned the captain's face of the blood and said in relief, "He ain't dead, nor anywhere near it, chile. The ball creased his temple, and it's bad enough, but a few inches to the right and he'd of been a goner for sure. Jus' you find somethin' to bandage up his head with, and he'll do."

Sorcha found she had to sit down in the grass rather suddenly herself, relief making her strangely light-headed. "Oh, Dessy!" she said and had to resist the weak urge to burst into tears.

Instead, she managed to regain her feet after a moment, ashamed of herself, and at Dessy's command, ripped the flounce off her by now far from clean petticoat for bandages. She helped Dessy bind up the wound, seeing that there was indeed a deep fur-row, raw and angry-looking, and still bleeding sluggishly, above the captain's left ear. But to her relief she could find no other signs of hurt anywhere else, and his heart, when she pressed her ear to his chest, was beating steadily.

But he had made no stir from the moment he had been shot, and she said worriedly, "Why does he not come round?"

"Concussion, mos' like," said Dessy cheerfully. "Don't you

worry none, chile, he's as strong as an ox. Has to be to've been a soldier so long."

Sorcha was not so sure the one followed the other, but she knew Dessy was an excellent nurse, and trusted her judgment. Still, that solved but one of the most pressing problems facing them at the moment. She might feel little better than a murderer if the captain should die. But he must be got somewhere to safety— they all must—and that was likely to present a dilemma of over-whelming proportions.

Sorcha straightened and arched her aching back, then looked around them helplessly, having not the least idea where they were. She felt very much like the exhausted chestnut, who still hung with its head down, cropping desultorily at the side of the road. The rain was thankfully beginning to lessen, but she could still see very little in either direction and had no idea of which way to head.

Annapolis lay back along the main road, but so might the sol-diers, and after the last half hour she had absolutely no inclination to ask for their protection. She had no clear idea how far they had come and did not immediately recognize where they were, but that was scarcely surprising. But to reach Annapolis all she had to do was to follow the road, so technically they were not lost.

Still, at least for the moment, that option did not seem open to her. Nor could they remain where they were, in the wet, when the captain clearly needed medical attention and at once.

His own army would have surgeons who must know how to deal with such wounds, but she could hardly retrace her steps all the way back to Bladensburg. For all she knew she was closer to Annapolis by now, and she cursed herself for having fallen asleep and being too weary to pay much attention to where they were going. Despite her resolve not to turn over the entire responsibil-ity to the captain himself, that seemed to have been exactly what she had done and the realization annoyed her.

On the one hand, of course, it would be a relief to turn the cap-tain over to his own army and be able to wash her hands of him. But she was inclined to reach the same conclusion the captain had, that in the present circumstances she could trust neither side completely. It therefore seemed that she was going to have to make a decision, and quickly, for now even the captain's life hung in the balance.

She knew as well as Dessy, moreover, that even if the bullet had not killed the captain outright, infection and fever were still a very real danger and killed as often as the initial wound itself. Luckily he did not seem to have lost too much blood, despite the crimson stains that covered both of them. Scalps bled notoriously freely, but he was unlikely to bleed to death unless a major artery had been severed.

Still, he needed a doctor and at once. And there was another factor as well that she had not sufficiently considered before. Were he to be captured by Americans, he would undoubtedly become a prisoner of war; and whereas before yesterday she would have maintained staunchly that American prisoners of war were always treated kindly, she was no longer as convinced that that was true. At least not enough to risk the captain's life on it.

For the first time she had to face the unwelcome fact that the captain had been right, and it had been unbelievably foolhardy to have set out on such a journey. At the time she had thought only of Magnus and reaching home again. But the consequences, so far, had been as unpleasant as they were uncomfortable, and there was no doubt that all must be laid directly at her door. She had dragged them all along with her on the strength of her stubborn will, just as Captain Ashbourne had accused her, and now, belatedly, the responsibility for all of their safety appalled her. Dessy, Elsie and her scrap of a baby, even the dog and her pups, not to mention the captain himself, all now depended upon her strength and ingenuity to get them out of the danger she had blindly led them into in the first place. It was far too late to wish she had taken the captain's advice and remained barricaded in some house in Washington.

For the first time it also occurred to her that she had no way of knowing whether Annapolis might have suffered the same fate as Washington. If she pushed on and managed to evade the troops of either side, she might arrive only to discover it burned to the ground or in enemy hands.

She said bitterly and wearily to Dessy, "Don't bother saying it! This has all been my fault. And if . . . if the captain d-dies, that will be my fault as well. We can't go all the way back to return him to his own friends and for medical help, on the off chance the British are where we left them. And I am beginning to think things may be as bad in Annapolis as they are here. Besides, we are all exhausted and frightened, and I am almost as afraid to go on as I am to go back."

"Tha's all true," confirmed Dessy calmly, "except the captain isn't likely to die."

Sorcha swallowed painfully. "I . . . only hope you may be right. But even if by some miracle he does not, it is my fault he was wounded at all. And I am afraid to turn him over to the British for our safety, and dare not turn him over to our own army for his."

Dessy accepted this without any comment at all, plainly waiting.

Sorcha smiled crookedly. "Well, it looks as if I shall just have to get us out of a predicament I am to blame for getting us into in the first place."

She looked down at the still unconscious captain, his face now cleaned of most of the blood and a bandage tied around his head in Dessy's neat work, and reluctantly jettisoned her own still strong instinct that she would find Magnus in Annapolis and they would all be safe there. "We can't go on," she admitted tiredly. "We all need rest, and he needs a doctor. We are assuming his wound is not serious, but we don't really know that for s-sure. Perhaps we can find someplace to stay for a few days, until he is . . . stronger, and it will be easier to know what to do. How are Elsie and the baby doing?"

"As well as can be expected for a chile herself who's just risen from childbed." Dessy chuckled richly. "Don't go worrying about that little babe o' hers. He's got as tenacious a hold on life as I've ever seen."

Relieved on that count at least and glad to have made any decision, whether right or wrong, Sorcha turned gratefully to more practical matters. She shaded her eyes from the rain with her hand, trying to peer down the track they were on, but a bend in the road close ahead made it impossible to see anything but rain and trees and gray sky wherever she looked.

It did not look promising, but Sorcha knew well that in the sparsely populated country, a track of any kind eventually led to some habitation, if only a remote farm. At the moment a farmhouse with a jolly farm wife and warm beds appealed strongly to her. Always assuming, of course, that they had not fled in the face of the British, which was all too painfully likely.

But at least they could get in out of the wet, and she would have no hesitation in breaking into an empty house and using what supplies she needed. Desperate times called for desperate measures, and these were desperate times indeed.

She and Dessy consequently turned their attention to getting the captain's heavy figure into the back of the cart. It was not easy, but Dessy was strong, and Sorcha herself motivated by fear and guilt, and they at last managed it. The captain did not stir, though they must have aggravated his injuries since his wound had started sluggishly bleeding again.

The last thing Sorcha did was to push the captain's shako and distinctive uniform jacket under the heavy mattress. There was no point in advertising his identity, though in truth by that time Sorcha was reluctant to give up his warm jacket, for it had protected her from at least some of the rain.

Elsie watched the procedure with wide eyes and made no comment, though the back of the cart was getting rather crowded. The dog thumped her tail weakly and lay curled up on the mattress, her puppies, their fears subsiding, having discovered the source of their sustenance. If she had been less worried, Sorcha might have laughed, for taken all in all, it was a fairly ridiculous assortment, as the captain had said.

And they were all depending on her to rescue them. She had not wanted to acknowledge earlier how much she had come to rely on the captain's calm good sense and formidable presence, but now removed, she missed them sorely.

Dessy joined her on the seat, and Sorcha picked up the reins and urged the tired horse on, hoping it would not drop dead between the shafts from exhaustion. She felt much the same, her eyes gritty from tension and lack of sleep, her body aching all over, and her brain sluggish, as if it were filled with cotton wool.

They were obliged to drive along the rapidly worsening track for some distance before Sorcha saw the first sign of habitation. She had begun to fear, in fact, that against all logic the track led nowhere, and they would be faced at the end of it with the necessity to retrace the whole way back. But she at last caught a thin thread of smoke rising from a distant chimney. The rain had stopped by then, and a bright sun was struggling to get out, or she might not have seen the smoke at all. But with difficulty she was able to make out a small building in the distance, which by the signs of the smoke, must be inhabited.

Her spirits rose like a comet, and she exclaimed, "Oh, thank God!" only then realizing exactly how frightened she had been.

Dessy too straightened, though she pronounced doubtfully as

they drew nearer to the house, "Looks like a poor enough place to me."

"I don't care if it's an earthen hut," said Sorcha fervently. "And someone must be there, or there would be no kitchen fire."

It was, as they soon saw, a small tavern, too far out of the way to attract many travelers, and far from commodious or luxurious. Probably it served a settlement of some sort in the opposite direction, but Sorcha was in no mood to be overly critical. She would have welcomed a barn at that point.

No signs of any life appeared at first, but even as Sorcha pulled up in relief in the muddy yard, a gaunt woman in a dirty apron and stained dress stepped out of the door, an ancient flintlock held menacingly. "What is it you want?" she demanded suspiciously. "We ain't open."

But Sorcha was not about to be turned away at this point. "What we want," she said crisply, "is food and beds. We have a wounded man here as you see, and a woman who has just given birth. We . . . we have come from Washington, where the British burned the town last night, as you may have heard; and we are trying to reach Annapolis, where my home is. But we need to stop and rest for a . . . a few days and to find a doctor."

The woman regarded her as if she were crazy, which no doubt was understandable. "Well, you cain't stop here," she said uncompromisingly. "My man's away from home, and the servants has run off the place in fright, and I ain't fetchin' and carryin' for no sick man and baby. You'll have to keep goin'."

Sorcha's quick temper was aroused, and she climbed stiffly down from the wagon, having to bite her tongue to keep from alienating the woman completely. "I seriously doubt there is anywhere else we could stay in this direction. Is there?"

When the woman shook her head with a certain grim pleasure, Sorcha's temper increased another notch. "I thought not. But there is no need for you to fetch and carry if that's all you're worried about. I have my maid with me, and she will do all that is required. Surely you cannot, in common decency, mean to turn us away? I have a man who may die unless he gets some help."

The woman seemed wholly unimpressed. "Well, he ain't goin' to die here," she pronounced callously, still keeping her flintlock raised. "So they burned Washington, did they?" It was the first flicker of interest she had shown. "Well, all I kin say is good riddance to bad rubbish. I've no truck with them redcoats, but like

Sodom and Gomorrah, any evil city that's burned to the ground is
no loss, to my way of thinkin'."

Sorcha could scarcely believe her ears, but she was well
enough aware that the countryside was filled with many such people, holdovers from the original settlers who had come to the new
land for relief from religious persecution. They tended to hold all
towns and civilizations in suspicion, and they scratched out an ex-
istence by supporting themselves on the land as best they could,
buying as little as possible from the outside world. But still, this
was an inn, for the crude, weathered sign was clearly visible, and
Sorcha was not about to let herself be turned away.

She said more firmly, "All that is beside the point, Mrs. . . . er
Mrs. . . . ?"

"Tigwood," supplied the woman ungraciously after a moment.
She was probably somewhere between thirty and forty, though
she looked older, and her hair was stringy and her whole appearance unkempt. Under ordinary circumstances Sorcha would not
have set foot in an establishment kept by such a creature, but
these were far from ordinary times.

In light, however, of what were likely to be her reluctant landlady's fundamentalist religious views, she thought it best to pre-
varicate a little, and so said with a patience she was far from
feeling, "Mrs. Tigwood, my . . . my husband was wounded fighting the British. He must have food and rest and medical attention,
and the rest of us haven't slept in over twenty-four hours." In fact
it seemed much longer than that. "You cannot, in Christian char-
ity, turn us away. I am prepared to pay whatever is necessary, but
I refuse to go on another step. The horse is exhausted and must be
rubbed down and fed."

"The stable boy's run off, too," said Mrs. Tigwood, not without
triumph. "I tol' you I'm the only one on the place."

"Then you will no doubt be glad of the company, with the
British in the vicinity. Have you . . . er . . . seen any British soldiers, ma'am?"

She held her breath for the answer, but Mrs. Tigwood merely
snorted. She had, however, lowered her musket slightly. "Huh! I
seen 'em earlier. Why do you think everone ran off? But how do I
know he's yer husbin?" she demanded suspiciously. "This is a
God-fearin' house, and I won't have nothing goin' on in it. I
know what folks get up to in them places like Washington, and
even Annapolis."

Sorcha was having increasing difficulty hanging on to her patience. It seemed incredible that the woman could be worrying about such things under the circumstances, but she said stiffly, "I am . . . Sorcha Ashbourne. This is Dessy, my maid. I promise you we will be no trouble to you."

The woman at last grudgingly lowered her musket completely, to Sorcha's relief. "They's only the one room, save for the attics," she said unhelpfully. "The darkies will have to go up there, for I don't cotton to 'em, and the attics is good enough for the likes of them. As for you and your . . . husbin, if such he be, I s'pose you can have the front room. But this ain't a busy inn, nor one that caters to the likes of you, and I won't waste my time cookin' persnickety food, or do any nursin', so don't expect it!"

Sorcha would not have trusted her in a sickroom. "The only thing we need is a doctor—and we do need that. Is there one nearby that we can send for?"

But Mrs. Tigwood seemed to delight in delivering more bad news. "There was one, though I don't traffic with doctors, and I've never had 'im out. But he's been called up to tend the wounded soljers, or so I've heard tell. And there ain't another closer than Annapolis."

Sorcha accepted this with a sinking heart, realizing that it was probably true. "Are we closer to Annapolis than to Washington, then?" she asked, clutching at straws.

Mrs. Tigwood seemed uninclined to commit herself on that point, but grudgingly conducted Sorcha inside. The room at the front of the house on the second floor was cleaner than Sorcha had expected from her companion's slovenly appearance, though small and comfortless and spartan in the extreme. It held an enormous bed, which took up most of the space, but had windows on two sides, at the moment tightly closed, and was musty and airless, as if it had not been used or even aired in a very long time. But she could scarcely afford to be fussy at the moment.

She therefore quite gratefully thanked the woman, glad to have found any refuge, however unwelcoming. The one bed might prove a problem, but she could not worry about that at the moment. She had said the captain was her husband instinctively, hoping to hide his nationality from the unfriendly Mrs. Tigwood and allay at least some of her suspicions. She had also given the captain's name, rather than her own, for fear he might regain consciousness and betray himself somehow before they could be away again.

In fact, the next few days seemed fraught with difficulty, but as she went back downstairs with her ungracious hostess, she could only worry about one day at a time. "Where is it your husband has gone?" she asked the woman curiously. "To fight the British?"

Mrs. Tigwood snorted again. "Huh! Tain't likely! A traveling preacher is my Jed, doin' the Lord's good work. He don't hold with killin' of any sort. Told 'em so when them recruiters came and sent 'em away with a flea in their ear, I kin tell you. Said this is America, and our ancestors came here to get away from government tyranny."

For the wife of a preacher, however fundamentalist, Sorcha thought Mrs. Tigwood remarkably uncharitable. She could not decide whether to hope for the return of the absent Mr. Tigwood, or to fear that he would prove even more unlikable than his far from amiable wife.

Chapter 12

Between them, with little help from their hostess, Sorcha and Dessy managed to get the captain out of the cart and up the stairs. He was appallingly heavy, and did not stir, despite such rough treatment. Once in the wide four-poster, lumpily covered with a patchwork quilt over a primitive mattress, which was likely stuffed with corn cobs Sorcha knew, he lay as one dead.

The bed, Sorcha also knew, was so big because in such country taverns a landlord would often put two or three strangers (or more) in a single bed together and think nothing of it. Aside from the bed, the room held a crude bedside table of rough, unfinished wood with the bark still on it, and an oil lamp on top which was likely to smoke, and a single hard wooden chair. She vowed to get the feather mattress from the cart up there as soon as possible, which would make their patient slightly more comfortable. But at the moment she had no wish to disturb him anymore and was not sure she possessed the strength to tackle it anyway.

It was also unbearably hot with the windows tightly closed and no air stirring. Sorcha thought briefly and longingly of a long cool bath, but went instead to force open the windows.

Mrs. Tigwood, standing disapprovingly in the open doorway, objected to that, but Sorcha ignored her. It helped a little, but the captain still lay with his eyes tightly closed, his firm mouth relaxed and a gray pallor under his sunburnt skin that she didn't like at all.

Elsie was soon installed in the attic, which was indeed much hotter than the room below, but Mrs. Tigwood flatly refused to admit the mongrel bitch and her pups into the house and consigned them to the barn. With no other servants on the place, and Mrs. Tigwood wholly unwilling, there was a good deal to do, and it was nearly an hour later before Sorcha could wearily climb the stairs again, after having seen the mother and her pups settled in a nest of straw, and rubbed down and baited the tired horse. She had taken the precaution of secreting the captain's scarlet coat and his shako in the barn's corncrib, for she did not trust Mrs. Tigwood not to spy on them and betray him if she ever suspected the truth.

Her own gown had long since dried on her, and catching sight of herself in a spotted mirror in the tiny hall, she could scarcely blame Mrs. Tigwood for being suspicious. Her hair was a riot of untidy curls, and her gown was by now torn with bloodstains all down the front of it.

But she found to her relief that Dessy had made the captain more comfortable at least, having washed off the blood and dirt and sweat, rebandaged his wounds with cloth presumably provided by their reluctant hostess, stripped off his own ruined clothes and topboots, and tucked him under a light quilt. Dessy reported that the furrow on the captain's temple still did not seem overly serious, but that his arm was getting hot and inflamed. The dirty bandage on the original sabre cut had chafed and cut into it, no doubt due to too much exertion, and fear of infection was likely to be their worst danger at the moment.

Sorcha knew as well as Dessy did that it was more often infection than the original wound itself that killed. But Dessy was a reliable nurse, and she seemed optimistic enough. Sorcha had never heard all the story of her remarkable life, but she knew that Dessy had once been owned by a doctor and had learned a good many of his secrets. She had, in addition, considerable lore from her native country, from which she had been forcibly removed when a girl. She had often cured Sorcha's childhood ailments with roots and herbs unknown to local doctors, and Magnus had had considerable respect for her healing skill.

Twenty-four hours later, little had changed. They had quickly settled into a routine. Dessy did the cooking, after the greasy meal

Mrs. Tigwood grudgingly offered them that first night, and looked after the fast-recovering Elsie and her baby. Sorcha fed and groomed the horse and looked after the dog, which she had christened Bess, and her pups. She also took the lion's share of nursing the captain, which in truth constituted very little at the moment, since he still lay unconscious and had scarcely stirred.

Between them they had on the second day dragged the feather mattress up the narrow stairs and put it on top of the other in an effort to make the captain more comfortable. Since Mrs. Tigwood had yet to set foot in the sickroom, Sorcha had taken the opportunity to spirit the captain's jacket and shako up and had no hesitation to hide both under the mattress, thinking it probably the safest place for them.

The first night Sorcha had dispatched Dessy firmly to bed in the attic, knowing how tired she must be. She herself had meant to remain watchful, for the captain's continued unconsciousness was beginning to worry her. But after fighting a losing battle to keep her eyes open, even in the room's one hard chair, she could not help eyeing the great stretch of empty bed beside the captain with longing. She looked again at his unconscious form, which had scarcely moved from the time they had laid him on the bed, and abruptly jettisoning such foolish considerations as propriety, climbed up onto the big bed, and collapsed on the far edge. She was asleep almost the moment she put her head down.

She woke the next morning, at first unable to remember where she was or why she was not in her comfortable bed at home. Then as realization struck her, she glanced fearfully at the captain, who had unwittingly shared his bed with her. The yard of faded quilt still lay safely between them, and he had not visibly altered his position at all.

She rose hurriedly, doing what she could to straighten her disgusting gown and regretting the portmanteaux she had so lightly discarded to make room for the dog. Luckily, Dessy, when she came down, wisely asked no questions about her sleeping arrangements or lack thereof.

Sorcha had clung, no doubt foolishly, to the hope that they might be able to set out anew that first morning. But the captain showed no signs of making a quick recovery. Dessy pronounced herself pleased enough with the progress of his wounds, though the sabre cut still looked inflamed to her. But there could be no question of going anywhere while he remained in that prolonged stupor.

Dessy then turned her attention to her charge. Without another word she somehow bullied or cajoled the detestable Mrs. Tigwood into unearthing an ancient tin bath. She set it up in a corner of the captain's room, suspending a large sheet for modesty's sake, and even produced, to Sorcha's astonishment, a change of clothes for her. "Good God," said Sorcha faintly, "I thought I had thrown out the portmanteaux containing all the clothes."

"It's a good thing I retrieved it then," said Dessy calmly. "That dress ain't decent, and I won't have you going around looking like a ragamuffin before that woman downstairs. Now don' come out till you's boiled."

Sorcha laughed, surprising herself, and had never put off garments more willingly. While Dessy stood guard, Sorcha gratefully washed off the worst of two day's sweat and grime and soaped her hair, which still smelled of smoke.

When she had emerged at last, feeling almost human again, Dessy wrapped the sheet around her as both towel and dressing gown. Sorcha swathed her damp hair in a rough huckaback towel like a turban, and as she emerged from her temporary dressing room, glanced somewhat absently toward the captain, as much to reassure herself he was still unconscious as anything.

It was then she almost got the shock of her life. The captain's blue eyes were open, and he was staring at her frowningly.

She must have jumped a foot and blushed fierily at being caught in so compromising a position. Then common sense belatedly took over, and ignoring her unconventional attire, she hurried to his side, exclaiming in heartfelt relief, "You're awake! Oh, thank God! How do you feel?"

He regarded her with the frown still between his brows, but after a pause said vaguely in a weak voice, "Where am I?"

"Somewhere between Bladensburg and Annapolis. I don't know quite where. Are you—?"

But he had already closed his eyes again and seemed to have lapsed into unconsciousness, for she could get no more out of him.

Still, it was enough that he had roused once and spoken to her sensibly, if briefly. She was relieved that she had not, after all, apparently been the cause of his death, and that was sufficient to get her through the next few days.

She dressed quickly with Dessy's help, again behind the makeshift screen, but he did not wake again. But as she sat in the hard chair by his bedside for much of the rest of the day, she thought optimistically that he was perceptibly nearer the surface, for even if his eyes did not open again, he groaned once or twice and seemed to become more restless. She thought even that was preferable to the deep unconsciousness that had frightened her so much, for at least he did not seem so lifeless.

She knew, unwillingly, that part of her fear that he would die was less concern for him than an ardent desire not to have to feel any guiltier about him than she already did. If he died, it would be her fault, and that was a responsibility she did not want to have to deal with.

It was all more than confusing, for only a day or so ago Magnus had been on a field of battle, trying to kill British soldiers. Perhaps he and Captain Ashbourne had even met briefly. If so, there was no question where her loyalties should lie. The fact that this British officer had been unexpectedly kind to her should not alter the fact that he and others like him had invaded her country and killed innocent citizens and even burned her own house to the ground. She had been raised all her life to hate and despise the British, particularly its soldiers, and she now had ample proof of her own that much of what Magnus said was true.

And yet she doubted that things would ever be quite that simple again. And that was but another reason to hope for the captain's speedy recovery, for she had a strong presentiment that the longer she was forced to remain in the company of her enemy, the more impossible it was likely to be for her to go on seeing all British as a faceless brutal enemy.

The thought annoyed her, for of course they were not all alike. It had been naive and simplistic in the extreme to think so. She wondered if all wars and hatred arose from just such absurd prejudices. The British had done much of which she disapproved and even hated, and their policy regarding their former colonies had been extremely shortsighted, to say the least. But it was individuals like herself and Dessy and poor Elsie, and the captain, who paid the price in blood and fear and fire and hatred.

She didn't want to harbor such thoughts or start seeing the captain as other than a responsibility to be gotten rid of as quickly as possible. She didn't want to get involved, to risk her emotions and perhaps even her liking, all of which would only make her feel even more guilty than she did now. But it seemed it was already too late. Even if by some miracle the captain regained consciousness again and returned to his army at once, it was already too late.

She studied him at leisure in the fast-waning light, able to satisfy her growing curiosity about him without fear of interruption, for she had sent Dessy early to bed again. His bare chest was surprisingly well-muscled and browner than she would have expected. He had a three days' growth of beard by then, and with his tousled fair hair and the bandages round his head and left arm, he might easily have passed for a young American backwoodsman, not the British officer she knew him to be.

That at least was fortunate, for the last thing she needed was for the odious Mrs. Tigwood to become suspicious. She wondered what was happening in the outside world, and if the rain had indeed put out all the fire in the capital. She tried not to think of Magnus, who if he was not dead or wounded himself, would soon be growing frantic about her own safety. But there was no help for it. At least not as long as her patient continued in that unnatural unconsciousness.

She went to adjust the bandage around his head, which he had slightly disturbed, and to check for herself that he was showing no signs of fever, when the door unexpectedly opened.

She looked up, surprised and wholly unconscious of the seeming intimacy of her position, at first expecting to see Dessy. But it was Mrs. Tigwood who stood in disapproval on the threshold, accompanied by a rough-looking man Sorcha had never seen before.

Sorcha knew a brief moment of fear, for her first instinctive thought was that the captain's true identity had somehow been discovered, and this man had come to arrest him. But he was not dressed in a uniform, and she made herself steady her leaping pulses and say with creditable outrage, "How dare you? What is the meaning of this?"

"There!" said Mrs. Tigwood in triumph. "What did I tell you? Who knows what else has been goin' on behind my back?"

The man was middle-aged and unremarkable-looking, tall and thin and dressed in homespuns dyed a greasy black that made him look very much like a crow. Sorcha had not the least idea who he was, but said, "How dare you burst in here like that. Who is this man?"

"He's my husbin, that's who," said Mrs. Tigwood even more triumphantly. "The Reverend Jedediah Tigwood. I told him the way you pushed in here, with yer hoity-toity airs, issuin' orders left and right, and with yer darkies and absurd tales of havin' escaped from Washington. I also told him that I don't believe for one minute that you and that man are married—at least to each other! The Lord knows what was goin' on in here the las' few days, but you ain't stayin' a minute longer, that I kin tell you. You'll git out o' here now, this minute, all o' you!"

Sorcha was so relieved that they had not come to arrest the captain that at first she didn't fully take in this new danger. When she did, she was incredulous. "Are you mad?" she gasped. "Can't you see that this man is unconscious and has been since he arrived?"

"So you say," said Mrs. Tigwood, by now well launched into her attack and obviously enjoying the scene she had precipitated. "I notice you don't call him yer husbin that time. Which is just as well, with no weddin' ring in sight, and nothin' to go by but yer tales of who you are. Fer all I know he's an escaped British soljer with a price on his head. Well, I ain't havin' him in the house, nor you neither. You kin jes' git out now, all o' you. I ain't cookin' and slavin' for the likes of you, sinners and agents o' the devil, I make no doubt."

Sorcha made herself control her growing temper with great difficulty. As much as she might like to leave this dreadful tavern and never come back, she dare not, at least for a few days. She therefore took a deep breath and said with as much reasonableness as she could muster, "Mrs. Tigwood . . . Mr. Tigwood . . . there are reasonable explanations for all of this. I am not . . . wearing my wedding ring for fear it would be stolen, but I assure you this man is indeed my husband. Why would I bother to lie about a thing like that? As for being an . . . escaped British soldier, the very idea is laughable. Perhaps I should tell you that my father is Magnus MacKenzie, United States senator from the state of Maryland, and no one hates the British more than he does."

She saw the disbelief written large in Mrs. Tigwood's face, but it seemed that her husband, who had yet to say a word, was looking thoughtful. So Sorcha tried appealing to him. "Oh, this is ridiculous! Everything I told your wife is true, sir. I escaped Washington when my house was burned. My . . . my husband is a soldier and was wounded, as you see. I was lucky enough to find him and brought him away. We are trying to reach my father's house in Annapolis. Perhaps you can tell me if you have had any word of its safety?"

"No'm," said that man in a piping voice that fitted ill with his calling. "They say the British are withdrawin', but I don't pay much attention to such worldly matters. But if my wife is took agin ye, mistress, there's little I can do. Powerful stubborn, is my Durie." He sounded oddly proud of her.

"But this is ridiculous!" Sorcha said. "Good God. Even if what she feared were true, my . . . husband is scarcely in any state for the 'goings-on' she seems to imagine. Look for yourself. If you are indeed a Christian man, as you claim, you can hardly force us out when my husband is still so ill."

"Now you jes' hold on . . ." began Mrs. Tigwood angrily.

But her husband was scratching his chin thoughtfully. He needed a shave and had a prominent Adam's apple, which bobbed as he swallowed or spoke. He peered at the captain carefully and at last pronounced in his piping voice, again scratching his jaw, "Wal, now, p'raps it's as ye say, mistress, and p'raps it ain't. But like I said, if my Durie's turned agin ye, there's little I can do. I've my reputation to think of, after all."

Sorcha had never been so angry, but she was shaken as well. It seemed ludicrous to her that these absurd fools could really chuck her out for such a reason, but anxious as she had been herself to be away again, now that she was faced with the very real possibility, she was forced to acknowledge how valuable even this unpleasant shelter had been. At least they had been safe, more or less out of the path of the war, and were all beginning to recover from their unpleasant ordeal. Besides, to move the captain at this point was too dangerous, even if she were not faced with no alternative but to jolt and rattle him in the unsprung cart over the worst of roads.

The reverend, seeming to read all that and more in her expression, at last scratched his jaw again and added, as if the notion had just occurred to him, "O'course, I dessay there is a way that might cool Durie down apiece and allow you to stay."

Both Sorcha and his wife regarded him with suspicion, but Sorcha at least was in no position to object. "What is that?" she demanded unwillingly.

"I've nothin' agin ye, missus, nor yer husbin, if sech he be," said Mr. Tigwood pacifically. "But again, iff'n my wife's took agin ye, I can't ignore that. But I think I might see a way ever'one can be satisfied. Jes' supposin' I was to marry ye again—fer a fee, of course, jes to make it all nice and legal. Then my wife'ld be satisfied, and there'd be no thought of havin' to leave, when your husbin is so porely."

"What?" cried Sorcha in dismay, which she hoped she was concealing. "You can't be serious?"

"Why, jes' think it over, missus. Iff'n yer married already, it won't make no difference if you go through another ceremony, quietlike. And iff'n ye ain't, then my wife will be satisfied. Either way ye kin stay fer as long as ye like."

"But I still won't cook fer 'em!" put in his intractible spouse.

"Having tasted your food, that is a blessing!" snapped Sorcha, knowing she was being petty and doing herself no good thereby, but unable to resist it. Her mind was working rapidly, but she did not much like the conclusions it had reached. She saw their game well enough and knew it for a not-so-polite form of blackmail. Her dislike of the Tigwoods—husband and wife—rose several more notches, but she could see little way out of it. It was, in fact, a nice, neat little trap, and having charged her a large fee, no doubt, for the marriage ceremony he would conceivably be in a position to blackmail her further later.

The worst of it was that were she to refuse it would merely support that dreadful woman's supposed suspicions. Nor did she dare call her bluff, either, much as she might long to, for she would not put it past either to stand by their word and throw them all out, even at that hour.

Still she tried feebly, saying, "Aside from being extremely insulting, I have never heard anything more ridiculous. If nothing else, my husband"—the word was thankfully coming easier to her with each repetition—"is unconscious and in no state to undergo a ceremony of any sort."

"No, he ain't!" pronounced Mrs. Tigwood triumphantly, staring at the captain.

Sorcha, too, looked down quickly and saw that the captain's eyes were indeed open again, as if all the noise had disturbed him. There was the same faint frown between his eyes, and he said in a disturbingly weak voice, "Who are all these people? What the devil is going on here?"

Sorcha bent over him, uncertain whether to be grateful or alarmed by this untimely return to consciousness. "Don't try to talk . . . darling," she said quickly. "I am sorry if our voices disturbed you."

His blue eyes stared up into hers with the same frown, but he obediently remained quiet. She bent over, and under the guise of adjusting his pillow said under her breath, "Quiet! Don't say anything more. Only tell me this, and quickly. Are you married?"

It seemed to take him a while to process the question, but at last he said vaguely in a voice even she had to strain to hear, "Married? Yes, of course." The frown was still between his eyes, as if his head ached, which no doubt it did, and on the whole she was thankful when he closed his eyes and seemed to relapse into unconsciousness again.

For what she was about to do appalled even her, and it would be just as well if he remained in comfortable ignorance of it for as long as possible, though it seemed she had very little choice in the matter.

She lifted her head and said deliberately, "Very well. If it is the only way we may remain, you may marry us again, however ridiculous and insulting your suspicions may be. Only be quick about it. My husband is extremely ill and needs absolute peace and quiet."

Chapter 13

Thus did she find herself joined in far from holy wedlock, in a mockery of a ceremony performed by a man she despised, to a virtual stranger who was her enemy, and married to boot. If she had not been so furious, it would perhaps have been funny. But as it was, the only thing she found to please her in the service that took place in the low-ceilinged and stuffy little room she had grown heartily sick of already was that it was mercifully brief.

She had not, like most little girls, fantasized often about what her wedding would be like, planning it down to the last detail. But not even she could have foreseen this furtive little affair, born out of blackmail and as legally unbinding as it was sordid.

In fact, the only other good thing to be said about it was that the groom remained oblivious during most of it, his hot hand a dead weight in her own and his eyes exhaustedly closed. Sorcha wished she could have been equally unconscious.

The Reverend Jedediah Tigwood, his nasty little wife beside him, wore his dusty blacks and held a prayer book, the leather cover cracked and the pages soft with much handling. He behaved throughout as if he were officiating at a joyous occasion, which did nothing to add to Sorcha's enjoyment. His Adam's apple bobbed continually in his scrawny, unshaven throat, and Mrs. Tigwood stood beside him in triumph, her mean little eyes glowing with malice. Sorcha wondered wearily what sort of twisted religion had produced such a specimen.

It was over thankfully soon, the captain having been roused sufficiently, and over Sorcha's objections, to make his responses, though it was clear he had not the least notion or interest in what was happening. Sorcha's own responses were made in a clipped voice, and she knew that her extreme temper and a strange and unexpected sort of shame kept her cheeks blazing, for she could feel the heat in them herself.

An awkward moment arose when it came time for a ring, and it was Sorcha who leaned over and slipped a signet ring off the little finger of the captain's left hand and with a feeling of reluctance put it on her own. As she did, she cursed the lack of foresight that had prevented her from borrowing Dessy's ring in the first place, thus forestalling all questions about her marital state.

Then at last it was over, and with a final smirk of triumph Mrs. Tigwood took herself and her husband off. It was long, however, before Sorcha could cool down enough to go to bed. She would not have taken part in such an absurd ceremony if she had believed for one moment it was legal, of course. But for the first time she began to hope the captain did not regain full consciousness too quickly, for so long as they remained in that dreadful house, things were likely to be more and more awkward.

Starting with Dessy. She had not a hope of keeping the news from Dessy, and so told her next morning, after an unrestful night, with a certain defiance.

After the first startled moment Dessy tactfully busied herself straightening the sheets on the bed and made no comment whatsoever. It was Sorcha who was driven to defend herself against an unspoken criticism by saying, "Well, I didn't have any choice, did I? Besides, such a ridiculous ceremony cannot possibly be legal."

Dessy deliberately did not look at her again, but remarked offhandedly, "It's sometimes surprisin' what is legal, when it comes to weddin's. Comes from the time, long before you was born or thought of, when travelin' preachers like this one had to do for a lot of folks, and couldn't always git there in a timely fashion, especially in winter. There was a lot o' bastards bein' born, poor little innocent mites, and so laws concerning such were deliberately fuzzy."

Sorcha knew all that, at least vaguely. In many places no license was required, and a surprising number of people were against the state being involved in marriages at all. "You're no comfort," she complained crossly. "Anyway, this one cannot possibly be legal, for the captain is married already. D'you think I'd have gone through such a ceremony if I hadn't known that?"

For the first time Dessy looked up, betraying some surprise. "He is? How do you know that, chile?"

"Because he told me so. I asked him before I would consent to such a ceremony. But I suspected it anyway, for there was a miniature of his wife in his jacket pocket. She looks blond and mealymouthed."

Dessy looked as if she were on the verge of saying something else, then apparently thought better of it. Sorcha knew from long practice that if Dessy had decided to hold her peace, there was nothing to be got out of her. But all she said was, in some amusement, "Now how can you possibly know that? Don' tell me he tole you that as well?"

"No. But she looks exactly the type a man like him would fall for. Beautiful and insipid, the sort who is tiny and helpless and who men fall over themselves to help over the least inequity of the road. But then it is only what I expected, for he is obviously a chivalrous fool or he would never have gotten himself embroiled in our problems in the first place." Sorcha did not know herself why she was being so scathing.

Again Dessy made no comment, though there was something in her calm dark face that for once made it difficult for Sorcha to meet her eyes. "I know, I know!" she said grimacing. "I confess that for the first time in my life, I would give anything to be helpless and foolish and have someone rescue me from the present situation, exactly like the females I've always despised."

"You're doin' fine on your own," said Dessy soothingly.

"I'll admit I don't feel very strong at the moment. In fact, I would give anything if we were safely home." Sorcha lifted her chin and added with unwonted humility, "The captain was right, blast him! We should never have set out on such a hare-brained adventure in the first place. I have endangered him, and you, and that poor child upstairs, all for the sake of my stubborn pride. In fact, if we'd listened to his advice, none of this would have happened."

"Hmmph. Marriage don' seem to agree with you," remarked Dessy, returning to her earlier task. "It ain't like you to be in the glumps, chile. Besides, you can't say we'd any of us been safe if we'd stayed in Washington. That girl upstairs, for one, would have been a deal worse off if you hadn't insisted upon rescuing her. Have you thought of that?"

"Oh, Dessy," said Sorcha, stooping to kiss her worn cheek. "What would I do without you? And I must admit that when I think of the past three days, having my house burned out from under me seems almost peaceful by comparison."

Sorcha, in truth more chastened than she wished to let even Dessy know, firmly believed that she had indeed at last learned her lesson. Despite Dessy's tolerance, she could not deny to herself that most of what had happened could be laid directly at her own doorstep. Impetuous—stubborn—determined to have her way—all the captain's accusations came back to haunt her, and she was hard-pressed to come up with much in her own defense. It was no more than Magnus had often told her—though the thought of him brought little comfort. When would she learn not to be so impetuous.

That being the case, even she was somewhat appalled when, less than two hours after making this noble resolve, her impulsiveness once again landed her in hot water.

It started innocently enough. She left the captain to Dessy's tender mercies and went down to take care of the animals, mistrusting that Mr. Tigwood's return was likely to relieve her of that or any other duty she or Dessy had of necessity taken on. But, as usual, occupation and solitude, both of which were in short supply in the dreadful little inn, did much to restore her to her usual optimistic frame of mind. She might have made a mess of things, but even considering everything that had happened, she found it difficult to wish she had gone meekly with Henry and sat out the war in tedious safety. The captain might not have been injured if she had, it was true, but Dessy was right that Elsie and her baby, and the poor pups and their mother, who was recovering from her burns and almost pitifully grateful to Sorcha, would have been a deal worse off if she had chosen that prudent course.

And even the captain was recovering, which did much to relieve her of her dreadful load of guilt. With luck he would return to his regiment in a day or two, without ever being the wiser about that absurd little ceremony he had unwittingly taken part in; they would reach Annapolis and find Magnus well and impatient to see her, and it would all soon be over.

Such thoughts cheered her up, and she returned to the little front bedchamber at last, her face glowing with exercise and heat, her gown again somewhat stained and creased, for it had not been designed for grooming horses and raking straw, and her hair in all probability untidy. She thought that if Mrs. Tigwood had been different, she might have begged the use of a workdress from her, despite Dessy's disapproval, for it was ridiculous to ruin her one remaining dress when she might have to be presentable sooner or later.

She was thinking such innocuous thoughts, grateful that she had not run into either of the Tigwoods, when she entered the room to find Dessy gone and the captain again unexpectedly conscious.

She came to an abrupt halt, fearing that her cheeks were even redder with embarrassment. She was all too aware of that unpleasant little ceremony the night before and profoundly hoped he had no memory of it. "Oh!" she exclaimed foolishly. "Y-you're awake again!"

There was still a frown between the captain's brows, but he looked stronger, she was thankful to see. "Yes." His voice was still weak, but also growing stronger. He took in her appearance with her high color and tendrils of hair escaping on her hot neck and added dryly, "You make a most charming picture."

She blushed even more hotly, which annoyed her.

She ignored the remark to quickly feel his pulse, which was more or less normal she was thankful to discover. The cut on his arm had become somewhat inflamed and was still worrying Dessy, and his cheek was a little hot. But then that might be merely due to the heat in the tiny room, which tended to grow almost unbearable by the end of the day.

"Thank goodness. I think you are much better," she said fervently. "How are you feeling?"

He endured these ministrations with a frown, his eyes still on her in a puzzled way, as if he wondered what she was doing there. "Damnably," he admitted, not mincing matters. "My head feels as if it were an anvil and someone is hammering on it, and my left arm is stiff and throbbing." He put up his sound hand to feel above his ear, and his own touch made him wince. "What happened? Was I shot?"

"Yes," she conceded reluctantly and added defensively, "but at least the arm is not my fault. The sabre cut you received in battle has become inflamed. As for your head, it is scarcely surprising if it feels like an anvil, for you have a large graze caused by a pistol ball above your left ear, as you have just discovered. You are suffering from concussion and have been unconscious for the better part of three days since we arrived here. In fact, you are fortunate to be alive at all, for a fraction of an inch to the right and the bullet would have killed you."

He took that in, frowningly. "Thank goodness," he croaked in obvious relief. "At least it is nothing serious then."

She looked startled, then was obliged to laugh despite herself. "Nothing serious, as you say. I begin to think you are even madder than Magnus, Captain."

"Am I to take it you consider the . . . er . . . bullet graze *is* your fault?" he asked weakly. "You said the sabre cut was not."

"No!" She was immediately defiant. "You were the one who would come with us, so it is all your own fault."

He took that in without comment. "Where are we, by the way?" he asked, looking around the stuffy little room with the frown still between his eyes.

"I am not much wiser than the last time you asked that question," she was obliged to admit. "Somewhere between Bladensburg and Annapolis. Though as it appears Mrs. Tigwood finds all cities dens of iniquity and never sets foot in them, she was unable to give me any precise clues. But at least we are not on a main road and have been relatively safe so far."

He frowned again, as if with an effort at memory, and asked rather blankly, "Mrs. Tigwood?"

"Yes. An odious creature. She is the landlady of the inn, thought a most reluctant one I will confess. I can't imagine how she and her husband manage to attract any customers, since both of them are as disobliging as they know how to be. She wouldn't have taken us in at all if I hadn't made her, and she is eager to be rid of us. But you needn't worry; she has categorically refused to help with the nursing and does no cleaning or cooking, so it is unlikely you will be bothered with her. In fact, I have every intention of keeping her away from you."

He had closed his eyes rather wearily, but he said now, as if untroubled by the thought of the odious Mrs. Tigwood, "She sounds a most unusual landlady. But don't worry on my account. This is an inn, you say?"

She supposed that it was scarcely surprising he should still be weak and was grateful he had not yet asked her any more awkward questions. She suspected relief was making her far more voluble than usual, but didn't seem to know how to stop. "Yes, if you can call it that. Her husband is less spiteful but still . . . unpleasant."

He opened his eyes again to look at her, and his gaze was somehow disconcerting, as if he were studying her for the first time. "Do I take it it was . . . you who brought me here?"

She blushed a little and again was annoyed at the telltale sign. "Yes, of course. After you were . . . wounded, it seemed I had no other choice. Though if I had known then what I know now, I might have tried to push on to Annapolis. Don't you remember? You have regained consciousness briefly several times since we've been here." On the whole she thought she would be relieved if he had little memory of what had occurred since their arrival.

But he had closed his eyes again, saying weakly, "I remember that. Vaguely. How long have I . . . we . . . been here?"

"This is the third day," she answered, once more slightly defensive, though even she scarcely knew why. "When we first arrived, you were in no state to go on, of course, and we were all exhausted. Besides, after our last encounter, it seemed safest to lie low for a while. You do remember that at least, don't you?"

He made a vague gesture and instead of answering her directly, asked weakly, "You said . . . Annapolis. In America?"

"Yes, of course." She eyed him in dawning suspicion. "Look here, how much do you remember? You do at least remember the British burning Washington, don't you? And the battle at Bladensburg?"

He closed his eyes again as if it was too great an effort to keep them open and remarked almost dreamily, "No. I don't know. It's all a jumble. I remember you. And being bumped over a very bad road, only I thought it must have been in Spain."

Then, even as she was goggling at him, he opened his eyes again and left her completely speechless by adding matter-of-factly, "But I don't seem to remember my own name, at least at the moment. Or yours. In fact, I don't seem to remember much of anything."

Chapter 14

For a long moment Sorcha could only stare at him aghast. It was the one thing she had not considered, but she saw now that she should have. The concussion, the long period of unconsciousness—it was scarcely surprising if he had temporarily lost his memory. At least she hoped it was only temporary. Her mind refused to consider the ramifications if it were not.

"Your name is . . . Charles Ashbourne," she said at last. "Captain Charles Ashbourne."

He frowned, but seemed to find no familiarity in it. "Thank you. And you are? It would seem, from the situation, that we know each other . . . well." Again he spoke matter-of-factly, but she had the unwelcome suspicion he was remembering something that, if his memory was in truth gone, a kinder fate would have seen that he had forgotten. But then she had been aware for days now that fate was most definitely not her friend.

She found herself blushing idiotically and was about to launch into the awkward explanations she had already been dreading when her mind leapt to a solution to her most immediate problems that was as daring as it was outrageous. She was well aware it was her impulsiveness that had gotten her into her present trouble in the first place, but it seemed fate had not abandoned her altogether after all, for she could not help but realize that his temporary amnesia might prove to be a blessing in disguise. She had been dreading the already complicated explanations she was going to have to make, and she was almost overwhelmed at having to inform him in one breath of who she was and all that had passed between them.

She had also been on pins and needles the entire time they had been in the inn that in his present weak and confused state he might blurt out something that would alert the Tigwoods to his true identity. At this point she would put nothing past them, and to turn in an enemy soldier, however apolitical they might be, was certainly something they might do—especially if they believed there might be a reward in it for them.

She couldn't help wondering if it wouldn't be better—not to mention easier all round—not to tell him the truth just yet. He could not blurt out something he didn't know, and since his very life might depend upon continuing the fiction that they were man and wife, in the face of the Tigwoods' already existing suspicions, it might be far less dangerous if only one of them was obliged to be acting.

At least she had the grace to realize that what she was contemplating was dishonest, and perhaps even dangerous, for she had no way of knowing if it might set him back in his recovery. But that seemed a small enough price to pay. It would only be necessary for a few days, after all, and at the moment she thought his physical safety must outweigh everything else.

Long afterward, of course, she could see how extremely foolish and even naive she had been to think that such a deceit could possibly work. It was fraught with all sorts of unforeseeable risks and almost bound to end in disaster. But at the time she was honestly thinking of him as much as herself and had the best of intentions.

And perhaps that alone should have warned her to be wary, for Mr. Tigwood could certainly have quoted scripture to good effect about the danger of good intentions.

But it did not. All these thoughts took place at lightning speed, so that his face had only had time to grow slightly more puzzled before she at last pulled herself together and answered him. She discovered her heart was pounding, for some reason, as if she had been running, but with an effort she was able to make her voice sound calm and even untroubled. "I am . . . your wife, of course. Now don't try and talk anymore. You have suffered a concussion, and it is little wonder your memory is erratic at the moment. Try and get some rest."

She had trouble meeting his eyes and feared she was blushing again, which was scarcely likely to convince him she was a wife of long standing. She could only hope he would put it down to natural embarrassment at the situation. She considered shedding a few tears, both to help convince him and perhaps put an end to what was likely to prove increasingly embarrassing questions. But at the moment such histrionics seemed beyond her. It was all she could do to remain calm in the face of what seemed to her, now that it was out and too late to recall, an outrageous and unforgivable lie.

But when she steeled herself to look at him, he was still frowning, and she saw that he had indeed apparently drawn his own conclusions for he was not in the least surprised. The state of dishabille he had seen her in, her very presence in his sickroom, must have prepared him. Besides, if he had truly lost his memory, however temporarily, and wasn't shamming it—and she could think of no reason why he should be—he had no cause at all to doubt her word, or suspect such a monstrous deception.

"I . . . see," he said at last. "I had guessed as much. This must be as . . . difficult for you as it is for me. I'm sorry. I don't even know your name."

"It is Sorcha. Sorcha MacKenzie Ashbourne," she supplied a little hollowly. His concern for her made her feel even more guilty, but now that she was committed, it was too late to be thinking of that.

"Sorcha . . ." He repeated it weakly, as if trying to force some recognition into his sluggish brain. "I'm sorry," he said again, weakly closing his eyes. "Obviously neither of us has ever had to deal with such a situation before. You are Scots? But then I suppose I should have guessed by the hair."

She found herself blushing again, ridiculously. "My father is. Or at least was. He came to America when he was sixteen, in time to fight the . . . I mean, in time to fight in the Revolution."

"Yes, I am forgetting this is America," he said, still frowning. "You called me captain earlier. I am also in the . . . army?"

"Yes, of course. The . . . the American army," she said rather defiantly, refusing to listen to her by-then loudly protesting conscience. When he frowned again, even more heavily, she added hopefully, "You *did* say you remembered nothing of the late battle, or the burning of Washington, didn't you?"

He rubbed his hand over his face as if he could force his sluggish brain to work. "No, nothing. Perhaps some vague impressions. It certainly seems right that I am a soldier. But did you say I am in the *American Army*?" he repeated more incredulously, as if suddenly more alert.

She feared her deception would be over before it had begun, for it seemed some memories were stirring at least. Otherwise he would not have found it so astonishing when she told him he was an American soldier, not a British one. She didn't know whether to be sorry or glad, but could only cling to her story for the moment, and so said somewhat desperately, "I . . . I . . . yes of course. What else?"

After a moment he merely remarked in the same exhausted voice, "Never mind. Tell me how we came to be here. And how I came to be wounded if it was not in battle."

That was scarcely a more welcome topic, but she did what she could to edit the truth and gave him a brief version of it. "You . . . you were wounded at Bladensburg, as I said. I was in Washington at the time, and when the British burned that to the ground—"

He had put up his sound hand to cover his eyes, as if the light hurt them, but he lifted it at that as if in surprise. "Wait a minute! You said that before. The British burned *Washington*?" Again he sounded incredulous.

"Yes, of course. They—did it in retaliation for our burning York earlier in the war," she repeated unwillingly. It seemed unpleasantly clear that despite his loss of memory, he remembered more perhaps than he realized and was having trouble accepting some, at least, of what she was saying. Again she was sorry she had ever started this, for it seemed she would be left at point nonplus very soon, and the truth was apt to be even more embarrassing then. "But . . . but that is unimportant. You came to find me when you discovered it, and . . . and after that we decided to go to Annapolis to find Magnus, my father, that is, who had also volunteered to help protect the capital. It was on the way that . . . that we were overtaken by a . . . by a troop of British soldiers, and one of them fired after us and that is how you came to be wounded. I . . . brought you and everyone else here, for we were all exhausted by then, and that . . . that is about it."

He had returned his hand to its former position and now said from behind it, "It would seem I am married to . . . a most remarkable woman. But who is 'all'?"

"Dessy and Elsie and the baby, of course, not to mention the poor dog who was burned and we rescued." She feared she was babbling foolishly. "But all of that is by far too long a story for the moment. You should be getting some rest."

"So it would seem," he agreed tiredly, dropping his hand away to once again stare at her uncomfortably. "For I confess I can make out little of what you have told me so far. How . . . how long have we been married?"

"T-two years," she said desperately. "But you are right. This is difficult for me as well. I think it would be better if we waited until you are feeling stronger." And God help her, she took refuge in her handkerchief, once she was desperate enough belatedly finding the histrionic ability she had earlier lacked. She could only hope he would believe her overcome with emotion and take pity on her. And surely if she were in reality his wife, it could scarcely have been pleasant to discover her husband no longer remembered her.

She was right, for he said instantly, and with a compunction she knew she didn't deserve, "Forgive me! It is just that it seems more than a little strange to find myself with an identity I don't remember, and in possession of a wife I can't recall. Especially so lovely a one."

When she winced involuntarily, he put out a warm hand to cover her own, at present guiltily shredding her handkerchief into her lap, and said quickly, "I'm sorry! That was clumsy of me. God! What a devil of a coil!"

She at least had the grace to feel thoroughly ashamed of herself. She made herself turn her hand to clasp his and said with what she hoped would be mistaken for wifely concern, "Oh, pray don't let us think about it for the moment. Surely, your memory will come back soon. You are just tired and need to rest. I should never have told you so much when you are still so weak."

He squeezed her hand weakly, but it did indeed seem as if he was at the end of his strength, for he closed his eyes again, his lean cheeks pale and a sharp pair of lines cut between his brows that she abruptly wished she could erase. "Yes, I am exhausted," he said in a thread of a voice. "And too weak at the moment to cut through so damnable a coil. At least it would seem I am possessed of a wife as generous as she is beautiful. If only I could *remember*!"

His head moved restlessly on his pillows and his hand tightened still more on hers, almost to the point of pain. But in a few minutes the frown smoothed out and his hand relaxed, and she was relieved to see he had fallen asleep again. And if her relief was largely for the awkwardness of his questions that she had escaped, at least some of it was in genuine concern for his health, which alarmed her almost as much as the lies she had told.

She had no choice, of course, but to confess to Dessy what she had done, for such a deception could scarcely be kept a secret. She did so a little defiantly, knowing what Dessy was likely to think, but Dessy's reaction was, as usual, predictable. She revealed neither surprise nor disapproval, and when Sorcha had at last finished, said merely, "Uh-huh. And what if he don't git his memory back? What then?"

"What I'm more worried about is that he'll get it back too soon," confessed Sorcha unwillingly. "He is already having trouble believing some of the things I told him, as if his memory is just below the surface and struggling to get out. You needn't scold me, for as it happens I'm sorry now I started any of it. But at the time . . . and anyway, I *have* been afraid he'll blurt something out in those wretched Tigwoods' hearing. Oh, Lord, what a coil, as he said. I almost hope he does get his memory back immediately, however awkward explanations may be."

"Well," said Dessy slowly, "it's true he might say something to give hisself away. And it's also true them Tigwoods is not to be trusted. *He's* even worse than she is, if possible. I been meanin' to warn you to stay clear o' him, for he's up to no good, if you ask me."

"No, of course he isn't," said Sorcha rather impatiently, having no desire to discuss the Tigwoods at the moment. "I agree that he is every bit as unprincipled as she is, but at least he is slightly more pleasant. He even had the grace to apologize to me for his wife's behavior."

"Hmph," said Dessy again. "That's what I mean. If you ask me, he's taken a shine to you, and I don't trust him. You jus' stay out of his way, chile, and I'll feel safer."

Sorcha promised, relieved to have gotten over the hump of Dessy's disapproval so easily. But she was far more concerned with her present predicament, and could only hope she would be more prepared for his questions the next time the captain awoke. To start it would help if she stopped blushing and stammering in his presence like a frightened schoolgirl, not a wife of two years' standing.

Luckily, he slept for some hours, in an exhausted state that spoke volumes about his continued current weakened condition. Now and then he muttered in his sleep and once turned his head restlessly, as if trying to find a cool place on his pillow. She went silently to turn it for him, herself baking in the hot little room, and bathed his forehead with a cool cloth.

To her surprise he pushed her hand away and said distinctly, "Don't! Go away!"

Amused despite herself, she was about to do so when his eyes opened slowly, and he looked up into her face.

It seemed to take a moment for them to focus on her and remember who she was, but she could see when he did so, for the frown came back quickly between his brows and he said in the vague, weak voice she was becoming used to, "Oh! It's you. How long have I been asleep?"

"For hours. You pushed my hand away just now when I tried to bathe your forehead. But I'm afraid this dreadful little room is hardly conducive either to your recovering health or comfort."

"Did I?" he asked, again passing his hand over his face. "I'm sorry. I must have been dreaming." He still seemed half asleep and only partly aware of who she was and where they were, but even as she watched, his blue eyes gradually seemed to come into focus and he looked more himself, as if, at least, some of his wits were returning. Perhaps too much, she was soon to discover. But now he said more strongly, "Good Lord! I do remember now. At least . . . I don't, and that seems to be the problem. Did you really tell me that we are married?"

She nodded, unwillingly. "Yes. D-don't you believe me?"

"Of course I do. I can see no reason why you would lie about such a thing." His eyes had returned to her in frank assessment, and she willed herself not to blush or look as guilty as she felt. "And . . . do we have any . . . children?"

She did blush then and said in pardonable annoyance, "No, of course we have not! We have only been m-married two years, and . . . and you have been away most of that time."

"Ah, yes, I am a soldier. I do seem to remember that. And that, if you don't mind my saying so, sounds like a genuinely wifely complaint. But perhaps that explains it, for you still blush so delightfully that I am surprised we have been married even so long as two years.

She blushed hotly again, cursing the brainstorm that had led her into such a ridiculous charade, and wondering where it would all end. It also occurred to her, unwillingly, that even a wife of two years would likely show more affection and relief at the recovery of her husband, even without his memory intact, than she was doing. Consequently, she made herself sit on the side of the bed and take his hand, hoping he could not feel how cold her own was. "If I blush, you must remember that it is . . . hardly pleasant to find myself married to a man who . . . doesn't remember me," she said quickly. "But never mind that. I think it would be b-best if we avoided all controversial topics for the moment. Tell me instead how you are feeling? Still as if your head were an anvil?"

He grimaced. "Did I say that? If so, it is more like a drum, now, I'm thankful to say." He was still watching her in a disconcerting manner, but he frowned and added, "Did I also dream it, or did you in fact tell me some rigmarole about Washington having been torched?"

It was the last subject she wanted to discuss with him, for it seemed to her that however blank his memory might be at the moment, he was dangerously near remembering a good deal more than she wished him to. Again she wished she had never launched herself into such a tangle of lies, which seemed increasingly to resemble quicksand, tripping her up at every turn and dragging her ever deeper and deeper.

"Y-yes," she said unwillingly. "The . . . the British burned the public buildings to the ground in retaliation for our having burnt York early in the war. But that is surely not important now."

He was still frowning, but he said slowly, "Perhaps you're right. That seems to ring a bell with me, however. And what was I doing at the time? I mean surely we did not simply stand by and let them do it?"

She wished she could find some way to get him off the wretched topic of the war. She wished Dessy would come in, or even the odious Mrs. Tigwood, or she could think of some excuse for cutting so unwanted a discussion short. "No, of course not! That is . . . you . . . I mean our troops . . . had made a stand at Bladensburg, and were unfortunately defeated there."

"I . . . see," he said again. "Is that where I was wounded?"

"Yes, you took a sabre cut there. That is why your arm continues so stiff."

"And you remained in Washington?" he asked incredulously.

"Did I at least not have enough sense to see my wife to safety before I went off to battle?"

This was growing more and more difficult. "You . . . you wished me to go, but I wouldn't," she said somewhat desperately. "Anyway, we . . . we believed Baltimore would be the British target, not Washington. And afterward, of course, you came as soon as you could to find me."

"I am glad to hear it. That relieves my mind of one of its worries at least," he remarked almost sardonically.

"What do you mean?" She was not in the least sure she wanted to know.

"Simply that I am beginning to wonder why you married me, my dear. I would seem to be a most irresponsible husband. But perhaps that explains one thing that had begun to puzzle me."

"W-what?" she demanded again, even more unwillingly.

He smiled ruefully. "Forgive me, but I confess I am finding it somewhat difficult to believe that we are a loving couple, as you have tried to convince me," he said, giving her the worst shock yet.

Chapter 15

She found she could think of nothing to say, which was fortunate, for he was not, as she had first suspected, rejecting her story completely. "Don't look like that," he added quickly. "I'm not blaming you. How could I? On the contrary, it would seem I have not been a very good husband to you already, my dear. And now this."

Again she felt the most complete fraud. But it might make things easier if he believed they were somewhat estranged. So she dropped her eyes and said as if unwillingly, "I . . . it is true that we . . . have not always seen eye to eye. But I daresay all . . . marriages are somewhat rocky at the beginning. Besides, you mustn't blame yourself entirely. We have both been stubborn and"—she could not resist, remembering his earlier accusation—"pigheaded. You didn't want me to remain in Washington and would have sent me to safety, but I didn't wish to go. And . . . and you did come back for me. So it is not all your fault."

He grinned weakly. "A more handsome admission than I suspect I deserve. Thank you. Which reminds me, that is another part of the story that makes no sense to me. Or did you not say something about others? Some . . . girl and her baby and a dog? Surely that cannot be right?"

"Of course it is!" She was glad to be on safer ground. "We stopped and rescued them, for we could scarcely have left either to burn—or to the tender mercies of the British. Elsie had just given birth and had been left behind when the family she belongs to fled Washington. And the mongrel dog had been badly burnt and was shortly to have puppies. Why are you laughing?"

"I'm sorry, my dear. I can't help it. It is all so ridiculous, you know. And you should not make me laugh, for it hurts too much. On second thought, perhaps you had better not tell me any more now, for it seems I am not yet strong enough to take it in. In fact, only one thing is becoming increasingly clear to me."

She was again half fearful of his answer. "And what is that?"

"That however much I may wonder why you ever married *me*, my dear, I have no doubt whatsoever why I married you." He took her hand in his weak clasp and unexpectedly lifted it to his lips and kissed it. The contact burned, and it was all Sorcha could do not to snatch her hand away and to allow it to lie submissively in his until he had closed his eyes tiredly again and gone back to sleep.

As if all that weren't bad enough, Dessy was soon proved right about the Reverend Jedediah Tigwood as well.

Sorcha had thought that his return would prove no help as far as the work they were obliged to do, but she soon discovered she was mistaken and could only wish she had been right. He took to turning up whenever Sorcha ventured downstairs, wanting to carry trays for her or perform any other service she might have for him. His manner was always obsequious, but she could not forget that first night and was as short as she dared be with him.

Even more to her disgust, he also developed a habit of hanging around the barn, lying in wait for her to come down and feed and care for the animals. There she was out of reach of Dessy's protection, and though she did not fear Mr. Tigwood, few things would she have liked less than to be obliged to fend off his advances.

He did not go so far—at least yet. In fact, he took care not to do anything Sorcha could technically object to. He remained just on the right side of acceptable behavior, though his brand of heavy gallantry was annoying. His eyes also betrayed him, for despite his calling they had a way of mentally undressing her whenever they rested upon her.

He also contrived to make it plain that he was at least as suspicious about her circumstances and her so-called husband as his wife was, which was the one thing that kept her from putting an end to his unwanted attentions at once and in a blistering way he was unlikely soon to forget.

For it was still an unwelcome fact that for the moment, at least, until the captain recovered enough to travel, she could not afford to alienate either of the Tigwoods too much.

So she held her tongue with difficulty and made fewer and fewer forays downstairs. When she did go, she made sure Dessy was nearby, and was even forced into taking the already over-worked Dessy with her when she tended to the animals.

For whatever her husband's failings, to which she seemed largely oblivious, Mrs. Tigwood had continued strong in her re-fusal to wait on her unwanted guests. That meant Dessy was obliged to do all the cooking; and with so many invalids in the house there was a great deal of toiling up and down narrow stairs with trays and cans of hot water and the like. Sorcha did what she could to help her, but between the problem with Mr. Tigwood and Dessy's own stubborn views of what was fitting for her charge, this was little enough.

At least Elsie was fast recovering her health and spirits, and her scrap of a baby was gaining weight and yelling lustily whenever something did not please him.

Dessy, who in Sorcha's view was fast developing an irritating partiality for the captain, took to taking the baby downstairs to en-tertain the captain. It might have amused her to see the captain, awkwardly holding the tiny black child in his one good arm, and trying to coax a smile from it, but Sorcha was less enthralled.

Dessy also fussed over the captain to a degree Sorcha thought ridiculous. She had always known that Dessy had an unworthy respect for strong and forceful men, notwithstanding her own husband's easygoing ways. But she thought Dessy spoiled the captain ridiculously.

The captain's memory had not returned, somewhat to Sorcha's secret and painful relief, but after that first painful interview his health seemed to be mending far more rapidly than Sorcha would have expected. He still complained of headaches and slept a good part of the day, but his arm was at last mending, and physically at least, he seemed stronger every day.

On the one hand, that was undoubtedly good news, for once he was recovered sufficiently to travel, they could leave that dreadful place forever. But on the other hand, what to do with him until—or if—his memory returned, was a problem that was increasingly

occupying Sorcha. She supposed she could simply turn him over
to his own army, but that entailed risks of its own. Besides, she
was far more anxious to find Magnus and reassure herself that he
was all right, than she was to go in search of the British troops.

She had half feared one or the other side would find them, but
they seemed far enough off the beaten path that no one came at
all, not even to drink ale in the dingy taproom downstairs. They
might have been the only persons left in the world, trapped together in that unpleasant inn, with no news at all from the outside
world. How the war was progressing or which side was winning
were all things she could only speculate anxiously on, for they
might as well have been on the moon.

The only good thing to be said was that after that fist day the
captain had thankfully not subjected her to any more catechisms,
seemingly content merely to lie there and watch her whenever she
was in the room. Sometimes his glance was quizzical, as if he
were on the verge of remembering something. And at other times
he watched her with an intensity that she found unnerving, as if
she puzzled him and he would like to get to the bottom of her. But
still the breakthrough that she both dreaded and longed for never
occurred, and though he was improving physically by leaps and
bounds, his memory remained blank and clouded.

He himself was made increasingly restive and impatient by that
fact and began to object to lying around in bed and leaving all the
work to her and Dessy.

Dessy pooh-poohed that and assured him confidently that after
such a blow to the head it was not unusual to suffer a temporary
loss of memory. The chances were the least little thing would at
last spark his memory, and in the meantime he was not to worry
himself sick or to let her see him trying to get up again when he
was still as weak as a kitten and likely to suffer a relapse if he
weren't careful.

He had subsided on that occasion with a rueful grin and since
Dessy spoiled him shamelessly, was wholly tractable in her
hands. She made special dishes to tempt his still poor appetite and
had even taken to regaling him with tales of Sorcha's own mis-
spent girlhood since there were no books in the house and he
claimed to be bored to death just lying there. But that at least was
a pastime that Sorcha did her best to discourage, for she thought it
dangerous, if nothing else. The whole situation seemed to her like

a house of cards needing only a whiff of wind to send the whole tumbling down.

As for herself, Sorcha didn't know whether to be alarmed that he would regain his memory too soon, or increasingly worried when he did not. The deception she was forced to live with, brought about by her own impetuous tongue, and the enforced intimacy of the whole ridiculous situation was definitely starting to wear on her. The captain made no demands on her and absolutely no attempt to take advantage of the situation. He was far too weak for one thing and far too much of a gentleman, she suspected, for another.

Indeed, he continued to assume that as his supposed wife she must be feeling his loss of memory as much or more than he did, and his concern only served to make her feel even more of a wretch. It was growing increasingly difficult for her to meet his eyes, and increasingly embarrassing to make herself convey at least the impression of a loving and worried wife.

Worse, her deliberate avoidance of the scarecrow-thin Mr. Tigwood, with his bobbing Adam's apple, threw her back into the captain's company far more than she wished, and more than his slowly gaining strength would have dictated. He dozed a good deal in a half-waking, half-sleeping state that Dessy pronounced to be just what he needed, easily aroused but by no means normal, and yet certainly no longer requiring a full-time nurse.

He also, despite his continued weakness, saw far more than was convenient at times, and Sorcha remained wary of his unnerving gaze.

Once she had managed to escape from the ever-vigilant Mr. Tigwood only by using the tray of soup she was taking up to the sickroom as a shield and insisting that it would get cold if she didn't hurry. The reverend's eyes were growing more and more bold as the days passed, and in the face of her avoidance of him, he had begun to use any excuse he could find to corner her. When he did, which was unfortunately not always avoidable, he had taken to brushing against her as if accidentally, though Sorcha knew that it was anything but an accident. He would insist upon holding a door for her, or taking the tray she was carrying, as now, and seldom missed touching her hand or her shoulder or worse. It was a contact that made her flesh creep and made her wonder if he really thought she was too stupid to know what he was doing.

This time he insisted upon carrying the tray upstairs for her, as if it had been an immensely heavy object, and thanks to his wife's laziness she had not been forced to fetch and carry far heavier things up the same stairs. He seemed impressed by her "quality," and Sorcha had once heard him trying to press Dessy about her, with particular emphasis on her wealth, her so-called marriage, and Magnus's being a senator.

That had not worried Sorcha, for getting anything out of Dessy that she did not wish to reveal was a complete waste of time, as she herself had discovered at an early age.

But still, she did not like the way the landlord's mind was running, and she was more eager than ever to see the last of the Tigwoods, both husband and wife. Unfortunately, she was still not eager to force the issue and could only put up with his unpleasant gropings for as long as it did not become too unbearable.

She was becoming adept at fending him off, however, and by dint of her tray and a freezing glance that she employed to good effect, managed to escape him once again. He gave in with an ill grace, but not without managing to brush her arm on the narrow stairs as she passed and leer down from his superior height, as if trying to see down her dress.

She thus entered the hot little room more precipitately than usual and stood with her back against the scarred panels of the door, still holding her tray of soup and seething. With each passing day his attempts grew more blatant, and though Sorcha did not ultimately doubt her ability to protect herself—with a pistol if she had to—and was even almost to the point where she would welcome such a confrontation, she could not afford a blowup just yet. Even for the satisfaction of letting Mrs. Tigwood see exactly what her lecherous and far-from-holy husband was up to, it did not seem worth being ordered off and risking the captain's safety. It seemed she would have to hold on to her temper a while longer and endure Mr. Tigwood's groping hands.

She had just straightened from the door, far from satisfied with the expedient solution about Tigwood, when the captain's voice, still not completely normal but every day growing stronger, asked with unusual sharpness from the bed, "What is it, my dear? What's the matter?"

She started, for she had expected him to be asleep. "N-nothing!" she said quickly, coming on into the room. "I have brought you some soup. Dessy made it specially for you."

He looked at her with eyes that, however little he remembered of his own identity, still showed an uncannily acute intelligence sometimes. Mindful of her role as a loving wife, and those too-intelligent eyes, she dutifully and somewhat awkwardly went to kiss him on the cheek, as she had developed the habit of doing, then straightened his pillows and covers for him, hoping she was not blushing too ridiculously. Once he grew strong enough to expect more than a peck on the cheek, she would be in trouble, but so far he showed no signs of wanting more, perhaps respecting the unusual circumstances and his belief in their fictional quarrel. She knew he believed that they were somewhat estranged, though he had never again questioned her about it. But she had clung to that belief as to a lifeline, as a way to explain the awkwardness that was inevitable between them.

And this time, too, he subsided and asked no more embarrassing questions, as if respecting her reticence. Instead, he dutifully ate some of the soup, though his appetite was still almost nonexistent. But she might have known from her earlier dealings with him that he was not easily fooled. When the soup was disposed of, or at least as much as she could coax him to eat, and she had thankfully picked up her tray again, more willing to face the dreadful Tigwood again than stay to meet that steady, frowning gaze, he said abruptly, "Don't go yet! It seems you are always rushing off somewhere."

She hesitated, not daring to refuse, and he added ruefully, "I fear I must be a sad burden on you, my dear. It seems to me you have lost weight and are looking paler even than when we first arrived."

She might have told him the reason, but of course did not. But she wanted no tête-à-tête with him, especially if he were in a talkative mood. Since that first day he had asked her very little, but he often wore a frown that she hoped denoted headache and not growing doubt of her story.

"Don't be ridiculous," she said bracingly, holding her tray as a weapon exactly as she had done with Mr. Tigwood, though for very different reasons. It was not his hands she feared. "It is you who hardly eats enough to keep a bird alive, and Dessy is likely to think you don't like her cooking if you don't watch out. In fact, I should have sent her up with this, for I notice you eat far more under her coaxing than you do for me."

He smiled at her nonsense, though it was only perfunctory.

"Dessy knows none of that is true. Sit down again a moment, will you?" he inquired politely, patting the bed beside him. "I want to talk to you."

She reluctantly did so, unable to think of a convincing excuse, though she perched unwillingly on the extreme edge of the bed, as far away from him as possible. "Five minutes, then. You should be resting. Whatever you may say, and however uncommunicative you may be when I ask how you are doing, I know that you are still weak and your headaches have not gotten any better. Have they?"

He shrugged ruefully and did not answer, which was an answer in itself. Instead, he said, "I may have lost my memory, but I am neither blind, nor a fool, you know. Something is troubling you, and has been troubling you the whole time we've been here. And it is far more than my health or my wretched amnesia. What is it? I realize . . . things may not be as easy between us as I, at least, would wish, but cannot you bring yourself to confide in me?"

She almost laughed, for between hostile armies and even more hostile landlords, it seemed she had reason enough to be troubled, without going into the awkward truth. But she seized the most believable—and least controversial—of reasons and said with a show of reluctance, "I *am* worried about your health—how could I not be? But I also still have no way of knowing whether Magnus is safe or not, and I confess that I can't help worrying."

"I'm sorry," he said contritely, quickly covering her hand. "I know it must be hard for you, and I have been little help. Quite the reverse, in fact, for I am the one who is holding you here. But if that's truly all that is bothering you, we could leave tomorrow. I am very well able to travel, I assure you."

"And a more absurd statement I have seldom had to listen to!" she retorted. "When you can scarcely stand or even sit up without becoming dizzy, and are obviously far from being well enough even to go downstairs, let alone sit in a bumping cart over bad roads for a distance of some twenty or thirty miles."

He was obliged to agree, though with a rueful smile. But he said instead in a voice that was clearly meant to be eminently reasonable, "At least there is no reason why you could not go yourself. It makes no sense for both of us to be tied by the heels here, especially when you are so anxious about your father. In fact, it would relieve at least one of *my* worries, for as you well know, I dislike your having to wait on me hand and foot, toiling up those stairs and doing jobs more suited to a servant than my wife. It is not in the least fitting, especially since I am well enough now, save for this damned continued headache. The . . . er . . . Tigwoods can easily do all that I require and I should be well enough to follow you in a few days."

She almost laughed again, for she thought he would soon repent his bargain if she were indeed callous enough to leave him to the Tigwoods' tender mercies. But she said merely, "If that is all you have to say, I would do better to take this tray downstairs and leave you to sleep, for you are being unforgivably nonsensical."

He sighed, but said merely, "I somehow suspected you were going to say that. I may not remember how we met or anything about our marriage, but I am fast coming to know you, my dear. And you are remarkably stubborn you know."

He paused then, frowning, as if listening to what he had just said, and seemed to find an echo in his head. He had said something very similar to her on that first night, she remembered, on pins and needles that his own words would come back to him. But after a moment he shook his head impatiently and gave it up. "Damn and blast!" he said instead, betraying one of his brief flashes of frustration. "At times I seem to have snatches of memory, but they always elude me. Never mind. Your Dessy—whom I like more and more, by the way—tells me that she has some experience of such matters, and the harder I try, the longer it may take my memory to return. She also tells me that very likely it will come back all at once, when I least expect it. I only hope she may be right."

When Sorcha made no comment, finding none to make, he smiled somewhat ruefully and added, "But I didn't mean merely to add to your worries, my dear." Thankfully he seemed to have forgotten his earlier question, which was a relief, at least. But her relief turned out to be short-lived. "Tell me instead, if you will," he said, "what do I do when I am not fighting wars? Do I pursue a trade of some sort?"

She looked quickly at him, but he was lying with his hand shielding his eyes, as he often did, as if the light hurt him. "In . . . W-Washington?" She was going to have to get better control of herself and stop stuttering whenever he posed an awkward question, or she may as well tell him the truth and be done with it. "You are a solicitor." Because of Geoff, it was the first occupation that popped into her head.

He seemed astonished for some reason. "A solicitor?" he repeated. "You mean, wills and such?" Something in him must have rebelled at the notion, for he added, "Good God! I sit in an office all day poring over dusty books?"

"Y-yes, but in truth, I fear you are not a particularly good solicitor," she said feebly.

He grinned at that. "I can readily believe it. It is the last thing I would have pictured myself doing. In fact, it is the damnedest sensation. I lie here and listen to you or Dessy telling me about my past, though you both are oddly reluctant to talk about anything that happened before this week," he added dryly, removing his hand so that he could better see her face. "And it is as if it all belongs to someone else. It is frustrating, to say the least. I possess a beautiful wife I can't remember, a father-in-law, a profession, a home and friends, no doubt, and yet it all seems no more real to me than if I had read it in a novel." His hand had again lifted to gingerly touch the wound over his ear, another habit he had developed.

She felt a renewed stab of guilt and again came close, as she had once or twice before, to confessing the whole to him. She feared it was hindering his recovery; but it would all be over soon enough. Surely, they could leave in a day or two, and then whether he had recovered his memory or not, she would tell him the truth and leave it up to him what he wanted to do. She had appeased her conscience for days now with that.

"Don't!" she said quickly and with more emotion than she usually revealed. "T-try not to let it bother you."

He gave a hint of his crooked smile. "That at least sounded very wifely. Don't worry, my dear. I am very hard to kill."

She stared at him in a sudden frown. "How do you know that?" she asked quickly.

He, too, frowned, the smile fading. "I don't know," he acknowledged at last. "Under the circumstances it seems a remarkably foolish thing to say. Only I have a feeling . . . no, it was there briefly, but now it's gone."

He sounded merely tired this time, and despite herself her face softened. She put a hand briefly to his lean cheek, a gesture she usually did not permit herself, and said softly, "Try not to let it worry you. It will soon enough be over. Get some sleep." She hoped devoutly she was telling him the truth, for both their sakes.

He captured her hand and brought it to his lips, as he had become wont to do. "It seems my sleeping is almost worse than my waking," he confessed ruefully.

She knew that he had bad dreams, for often he twisted and turned restlessly, muttering in his sleep and obviously finding it anything but restful. She found pity stirring in her and for once did not hurry to pull her hand away, though usually she shrank guiltily from such gestures.

He also seemed surprised, but kissed it again, turning it over to hold against his cheek. "Poor darling!" he said lightly. "But I will make this up to you one day. I promise."

Despite his words he still looked tired and ill and dispirited, and not for the first time she had to resist the urge to reach out and smooth away the lines between his brows with her fingers. It was growing harder and harder all the time to remember this man was her enemy—and one upon whom she was practicing a most dangerous deception.

Chapter 16

That stopped her, for she realized in alarm that it was days since she had remembered everything that divided them, and that he was indeed still her enemy. In fact, it was increasingly difficult to accept that he was her enemy, whatever color uniform he might wear. It somehow had not even occurred to her until then that in sheltering the captain she was in effect betraying her own country. Magnus might even now be dead or severely wounded at the hands of a countryman, or even a friend, of the man she was now hiding and nursing back to health. And yet even if that should prove to be the case, she knew she could not have done any different. Not only had he risked his own life to help her, but he was no longer merely an enemy soldier to her, or even a stranger who had gone out of his way to be kind to her. In fact, for the first time she acknowledged that if she were not careful, she was in considerable danger of liking him too much.

She quickly shied away from the thought as if from a sore tooth. It was important to remember all that the British had done and were guilty of, from the burning of her own home on. She tried to stoke up the fires of the old hatred against the British, spurred on by Magnus's countless tales of British atrocities. But it no longer seemed to work.

Instead, she reminded herself that in a few days' time, with any luck, he would be back with his regiment and she would be in

Annapolis to find Magnus waiting for her, and all this would be forgotten. Nothing was more certain than that she would never see Captain Charles Ashbourne again. She would return to her old life, and the war would soon end, so things could go back to normal.

Yet it all rang hollow, somehow. Things might go back to normal, and she might well return to her old life. But she was not sure she would be the same, ever again.

She supposed she must be staring at him unnaturally, for his hand tightened on hers and he asked almost quizzically, "What are you thinking about, my dear? You are looking at me most oddly."

She blinked and with haste brought herself back to the present. "Nothing," she said hurriedly. "I m-must get this tray back downstairs again or Dessy will be forced to do the dishes. The odious Mrs. Tigwood does as little as she can get by with."

He frowned, but immediately let her hand go. "Yes, of course. The last thing I want to do is to add to your work. Or Dessy's either, for that matter. But I take it you don't find our . . . hostess particularly amiable? That is not the first time you've spoken of her disparagingly."

"She!" retorted Sorcha, grateful for the excuse to rise and busy herself gathering up the tray and put an end to the tête-à-tête. "She is a despicable woman, and if it were possible, I would like nothing better than to tell her what I think of her so-called Christian behavior. She only took us in grudgingly and dislikes having us here, chiefly I believe because of the extra work it causes her, though she takes good care to ensure that is little enough. I'm sorry to say it is Dessy who bears the brunt of it, for which you should be grateful. Your appetite would be even worse if you had to eat Mrs. Tigwood's cooking, I can assure you. As if that weren't bad enough, she has started having to come with me whenever I go out to see to the animals because that wretched—" Then she broke off, realizing too late where her unwary tongue was leading her. She had been so shaken by her thoughts that she had rattled on unthinkingly.

"Because that wretched—?" he prompted her, still faintly smiling.

"N-nothing! I've forgotten what I was about to say," she said hastily, and she feared not very convincingly. "Now try and get some sleep, without worrying about the odious Mrs. Tigwood and her equally odious husband."

He certainly seemed not to be convinced, for he had begun to frown a little, and he ignored that last advice. "That sounds ominous. What does the odious Mr. Tigwood do?"

She blushed and wished she had never started this. "Nothing," she said, again cursing her too ready tongue. "It is only thanks to his intervention that Mrs. Tigwood has consented to wait on us at all, so I should be grateful, I suppose."

"But you are not. I think I must meet the so obliging Mr. Tigwood. And soon," he pronounced rather grimly. "Damn this whole situation! Perhaps you should bring him up here so that we may have a little chat—and the sooner the better."

He looked, for a moment, surprisingly formidable, and for the first time it occurred to her she might have another resource to protect her against the odious Mr. Tigwood. Then she instantly dismissed the thought, thinking that he was far too weak to be a match for the leerily annoying Mr. Tigwood, who for all his thinness looked unpleasantly strong. Besides, the last thing she wanted was an exchange between the already suspicious Mr. Tigwood and the equally puzzled captain, whose memory might still evade him but who might remember everything at the most inconvenient moment and blurt it out.

She had no way of guessing, of course, looking at him in his weakened state, his head still bandaged and his arm all but useless, that she would indeed soon have cause to welcome his rescue yet again. And in her present mood it was doubtful if she would have welcomed the news if she had. It seemed to her that the sooner they all were away from the wretched inn the better, and not merely for the sake of the captain's safety.

For another day or so things remained quiet. Once the captain had begun to recover, Sorcha had prudently taken to sleeping in the attic, however crowded and uncomfortable it might be. She took care every evening, however, that the Tigwoods had retired to their own bedchamber down the hall and would not hear her creep up the stairs.

She had more or less managed to remain out of Mr. Tigwood's way. But since with the captain's improving health she had also taken to spending as little time as possible in his company, to Dessy's unspoken curiosity, it was becoming more and more difficult to find a haven in that uncomfortable little inn. She began taking long walks with the excuse that she needed the exercise and in truth hoping to tire herself out. And if she returned from them in no better humor than when she left, and was not sleeping particularly well, despite such exercise, she trusted that Dessy was too taken up with the two invalids to notice.

Though that was by no means certain. Dessy had begun to watch her oddly, and more than a little curiously, as if she were waiting for something, though Sorcha could not begin to guess what. With the continued recovery of both of Dessy's patients Sorcha was by no means grateful for the renewed attention of her old nurse.

But now Sorcha saw with a stab that Dessy herself was looking tired and every year of her age, which was nearer to sixty than fifty. It was little wonder, considering all they had been through, and the unpleasantness of their current surroundings. Like Sorcha herself, Dessy had no way of knowing what had become of Ham and must be fretting over it. She was always deeply reticent about her private life and had a dignity many of the Washington matrons might envy, but she must be as worried and frightened as Sorcha was.

Sorcha took another look at her and sent her to bed early. They were seated in the kitchen late one evening, where Dessy had stood over Sorcha until she had eaten, for Sorcha's appetite seemed to be as nonexistent as the captain's lately. Dessy had also taken to escorting her most places she went in the house, for she mistrusted their landlord even more than Sorcha did.

"And no excuses," Sorcha said firmly, seeing Dessy about to argue. "With Elsie and the baby to look after, not to mention the captain, and all the cooking to do, you look as if you need to sleep for a week. Do you think it would be of any help to me to have you ill as well?"

Then she stooped and gave her a swift kiss. "Go to bed," she ordered softly, "and don't come down again until you are completely rested. Just imagine what I would do without you. If you are worried about these few dishes, I'll do them. Or we'll leave them for Mrs. Tigwood in the morning. She does little enough as it is. I . . . I'll be up shortly."

Dessy smiled wearily and consented to go, which was a measure of how exhausted she must be. Usually she was as stubborn, in her own quiet way, as Magnus was. Where he blustered, she stood firm, her arms quietly folded and her face unreadable, and calmly did what she thought was right. No amount of argument usually managed to sway her.

Ham, her husband of more than thirty years, was in many ways her opposite. He was lighthearted and easygoing, with a grin that lit the black moon of his face to staggering brilliance, and prone to enjoying private jokes of his own, his big shoulders shaking in silent laughter. He served the volatile Magnus patiently and without question, as devoted to him as he was to his wife. He was simple and childlike and Sorcha adored him, but he himself realized without resentment that his wife was smarter than he was and took her advice on most things. Together they were a perfect couple and had made Sorcha's childhood as solid and secure as it could be under the circumstances. She indeed did not know what she would do without them.

Thus it was that Sorcha unwillingly climbed the stairs to the hot little attic unescorted, for once. Mr. Tigwood and his wife had taken themselves off to bed more than an hour before, so for once she felt relatively safe. She reached the landing on the second floor, carrying a rather malodorous lamp that cast strange shadows before her, since the amenities at the inn did not stretch to wax candles.

There a looming shape made her jump in nervousness she would not have experienced a week before. It seemed all her experiences were beginning to tell on her, and she was instantly annoyed with herself when she realized it was nothing but her own elongated shadow on the wall before her.

Her relief was shortlived, however. The next minute Mr. Tigwood peeled himself off the wall, where he had evidently been waiting for her, and she realized immediately that he had obviously been drinking. She could smell the cheap whiskey on his breath, probably homemade, even from a distance.

She glanced over her shoulder unwillingly, aware of the silent house and the stifling darkness on the landing that her lamp did but little to dispel. She was not precisely afraid, for the house was full of people who would come if she called—including his wife. But she was in no mood for another encounter with his probing hands and hot eyes, and her heart sank a little.

"What do you want?" she demanded sharply, though in a lowered voice, for fear of waking up the captain asleep not ten feet away behind one of the doors on the landing.

"Now, now, li'l lady," he said and grinned, his Adam's apple bobbing and his breath even more potently disgusting. "Jes you keep your voice down. I've somethin' to show you I think you might be interested in."

"There is nothing you could show me that I would in the least be interested," she retorted, wanting only to have this unpleasant encounter over. "Especially at this time of night. Now I am tired and I am going to . . ."

But her voice died out as she saw him produce a sabre from behind his back, which glowed dully in the insufficient light. He himself carried no lamp—no doubt to keep his hands free. And she thought she would not hesitate to use hers as a weapon if it came to that.

But now she gazed at the sabre in dawning horror, suspecting what it must be. "What . . . where did you get that?" she demanded a little hollowly. She had carefully hidden the captain's coat and helmet, but she could not now recall if she had done the same for his sabre, or if he had even been wearing one.

But it was all too evident from Mr. Tigwood's leering expression that he thought he had the upper hand at last.

"Shh!" he warned her again. "I somehow don't think you'd want my wife to hear what I have to say. Or that so-called husbin of yours. Powerful agin the redcoats, is my Durie."

Sorcha's heart was pounding suddenly in her throat and her mouth was dry. Her thoughts were jumbled, but she could do nothing or make no plans until she knew exactly what the danger was. If he suspected the truth—as she must suppose he did—he might again merely be after money, in which case she could manage to shut him up, at least for the present. In fact, she profoundly hoped it was only money he wanted.

But she did not like the look in his eyes, or the way he stared at her, as if she were a prime piece of horseflesh he was thinking of buying. It might indeed have to be the lamp, full of hot oil, and she would have no hesitation using it if necessary, though her hand was shaking so much the shadows wavered even more, making the whole scene seem like something out of a fantastic nightmare. She wondered rather ridiculously if she might be able to wrest the sabre out of his hands and use it on him.

"What do you want?" she repeated in a whisper she hoped was merely disdainful and did not betray her true emotions.

He grinned again, wolfishly. "Now, ma'am, we both know that

there man inside there ain't your husbin. Leastways he wasn't till I married you mysef. I'm beginning to regret that, but you cain't always see far enough ahead. What he is is an escaped British soljer, unless I much mistake, and that means what you're doing is treason. I suspected as much from the first, and so did my wife. She told me he don't talk like an American, and she was suspicious some hanky-panky was goin' on. But it wasn't till this afternoon when I found this buried in the barn that I knew for sure."

"Then someone else put it there," insisted Sorcha, trying to remain calm. "It may be American, for all I know. Or belong to you yourself."

"It's British, all right," he said confidently.

"If it is, then my husband must have found it and kept it as a prize of war." But she knew she was fighting a rear guard action.

He grinned again, most unpleasantly. "Now you got me wrong, l'il lady. Me, I don't care what side he fought for, or where he got it. Don't the Lord say we are all children in his eyes? The trouble is, I don't think anyone else is likely to be so tolerant as I am. Especially the army you tell us was so soundly whipped by the redcoats. But you play your cards right, and I ain't aimin' even to tell Durie, though the Lord also says a husbin and wife are of one flesh." The pious words almost made Sorcha gag under the circumstances. "But I would naturally expect somethin' in return."

Sorcha almost shuddered at the meaning in his alcohol-laden voice. "How . . . much?" she demanded unwillingly. "How much is the price of your . . . silence?"

He chuckled and loomed closer in the dark. "That's somethin' we kin discuss later. Now I'm interested in a more . . . immediate reward. A high-spirited gal like yoursef must be feeling mighty . . . lonely. After all, he ain't likely to be worth much to you in his present condition. Seems to me I'd even be doin' you a favor, like." He grinned again leeringly at her and put his hot hand on her arm.

She struck it away without reflection, though what he was threatening was more than alarming. Blackmail was one thing, though she would trust him about as far as she could throw him. But the captain's life might very well lie in the balance, and she dared not spurn him as she longed to. Even that instinctive act had been a mistake, as she very quickly saw.

For his expression changed instantly, the somewhat fatuous and unpleasant leer hardening. It seemed to her for a moment, in that fitful light, that he was not the negligible if annoying menace she had thought him. But she refused to give in to the thought. She was not afraid of the Reverend Jedediah Tigwood.

"It seems to me you ain't in any position to be so high and mighty and put on them airs anymore," he almost snarled. "Or perhaps you ain't thought it all through. Not only would that red-coat you been shelterin' end up at the end of a rope, most like, but feelin's are runnin' mighty high at the moment, as you know. The chances are you might even join him, for aidin' and abettin' an enemy. Have you thought of that? At the least you kin count on being arrested and disgraced, and that fine father you're so proud of would be, too. Scarcely a desirable thing for a senator to have a traitor for a daughter, now is it?"

She did not take him seriously on the threat against herself—at least too seriously. But the captain's fate, especially after the burning of Washington, was a different matter. She very much feared he might be right, for it was the thought that had driven her all along in disguising his identity.

But she hissed, in spite of everything still absurdly mindful of waking the captain, "Keep your distance! And it seems to me that if I was to tell your wife about your . . . little suggestion, you might find yourself in some hot water as well."

He chuckled and without warning reached out and grabbed her arm again in a bruising grip and pulled her toward him, triumph showing in his face, made even more unpleasant by the flickering light of the lamp she still held. The benefit of his breath at close quarters was almost more sickening than his touch. "She'll do as she's told," he said confidently. "Women-folk like to think they're clever, but you're jes like all the rest, l'il lady, believe me. All you need is a man to show you what's what and bring you down a peg or two, and I don't mean an invalid or a limey neither. In fact it'll give me great pleasure to do just that."

His grip on her arm was unexpectedly strong, and his face leered so near to her own, with the full burden of his whiskey-laden breath, that she was made almost physically sick by it. Worse, she was in imminent danger of dropping the lamp, which might at least put an end to the present horrible scene, she thought with an ill-timed humor, but another house burning down about her ears seemed a little too much, even for the circumstances.

He had managed to pull her against him, even hampered as she was by not wishing to drop the lamp or pour hot oil over herself, at least, though she was by no means as concerned for her assailant's safety. He was much stronger than she would have believed, and though she struggled determinedly, he seemed to possess a dozen hands and arms, all long and sinewy. One of them was fumbling at the front of her gown, and with a sudden move he managed to rip the neck of her dress away.

That almost made her laugh again, though it was no doubt hysteria rather than true amusement, for it seemed to her she had been in this precise situation before. Only this time the captain was unlikely to rescue her. And, far less amusingly, his own fate might very well hang in the balance.

But oddly enough, the damage to her only remaining gown made her furious, as well. She managed to land a telling blow to Tigwood's head, knowing even as she did so that she should be trying to placate him until he passed out, or put him off with vague promises until they could be out of there.

The trouble was he did not seem likely to be put off with vague promises, and even to save the captain she was not about to give in to his horrible demands. She wondered again if she could manage to grab the sabre and stab him with it, and was just concluding it would have to be the hot oil, when an unexpected voice demanded harshly from behind her. *"What the devil is going on here?"*

Both of them were so startled, the reverend momentarily loosened his hold on her, and she was able to wrench herself out of his grasp, panting a little in her relief. The captain stood in the doorway, his face in the lamplight unexpectedly hard. Despite his hastily dragged-on breeches and his bare chest and bandages, he looked surprisingly forbidding, and Sorcha remembered that he was indeed a soldier, after all.

Her first reaction was, in fact, profound relief, only subsequently overlaid by a new worry. He was not well or fit and would be no match in his present condition against the wiry Mr. Tigwood. Besides, the last thing she wanted was for Mr. Tigwood to repeat his accusations to the one they most nearly concerned.

But it seemed Tigwood shared her doubts about the captain's present physical prowess, for once he had recovered from his initial surprise, he laughed insultingly. "Nothin' that need concern you. In fact, you'd best hope this l'il lady don't turn too finicky, for your life may depend upon it." He again deliberately put his hand on her arm.

An unexpected metallic click startled Sorcha and seemed to penetrate even Tigwood's whiskey-soaked brain, for he jumped a foot.

"Yes," said the captain softly, holding a pistol cocked and aimed steadily at the landlord's heart. "At this range I would scarcely miss, and I am fast conceiving a desire to rid the world of someone I think it could very easily do without. Now *unhand my wife!*"

Despite herself Sorcha was not even much surprised when the reverend sullenly did as he was told. She was almost dizzy with relief, but not for one second did she delude herself that the problem had been solved. It had merely been postponed to a moment when the captain wasn't conveniently near. The captain may have won this round, but little though he knew it, he was in the gravest danger from the despicable creature eyeing them both with so much dislike.

And indeed Tigwood could not resist a parting shot. "We'll discuss this some other time, ma'am, don't think we won't!" he said with menace. "I meant everything I said, and don't you forgit it."

Chapter 17

She had no reason to disbelieve him, but could only be grateful to be free of his groping hands and horrible hot breath. She shuddered and did not need a second invitation to put a door between her and the Reverend Jedediah Tigwood, surely one of the most unworthy ministers of God in the world. Again she wondered how he managed to square his acts with his strange religion.

Once the door was safely closed, she said breathlessly, "Thank you! It seems you come to my rescue once again!"

The captain calmly lowered his pistol and uncocked it before laying it down. But he frowned at that. "Again?" he asked blankly.

She was sorry not to have more guard over her tongue and said quickly, almost at random, "N-never mind! W-where did you get the pistol?"

"I always feel safer with a pistol within reach," he said with equal calm, in another of those statements that never failed to alarm her, for they showed his memory was indeed just below the surface. For the first time he seemed to realize that Tigwood had torn her dress, however, for some of the calm seemed to leave him.

"The brute has torn your dress. Hell and damnation! I am beginning to wish I had killed him. You little fool, why didn't you tell me this was what you meant earlier? And what did he mean by his parting remark? What does he mean every word of?"

She shuddered again and was strangely tempted to tell him everything. But it would entail endless explanation and discussion, and quite frankly, at the moment she was not up to either. She felt strangely chilled despite the warm night, and answered only the first of his remarks. "Y-yes! He has torn my dress," she said, her teeth beginning to chatter for some reason. "And it is the l-last one I have, b-blast him!"

He laughed unexpectedly. Then he took another look at her and said abruptly, again, "Hell and damnation! *Blast* this weakness! Come here."

He held out his arms and for some reason she walked straight into them, deep shudders beginning to take her. "I . . . I d-don't know w-what's the m-matter with me," she said, trying to control the weakness she despised.

He was holding her tightly against him, her head beneath his chin, and his cheek on her hair. "I do," he said calmly. "Shock and delayed reaction. I have seen it hundreds of times. You have had all the burdens on your slender shoulders, my dear, and despite your conviction you can do anything, you are only human, I am glad to discover."

She was indeed all too human, for she was having to fight against bursting into tears and clinging to him like the weak-willed women she had always despised. He held her strongly—in both arms, though she failed to notice it—as if he would never let her go, and said softly against her hair, "Poor Sweetheart. Poor darling! It's over now. Don't worry. You're safe now."

Sorcha knew she should get control of herself. To give in to weakness at this late date would be to give way completely, and she could not afford that. Despite his show of strength now, ultimately everything still depended upon her. And Tigwood would still have to be confronted on the morrow.

But his caressing words and the feel of the hand that gently stroked her tumbled hair, far from comforting, seemed likely to undermine all her strength. Magnus was more of the school that one stood up and never cried, and expected her to fight her own battles. Even Dessy was seldom physical with her love; only Ham occasionally had ridden her on his back or given her a quick hug. She would not have thought the mere fact of physical contact could affect her so profoundly, for usually she had no liking to be casually touched.

Now, however, she wanted to weep and go on weeping, out of delayed fear and horror at all that had already happened, as he said, and dread of the future. It was all too tempting to let go of her burdens, at least for a little while, and give in to the hypnotic stroke of his hand in her hair and his arms tightly around her.

And she could not afford to do that. Still, she weakly closed her eyes and leaned against him, finding his warmth reduced the shudders, and that being in his arms was strangely comforting, like rocking in a boat out on the bay.

"Poor baby," he said again, his good arm for some reason tightening around her. "You are exhausted and no wonder. I should be horsewhipped for leaving it all to you and expecting you to carry all the burden. But now it is my turn to take care of you."

Without warning he lifted her bodily in his arms, despite the still only half-healed cut in his left arm. That belatedly got through to her, and she protested, though it seemed her tongue was oddly tangled, and scarcely did as she bid it. "No, no. Your arm! I am too heavy besides."

"My arm is better every day, and you are far from being too heavy, especially lately." He sounded amused, and with unexpected gentleness deposited her on the bed and began to calmly undress her, as if he had done it every night for the past two years they were supposed to have been married.

That almost made her laugh, for it seemed impossible he could really believe all her lies. But she seemed to hear his words as if only through a haze, and was scarcely aware when he removed her dress. At least he made no attempt to go any further, leaving her in her shift and petticoats, and merely tucking her between the rough sheets, as if she had been a child. She knew she should resist, especially since the bed was unaccountably comfortable, in place of the hard mattress she had lain on in that same bed for a night or two, and still lay on upstairs in the attic with Dessy. Part of her brain knew she was lying on the feather mattress she herself had hauled up there, but it was only a vague realization, for her brain seemed fuzzy, and nothing seemed real or important at the moment. All she knew was that she had never been more weary, and felt as if she were drifting in a cloud.

Whether or not he had been aware of the acre of quilt she had been careful to keep between them in the huge bed, she soon dis-

covered there was no acre now. The next moment the lamp had
been turned down, and he had slipped in beside her and taken her
in his sound arm again, holding her safe.

Again some sliver of consciousness recurred to trouble her, but
it was an effort to keep her eyes open—an effort to think of anything beyond never feeling so comfortable and wanting to sleep
for a week. Perhaps if she did, when she woke up, it would all be
over. That thought was so comforting she gave up making either
effort and welcomed sleep as a gift.

What happened next was no doubt inevitable. Had no doubt
been inevitable from the moment she first launched herself on so
desperate and foolish a masquerade. He was, after all, still in that
foggy half world that she had deliberately created, and thus not to
be blamed. The blame was hers alone, for she should have known
from the beginning exactly what fire she was playing with, and
that she was sooner or later bound to be burned.

Even in his weakened state he was undoubtedly a great deal
stronger than she was, but afterward, when it might have helped,
she could not even salve her conscience by claiming he had
forced her. She was the one, God help her, who even precipitated
the whole, for perhaps he had meant no more than to hold her
close during the night in comfort, and sleep innocently enough
beside her. But she woke some long time later with a strangled
cry, the dawn already turning the blackness to gray shadows. Her
dreams had been tumbled and restless, and she could not for a
moment even remember where she was.

Then a sleepy voice said over her head, a familiar hand coming
again to stroke her hair, "It's all right, love. Just a bad dream. Go
back to sleep."

She herself seemed still to be in that cloudy world where her
mind refused to function, and her recent nightmare was still in as-
cendance. Her heart was pumping and her mind full of dread, and
the hand was again something to cling to in a tumbled world.

"What . . . ?" she said foolishly, already half asleep again, re-
laxing under that caressing hand and finding herself unexpectedly
comfortable in the crook of his arm, her cheek pillowed against
his smooth, warm skin.

"You're safe, sweetheart," the voice said again and gathered
her even closer against him. "I'm here and I won't let anything
hurt you."

Foolish words, but she allowed herself to subside, half believing them. No one had held her like that since she had been a very small child and told her she was safe, and in her present half-waking, half-dreaming state, they were magical words, and absurdly comforting.

She should have gotten up then, and returned to her own hard bed upstairs. But she could hear the strong beat of his heart under her cheek and she clung to the shreds of sleep as to a too-short blanket, no doubt because to wake up meant to face reality and have only herself to rely upon. It meant facing Tigwood again, with his hot leering eyes and groping hands and his threats, and responsibility for the captain's safety, not to mention the disturbing truth about herself she had no desire at all to admit. And it meant finding out once and for all about her father's fate, and that of Ham and Geoff as well. It was little wonder she closed her eyes and burrowed against him, desperately trying to cling to the last welcome shreds of oblivion.

The captain's hand moved rhythmically in her hair as it had done earlier, and again it lulled her successfully back toward sleep. She sighed gratefully and moved more warmly against him, feeling comforted and safe. Afterward she could only wonder if she had deliberately rejected any conscious knowledge of the risk she was taking. But then she thought in her own defense, he had held her earlier without anything happening, so he was probably still too weak and ill to be any threat to her.

Or perhaps she had deliberately and knowingly provoked what followed. Again, long afterward, she could not wholly acquit herself of that shameful suspicion. She certainly sighed again and ran her hand over his warm bare chest, even then sinking into the blackness of sleep she so much sought.

But one must pay the price for arousing tigers, even unconsciously, and all along she had underestimated Captain Charles Ashbourne. His reactions, in his muddled mental state, were no doubt completely normal. He groaned, and his arm tightened about her, and he caught her hand up and pressed it to his lips, kissing the palm hotly.

Even then she remained perhaps willfully oblivious to her danger. The sensation he caused was oddly pleasurable, but she still clung obstinately to her dream world, and no alarm bells at all went off in her head as they should have done. She sighed again and stretched against him, and he had every reason to interpret that as complaisance on her part, even open encouragement.

He certainly groaned again, then gathered her even closer, beginning to plant kisses on her hair and face, and muttering, "Oh, God. I have been wanting to do this almost from the first moment I opened my eyes and saw you. It is the one thing that told me your story must be true, for I could scarcely keep my hands off you." He groaned again and pressed kisses lower on her face, her cheek, her nose, adding, "And how ridiculous it has been to be forced to lie here, finding myself every day falling more in love with my own wife all over again."

Somewhere below the surface a few alarm bells did go off at last, but she ignored them, still clinging to her willful dreamlike state, perhaps in protection against the guilt and shame she might otherwise be feeling. For there was no denying that she had no one to blame but herself for his present confused state, and that, by his lights, his actions were completely normal.

And even that was not the whole story, for underneath it all a shameful curiosity and slowly stirring excitement of her own was building, and would not be denied.

However that might be, instead of pushing him away, as she should have done, she raised her face to him, admittedly curious to discover what it would be like to be kissed by him. And if at the time it seemed harmless enough, it was but another in a long string of dangerous follies that she was guilty of committing.

Certainly she knew little of a man's passion, especially one who had no doubt been celibate for too long, and thought he had every right to take what she was seemingly offering. He groaned again and found her lips, and she quickly discovered that kissing him was very different from the few kisses she had exchanged with Geoff, who was almost her brother. But this man needed a shave, despite the fact he had long since demanded to be brought a razor and had begun to show concern for his appearance. Her cheek burned from abrasion with his cheek, and the kiss he was giving her was certainly neither chaste nor brotherly. And everywhere his lips—or hands—touched trailed fire.

Perhaps she did belatedly rouse to danger then. She tried to reassure herself afterward that she had tried to stop him. She had tried. But it was far too little and too late, and she was conscious all the time of his injuries, and ridiculously worried, even then, of not wanting to hurt him.

But that was only half the truth, and she knew it. She was exhausted, frightened, and overburdened, and had seen far too much of horror in the past days, and what he offered was an escape, no matter how brief or foolish—or how much she might come to regret it in the end.

Besides, she had not known she could feel like this; not even guessed that she could be so easily shaken to her soul by the feel of a man's mouth on hers, or that her toes would actually curl and her pulse start racing and her skin become so hot she might have had a fever. Or that she could moan and mindlessly open her mouth to him, or impatiently turn her head so that their mouths fitted more completely together.

It was all shatteringly new to her, and if he had been rough or too demanding, she might even then have come to her senses. But he was gentle and coaxing, as if she were infinitely precious, and everywhere made clear his delight and deep satisfaction with her. He did not rush her or hurry, which he might easily have done. It was as if he knew her inexperience, which of course he could not have done. But she had never guessed a man could be so gentle or so patient, and that realization swept her along as much as her own folly.

Even while he was kissing her, his hand found the ribbons of her chemise and loosed them. She did try to protest then, but her words got lost in his mouth, and she was far beyond rational thought at that point. He thought her his wife—her own lie come back to haunt her—and it was all too fatally easy to accept the part in private as well as in public. Their enforced intimacy, her concern for his safety, her reluctant gratitude for all he had done, all played a part, of course. But she had to acknowledge bitterly afterward that that was only a small part. It would not have happened if she had not wanted him as much as he wanted her at that moment.

Whatever excuses she might give to herself later, all that mattered was that at the time her puny protests were overborne with an almost ridiculous ease. She tried to pull his hand away, but he merely clasped it and returned it to his lips, and she weakly turned it against his face, her eyes tightly closed and already beginning to drift on a dangerous and rising tide of passion.

When his hand returned to its former task, she made no further objections, puny or otherwise. And when his hand, and then his lips, found her breast, she arched against him and moaned again, lost to all rational thought.

That he was a skillful and practiced lover there could be no doubt. Even afterward, when it might have helped in salving her conscience, she did not make the mistake of trying to delude herself that what he had in mind was love, despite the sweet names he whispered into her throat. Of her own motives she did not care to delve too deeply, and if she tried to reassure herself that it had been as much mere curiosity on her part, and the unconscious seeking of quick relief through passion from all that had happened, for a time she at least partly succeeded in making herself believe it.

Whatever her excuse, some part of her she hadn't even known existed gave him back kiss for kiss in that hot dawn, and made no further objection as first his hand and then his lips went lower, tantalizing, coaxing a response from her, and everywhere succeeding beyond her wildest imaginings.

And everywhere she touched him his skin was like fire, and he groaned heavily and said, "Yes. Oh, yes, my sweet love, my darling. Oh, God, you are beautiful . . . so beautiful. How could I have forgotten this . . . or this . . ."

And the new, wanton part of her did not want to listen to the old, rational part, and willfully thrust its warnings away to trail kisses across his hard brown chest, and press herself tightly against him, wanting more and still more of his burning touch, the sweet brush of his lips.

No, he did not force her; though there came a time when undoubtedly things had gone too far for turning back; and a man, even as gentle a one as he had proven himself to be, became suddenly a stranger—as perhaps all men become that first time. In the throes of his own passion his hands became hard and demanding, where before they had given only pleasure. It was frightening to one who was woefully ignorant on the subject, and she did try to resist then. But he stifled her small cries with his lips, and if, much too late, she grew craven, and wished she had not dared to rouse the sleeping tiger, in herself as well as in him, at least she had too much pride to compound her problem by laying the blame on him, or crying and pleading with him when it was far too late, and afterward claiming that he had taken her without her consent. Force and seduction, and her own surprising reactions to a man who was her enemy, were so inextricably bound together that she could not exonerate herself, much as she might have liked to.

And if she learned more of a man's passion, and of her own, than she had wanted to know, that was also to be laid directly at her own doorstep. And to her complete shame, when the ultimate moment came, she did not weep or beg, but clutched at him and cried out his name.

It was merely and cruelly ironic that the name he himself cried out was not her own at all. "Lisette!" he groaned. "Oh, God, Lisette."

If she did not weep when it might have saved her, she did when she lay in the warm dark afterward, long after he had fallen into an exhausted sleep, his body gone slack and his heartbeat at last reduced to a slow, steady drum. The useless tears came then, slow and bitter and full of recrimination. Nor did it help to know that the lie she had enacted had borne its inevitable fruit, or that she should have seen the danger long since. She was a greater fool than she had believed herself, on all counts, despite her much-vaunted intelligence.

It was no doubt even more of an irony that her original lie, and the fact that they lay, still entwined, when the soldiers burst in on them the next morning, undoubtedly saved the captain's life.

She wakened from an exhausted sleep with the tears dry on her cheek only an instant before disaster struck. Even so it was almost as ludicrous as it was frightening, for the soldiers, plainly summoned by a triumphant Mr. Tigwood, bent on revenge, were scarcely more than boys in faded and ill-fitting uniforms obviously hastily donned. They were clearly determined and pointed their muskets in menace at the bed where the two sleepers were obviously no threat to them, but they were unsure of themselves as well, which at least played into her hands somewhat.

She clutched the sheet about her, the fogginess of the night before thankfully cleared by the sharp threat of extreme danger, and managed to appear both bewildered and angry in turns. She dared not even glance at the captain beside her as she explained that the sabre, which Tigwood triumphantly waved, and which seemed to be what had convinced the soldiers in the first place, was a prize her husband had taken at Bladensburg.

All in all, she thought she did it very well, despite the fear that had her palms sweating and her heart beating so rapidly she

feared even the soldiers could hear it. She lied without compunction; but in the end it was the captain, who was not lying, who obviously convinced them. So perhaps she could comfort herself
with that, at least.

For if he had been lying, too, and as acutely aware of his danger as she was, it was doubtful if he could have been so convincing as he was. By the end the poor young soldiers were red-faced
and apologizing, having been raked most thoroughly over the
coals by a superior officer. Not even his weak state nor the disadvantage of being found in bed with nothing but a sheet to cover
himself did anything to diminish his obvious authority, and she
was again reminded of the man she had first met, so long ago, determined and more than a little formidable.

Dessy was summoned hastily to the scene, half-dressed and
groggy with sleep, and had helped as well, of course. She had
looked at the two of them together, the captain's arm protectively
around Sorcha, and assumed a look of stolid stupidity that none of
them, fortunately, thought to question. She, too, swore without a
blink that the captain was her master and had been married to her
mistress for two years. She swore as well, when asked, that Sorcha's father was indeed a United States senator, and no one hated
the British more.

That had perhaps been the deciding factor, but the poor young
soldiers, inexperienced and out of their depth, had already been
convinced, and ended up embarrassed. Then at last they had gone,
muttering in their ill-fitting hand-me-down uniforms, refusing to
listen to the still protesting Tigwood.

But perhaps the ultimate irony was that the unpleasant little
scene had precipitated the captain's return of memory at last, as
Sorcha had always been afraid it would. With the soldiers gone,
they were left staring at each other, the captain in increasing be-
wilderment, and it was not long before everything had come back
to him, as he afterward described it, like a door suddenly opening
and a flood of light coming through.

He remembered having rescued Sorcha in the streets of Washington and having come with them to punish his superior. He remembered the wild ride and Elsie and her baby and the ridiculous
dog, as well as the search for her father and setting out for Annapolis.

He remembered it all, in fact, except everything that had happened from the moment he was grazed by the ball and knocked

unconscious. And that included the almost week they had spent in the inn as man and wife, and everything that had occurred until the moment he woke up to find the soldiers pointing their muskets at him.

And it was merely a fitting end to it all that it had taken Sorcha until the moment when the soldiers erupted into the room to realize that she had been lying to herself even more than to the captain the entire time. She had committed the ultimate folly of falling in love with Captain Charles Ashbourne, her bitterest enemy and married to another woman, and who was almost embarrassingly grateful to her for saving his life.

But did not remember anything at all of the night she had just spent in his arms.

Chapter 18

"Oh, Charles, do stop flirting with Caroline and pay attention," complained Lady Babworth in her fascinating voice. "You simply have to help us."

Charles Ashbourne, late of His Majesty's 85th, drew his attention from the very mild conversation he was having with Miss Groton, a pretty brunette who was one of Lady Babworth's disciples, and as usual could not help smiling a little at the lovely picture Lady Babworth made. At the ripe age of seven-and-twenty she was an extremely wealthy widow, and her brief marriage to a man more than twice her age seemed not to have altered the fatal fascination she had always exerted over her court—or noticeably dampened her spirits either, for that matter. Once the prescribed period of strict mourning had thankfully passed, she had quickly taken her place again as the most sought after beauty in London, almost as if she had not been married and conveniently widowed in the space of a few years.

She was dressed, as usual, in the height of fashion, wearing an extremely becoming (and no doubt wickedly expensive) ball gown of gauze and silver embroidery over her favorite sea blue taffeta, which was cut very low to display her lovely white shoulders and a king's ransom worth of diamonds and sapphires she was wearing. But since she had wed her aged lord almost exclusively for his money and his title, it was good to see, Ashbourne thought dispassionately, that on the whole she had not been cheated.

She was also surrounded, as always, by her usual court of admirers as well as a few select and loyal females who were content to sit admiringly at her feet and did not seem to object to seeing her take the lion's share of the attention and admiration in any room she graced. They were all gathered at a select Christmas house party given by Lord Castlereagh, the Foreign Secretary, at his immense country seat that could easily have housed a hundred guests and their servants, not the mere thirty or so who had been invited for the holidays. They were presently waiting in the long gallery, heavy with brocade and gilded frames, and looking festive in the light from a hundred candles, for dinner to be announced, which seemed to have been unaccountably set back for some reason.

Charles had at first been surprised to be invited to join so august a party, for after so many years spent abroad he no longer felt much at home in such elite social circles. But once he had realized Lady Babworth was among those invited, it seemed clear that she must have wangled an invitation for him. She had ambitions of his going into politics, and not all his assurances that he had neither the interest nor the aptitude for such a career had so far fazed her. And since she was very used to getting what she wanted, she had merely laughed and abjured him not to be a fool, for Lord Castlereagh assured her he was exactly what the party needed.

However far Charles might be from believing that, he obediently turned his attention to what Lady Babworth was saying. "If it is a social question, my dear, I fear you had best look elsewhere," he warned her in amusement. "I am scarcely up to snuff myself yet, you know. In fact, I often feel I have been away far more than four years."

"Darling, you are always much too modest," insisted Lady Babworth. "I keep telling you you undervalue yourself shockingly. Besides, you are exactly the man we need in this particular emergency, for you are the only one among us to have been to America."

Charles's ears perked up a little at that. Since his return to England after Waterloo, America had seldom been mentioned, at least in his hearing. It seemed most people preferred to dwell on the glorious and bloody victory over Napoleon, which had proved once and for all that Wellington was the better general, and had led to the second abdication of the usurping French emperor and his speedy incarceration on a desolate little isle from which he was unlikely to escape a second time, than on a war that left a bitter taste in many people's mouths. Their own country's less than admirable behavior in burning the American capital, not to mention the two bloody and humiliating defeats at the upstart Americans' hands that came afterward, first at Baltimore and then at New Orleans, seemed to have vanished from the public consciousness as if they had never occurred.

But he said, "Yes, I was in America. What is the problem?"

"It is merely that Lord Castlereagh has felt himself obliged to invite two bumptious Americans here for the week," complained Lady Babworth. "It seems the father is here on official business of some sort, though after all that has happened I would have thought that the less we have to do with that ungrateful country the better off we shall all be. But you know how dear Castlereagh puts his duty above everything else—even his guests comfort, it would seem. Really, it would be bad enough even if they were presentable, for no one has the least idea what to say to them. But I have met the daughter and found her to be rude and ill-mannered and dreadfully common, poor thing. But then what else can you expect of such a rude and primitive country?"

Charles was again amused, for it was an attitude he had run into often since his return. He correctly diagnosed that either the unknown daughter—and if Lady Babworth had taken a dislike to her, she was sincerely to be pitied, though she might not yet realize her danger—was perceived as a potential threat to Lady Babworth's position as the acknowledged reigning beauty; or else she had made the mistake of not being properly impressed. Charles began to develop a mild desire to see the Americans for himself.

Surprisingly, however, it was young Lord Longstowe, one of the newest and most smitten members of Lady Babworth's court, who remarked seriously, blushing a little at his temerity in daring to contradict his goddess, "Oh, I don't know. I th-thought she was rather nice. And v-very pretty."

Lady Babworth raised delicately arched brows in astonishment. "Pretty! Darling, you must be mad. Much too overblown for my tastes, aside from being a rustic with not the least notion how to go on in polite society. We shall be lucky if she doesn't drink her soup from her plate."

Charles observed with some sympathy that young Wiffy Longstowe would not remain one of the favored few for long unless he grew more tactful. For he blushed hotly again and said even more ineptly, "I-I m-mean, of course not pretty in . . . in any accepted way. But I confess I feel a little sorry for her, for it c-can't be easy to find herself in a . . . a c-country that was her e-enemy until very r-recently."

Charles made a mental note to cultivate young Longstowe, who would seem to have unexpected depths. But Miss Groten said brightly, "Well, I certainly don't. Feel sorry for her, I mean. I am surprised Lord Castlereagh would invite them here, or that they would accept for that matter."

"Who is this poor unfortunate?" inquired Charles. "And what has she done to incur so much displeasure?"

"That is what I have just been trying to tell you," said Lady Babworth with some impatience. "Really, Charles, since you got back you are very changed. Haven't you been listening to a word I said?"

Charles hadn't, for he found the endless gossip and feuds and scandals that absorbed everyone and which had changed surprisingly little in the four years since he had last been in England, of far less compelling interest than everyone else seemed to. But it would only offend people to say so and do nothing to solve his own immediate problem. So he smiled ruefully down into Lady Babworth's beautiful, restless face and said obligingly, "I'm listening now. Tell me again."

"Honestly, Charles!" Lady Babworth was mildly annoyed, for she no doubt sensed that since his return some four months ago he was by no means as blindly admiring as he had once been. She did not understand the reason, but it had clearly piqued her vanity, and she had redoubled her efforts to re-ensnare him. Charles had gone along, quite simply because he didn't care enough, one way or the other, to resist.

But Wiffy Longstowe, whom Charles had already discovered, to his private amusement, seemed to have developed something of a hero worship for him, was even swifter to rush to Charles's defense. "W-well, of course he is different! We must all seem a-awfully futile to him, after all he's been through."

"Well, no," said Charles gently, thinking Wiffy was like any number of young ensigns, still green behind the ears, whom he had whipped into shape over the years. And that a few months under him would have been all young Longstowe needed to mature into an assured and likeable young man.

"Oh, pray don't talk to me anymore of the war!" begged Lady Babworth. "I am sick to death of it! That's all anyone has been able to talk of for months now."

"Yes, let us rather talk of this rude and overblown female, whoever she may be," said Charles. "Who is she, by the way?"

"I just told you. The daughter of some American here on official business."

"Yes, so I gathered. But what do you expect me to do?"

"Tell us if all Americans are so . . . so rustic and uncouth," said Miss Groton immediately. "None of us has ever met one before."

Charles smiled despite himself. "Well, I naturally did not get on speaking terms with many of them," he pointed out. "But I didn't find them particularly rustic or uncouth."

"Really, Charles! Of course they are," insisted Lady Babworth. "What else can you expect, coming from such an upstart country?"

"Besides, didn't you have some adventure or other, where some American female saved your life?" persisted Miss Groton, whose intellect did not seem to be too bright.

Charles was rather annoyed, for it was not a topic he much cared to talk of. "Yes, that's right," he said pleasantly and without encouragement.

Miss Groton refused to take the hint, however. "Good gracious! How romantic! What was she like?" she demanded in fascination.

Charles again hesitated, but he supposed that in fairness to the two unknown Americans he owed it to them to dispel at least some of the more obvious misperceptions. It was ridiculous that he disliked talking of it, anyway.

So he reluctantly recounted an expurgated version of his adventures in America, including the ridiculous ride and the rescue of the black girl and her baby, not to mention the pregnant dog.

Miss Groton listened to it all thrillingly, though Lady Babworth exclaimed at that point, "Charles! Really, darling, don't be coarse."

"Oh, no!" insisted Miss Groton. "I declare it is better than any novel! So that is how you got that scar! But it seems to me she must be quite brazen. I mean, she actually dared to claim you were her husband? And remained with you all that time while you had lost your memory? I daresay it was very brave of her, but still, I am sure no well-bred English girl would dream of doing such a thing. As for her refusal to evacuate the city when everyone else did and setting out to go all that way alone in the middle of a war, no less, she sounds most unfeminine! Do you suppose all American women are like her?"

Despite himself Charles was annoyed at this provincial view of the matter. It was one of the reasons he disliked talking of it, since most listeners tended to be more critical than impressed by such a tale of heroism. "She was hardly alone, since she had her maid with her, not to mention the objects of pity she insisted upon rescuing. But she does indeed possess a great deal of courage. As for her being brazen, I am unlikely to find fault with her, since I would undoubtedly not be standing here today had she been even a whit more conventional. But I somehow doubt that most American women are in the least like her. She was a . . . most unusual woman."

"Good Lord!" said Miss Groton, eyeing him rather curiously. "Have you heard anything from her since?"

"No," said Charles regretfully. "I wrote to her when I returned, of course, but I have had no reply. Under the circumstances we . . . parted rather hurriedly, I'm afraid, as soon as I had seen her safely—and belatedly—to Annapolis. Keep in mind I had just recovered my memory, or at least the better part of it. There are still annoying gaps that I am warned may never be filled in. But since I was in considerable danger of being arrested as a spy or worse, our . . . good-byes were of necessity rather hasty and unsatisfying. I don't even know if she found her father alive, as she was understandably so anxious to do."

He frowned, for their parting had indeed been unsatisfactory. They had packed up and left the little inn that very morning, fearful that the young soldiers might even yet change their minds and return, as well as the landlord's continued malice. Charles, still damnably weak and his brain reeling in confusion from the combined lingering effects of the concussion and his suddenly regained memories, not to mention the lost days at the inn which, more than a year later, still stubbornly refused to return to him, had scarcely been a reliable protector or companion. The journey had largely been accomplished in a tense silence, all of them half afraid they would again be waylaid. And they were all exhausted by the time they had reached Annapolis in the small hours of the next morning, and parted most hastily, since the town was discovered to be still standing, and in the possession of American troops. She had been oddly withdrawn and had not wanted to hear his thanks, and had almost fled from him, and he was left to look after her in frustration, concluding that she was glad to be rid of him.

Charles had managed to rejoin his regiment a day later and had been just in time to take part in the ill-fated attack against Baltimore, weak though he still was. And after that there had been scarcely a moment to draw breath for many months, given the even more ill-conceived attack against New Orleans, the defeat, and the belated discovery that the battle had been fought after peace had already been declared. Then had come the hasty recall to Europe and another unpleasant sea voyage, culminating in the battle of Waterloo, which was the worst he had ever taken part in, even after his experiences in Spain and America.

"Really, Charles," drawled Lady Babworth mockingly, recalling his wandering attention to the present, and seemingly not best pleased at this paean to another woman, however far away. "Caro is right. It all sounds ridiculously like some gothic novel. Either that or a fairy story. I had no idea you were such a knight-errant. I hope she was properly grateful to you for all you did for her?"

He grinned reminiscently. "Not in the least. She had been reared to despise the British, you see, exactly as you have . . . er . . . been taught to dislike Americans. Only the direst of emergencies made her accept my help in the first place, and it must have gone very much against the grain with her to be obliged to remain with me when I was shot, and in effect, save my life. I remember very little of that period, unfortunately, but I gather that it was most unpleasant, and she made a considerable sacrifice to protect me. As far as gratitude goes, the boot's very much on the other leg, I fear. It is I who will be eternally grateful to her." He added quietly, "I only wish there were some way I could repay that debt, but I doubt I will ever see her again."

Lady Babworth seemed to dislike this even more, for she remarked somewhat waspishly, "It is very clear that you admired her, Charles. And what did this rustic heroine of yours look like? Or perhaps I can guess. She must have been a little beauty indeed to make you go so far out of your way to help her."

His smile grew, for he could not help instantly bringing up a mental picture of Sorcha. He had a host of them: Sorcha defiantly refusing to admit she had taken on more than she could handle;

Sorcha white-faced and with huge eyes searching through that carnage for her father; Sorcha defying her own soldiers, and thus saving his life once again, though it must have cost her a great deal to do it.

But he said merely, "I daresay you would not have found her classically beautiful, no."

He discovered, somewhat to his surprise, that the circle had grown, several more people having joined them to listen to his tale in apparent fascination. Now an older woman said with a sigh, "What a fascinating story! It is indeed just like a novel! I daresay you are right and you will never see or hear of her again, but what a shame. I declare I have never heard anything so romantic in my life."

Almost as if on cue, the door opened and two more guests were ushered in, no doubt the reason for the delay of dinner. Charles had heard two more guests had arrived late that afternoon, perhaps the very Americans Lady Babworth had complained of.

Like everyone else he turned somewhat curiously to look. He heard Miss Groton giggle and say under her breath, "Oh, Lord! It's her! Did you ever see such a gown? And that hair! I am sure that cannot be its natural color."

For a moment Charles, from where he stood, could see nothing but a big, slightly red-faced man with unruly ginger hair who was talking to their host, who had gone unhurriedly up to welcome them. Then he moved slightly, and Charles at last caught a glimpse of the woman behind him.

He froze, scarcely able to believe his eyes, and feeling oddly dizzy of a sudden. He had long since ceased to suffer from the headaches that had plagued him for months, but now he felt the pain of his old wound again and almost put up his hand to touch it, as if expecting to find it still raw and new. It was a most extraordinary feeling, for in those few moments he felt almost as if the elegant drawing room in which he stood had somehow been swept away, and he stood in a very different room, small and airless and with primitive furnishings, half a world away.

It lasted only a minute, in which he felt displaced and disembodied, as if he were groping to find his way through a fog.

For the woman who had just quietly entered in the wake of the bluff man and who stood looking about her just a shade defiantly, as if aware of the whispers she was provoking, was without any possibility of doubt Sorcha. A transformed Sorcha, no longer in a torn dress and her hair in an untidy tangle, but looking unexpectedly beautiful in a green velvet gown that brought out the color of her eyes and made her hair, already turned to flame by the myriad of candles, look even more unusual.

After a stunned moment he started eagerly toward her, forgetting everyone else in the room. It was then the butler stentoriously announced their names. "Senator Magnus MacKenzie, from America, and his daughter, Mrs. Warburton."

Chapter 19

Sorcha found the protracted dinner party every bit as bad as she had expected it to be. Not only did she dislike such gatherings in general, especially when she knew no one present—and knew herself as well to be the cynosure of too many critical eyes; but despite the diplomatic nature of Magnus's assignment in England, she had never learned to hold her tongue when annoyed or angered. Which happened all too frequently among a people that either expected her to eat with her knife and live in a hut, or seemed to hold her personally responsible for the late war between their two countries. It had been swiftly borne in upon her since her unwilling arrival in England that if she had always disliked and mistrusted the British, that sentiment was returned in full measure.

In fact, she had begged Magnus to leave her at home when he had first announced so unexpected a posting. But he was oddly adamant, and it had taken more energy than she then possessed to hold out against a determined Magnus. She had come, willy-nilly, and found it every bit as bad as she had expected. Only one circumstance made it at all bearable, and that had proven little enough comfort, after all.

The English themselves, with their stilted manners and absurd preoccupation with rank and privilege, she found largely baffling. They seemed to care more for ceremony than anything else, and birth counted far more than intelligence or virtue or kindliness. If you could not trace your lineage back to the Conqueror, neither wealth nor wit would save you. Fools that back home would have been despised or even heartily laughed at here need only possess an exalted title, and inexcusable folly became mere eccentricity, intolerable rudeness a proper awareness of one's worth, and seemingly every debauchery overlooked. More, they looked down their noses at those unfortunates less nobly born and took what Sorcha thought an exaggerated and undignified acknowledgment of their natural superiority entirely for granted.

Lord Castlereagh, their host, was not quite so bad, and Sorcha had developed a certain grudging liking for him. He had issued the invitation no doubt out of obligation, but kindly took her into dinner himself, in defiance of far stronger claims of precedence, and sat beside her at dinner, dividing his attention between her and a haughty dame on his left who had been briefly introduced to Sorcha as a marchioness.

She had at least grown used to such dinner parties by then, with their elaborate formality and endless courses, though the first one she had endured had amazed her. She disliked formal affairs even at home, but nothing had prepared her for the length or grandeur of such English state occasions, and even informal parties, which Lord Castelreagh had assured her this was, would have put to shame the grandest dinner party at home. Even the length of the table, with its snowy napery and burden of silver plate, had to be seen to be believed, as did the heat and noise of so many polite voices raised in discreet conversation, or the splendor of the gowns and jewels worn by the ladies, made even more dazzling in the candlelight, and the liveried footmen ranged behind the diners, ready to refill a glass or whisk a soiled plate away at a moment's notice. To Sorcha it all seemed designed for show, not mere eating or even entertainment, and the hauteur or jaded boredom on most faces easily bore that impression out.

Nor did this night prove any exception. Dinner seemed interminable, and she was relieved when the ladies at last rose to leave the gentlemen to their port and cigars, though in general she found the English women she met even less likeable than the gentlemen. But she was used by then to their barbs, always couched in the politest of terms, and was again rescued by her hostess, a kindly lady who sat talking to her on unimportant topics until the tea tray signaled the return of the gentlemen.

It was then that Sorcha received the shock of her life. Not the

least of her reasons for not wishing to go to England was the risk
of encountering Captain Charles Ashbourne again, after all that
lay between them. And if she despised herself for such weakness,
she had been relieved to discover that though England seemed a
great deal smaller than America, she had as yet not run into him,
or even anyone who knew him. But then, for all she knew, he had
been killed in one of the ensuing battles, like so many friends and
acquaintances. And if that thought brought more pain than it
should have, she was the first to acknowledge her folly.

Besides, even if he were still alive, nothing was more likely
than that she scarcely held a place in his memory by now. She
had had ample time to be relieved that he had no memory of the
week they had spent together, with its bitter culmination. In fact,
her worst fear now was that his memory would return to him,
which would invite all sorts of complications she could well do
without.

Her surprise and shock, then, to see him calmly enter that formal room produced almost the same effect on her that it had on
him, if for very different reasons. For a moment she felt her heart
leap suffocatingly into her throat, and her pulse pounded so
loudly in her ears that she could no longer hear the platitudes her
kind hostess was murmuring to her. She felt her cheeks burning
betrayingly as well, and knew she had to get a hold on herself and
quickly.

Fortunately, he had not yet seen her, though he seemed to be
rapidly scanning the room in search of someone, so she had a moment at least in which to recover herself and take him in unob-
served. He was not in uniform, but in distinguished dinner
clothes, and she was a little surprised to see how natural he
looked in them, and how well he fitted in these elegant surroundings. It made her more aware than ever how primitive he must
have found his time with her, and was ample evidence, if she had
needed any more proof, that their worlds could not have been further apart.

It seemed she had forgotten, as well, exactly how handsome he
was. She had seen him only grimed and ill-tempered, or ill and
unshaven, and even then he had possessed a potent charm. Now
in full health and in the formal clothes that so well became him,
he looked almost a stranger, and she seized upon that thought
with gratitude. He was a stranger, notwithstanding the week they
had spent in each other's company in that dreadful little inn in

such forced intimacy, and she had only to remember the fact. Her heart might still be jumping uncomfortably, and her feet feel as if they did not belong to her. But with any luck—though she had long since realized bitterly that luck was very much her enemy—he had not regained his lost memories. The house party, that before she had contemplated with considerable dread, had by now assumed the proportions of complete disaster; but she had only to keep her wits about her tonight, and she would escape as soon as humanly possible.

Then he had seen her, and she discovered unwillingly that she had also forgotten how charming was his smile. It flashed warmly and spontaneously across the room at her and he made his way quickly toward her as if she were the only person there, thus destroying any hope, admittedly weak, she might have cherished that he had forgotten her completely.

She had her emotions enough in hand by then to watch his approach with at least the semblance of calm. For his part, his eyes held a warmth she also did not remember, and he said as soon as he had reached her, "I began to think dinner would never be over! You could have knocked me over with a feather when I looked up and saw you entering the room before dinner. What are you doing here? Somehow I never thought to see you in England."

There was nothing in his eyes but warm friendliness. No hint that he remembered that last night in the inn and its bitter aftermath, for which she could only be grateful. She made a further effort to pull herself together and answered somehow, though she could not afterward remember what it was she had said.

Lady Castlereagh was looking between them in curiosity. "Do you know Lord Charles?" she asked Sorcha in surprise.

That gave Sorcha another jolt, for she had certainly never heard the title before. But it was Charles who answered, still with that warm smile. "Indeed she does, ma'am, for she saved my life once. You can therefore imagine how delighted I am to see her again."

Lady Castlereagh looked between them again and rose immediately. "Then you will be wishing me at Jericho, for you must have lots to talk about," she said cheerfully. "I will go away, but only if you promise to tell me the whole story sometime. It sounds most intriguing."

She was gone on the words, and they were left together. Charles took her place beside Sorcha on the sofa and said softly,

"Indeed we do. You are well? But I need not ask, for you are looking even more beautiful than I remembered you. I had not remembered, for instance, that your hair was quite so fiery, or your eyes so green. Odd how one's memory plays tricks on one, isn't it?"

"Considering what I must have looked like the last time you saw me, it is scarcely remarkable!" she retorted, put a little more at ease by the familiar raillery. "*I* had not imagined that you would look so at home in a formal drawing room, either. And what did she mean by calling you *Lord* Charles?"

He laughed. "Now I know that it is really you, for I see that you have lost none of your spirit. As for the title, I seldom use it. It comes from being the son and brother of a duke, but I assure you I am quite unimportant myself. What on earth are you doing here? When did you arrive? Tell me everything! But first— though again I need not ask—you found your father safely, I take it?"

She glanced toward Magnus, wishing he would come and rescue her. But he seemed to be occupied in flirting outrageously with a shapely brunette in a spangled gown and had not even glanced in her direction since he had entered the room. "Yes, of course," she answered, fearing she sounded stilted. "Luckily, he emerged unscathed and guessed where I would go." She made an effort to sound more natural and added, "You . . . you were not court-martialed then?"

He laughed again. "No. Though it was a near-run thing, I must confess. For a while I would not have cared much, either, as you know. I still can't believe you are really here. And to think I was dreading this house party. You can't imagine how often I have thought of you—and at the oddest moments, too—and wondered how you were doing, and what had become of Dessy and Elsie and her baby, and even that absurd dog and her pups that you insisted upon foisting on me. It all seems so long ago, almost as if it had happened in another life."

She thought he was lucky to think so, but said merely, "They are all well. Magnus agreed to buy Elsie and the baby, since they had taken a liking to Dessy, and gave them both their freedom, you will no doubt be glad to learn. I kept the dog as well, and one of the pups, though Magnus was considerably less enthusiastic about that."

Again he smiled down at her with unexpected warmth. "Did

you? That hardly surprises me. I may have cursed when you saddled me with such an absurd assortment, but I never doubted the warmth of your heart. And Dessy? She is well? I look forward to seeing her again."

"Yes, of course. She . . . she remained behind in London, however."

He seemed surprised. "Did she? Then I will look forward to calling on her there. I must confess I would never have expected, given your views, that you or your father would ever consent to come to England. But I hope your visit is to be a lengthy one. When did you arrive, and why, by the way, have I not heard a word of your presence until now? I can't believe you have changed so much that news of a disturbance has not reached my ears."

She ignored that. "We arrived two weeks ago after a most unpleasant crossing."

"Ah, then that explains it. I thought you looked thinner than I remembered. You have my sympathy, since I well remember my own crossings with something less than enjoyment. Were you most vilely unwell the entire time?"

She was grateful for so neutral a topic and spoke more naturally. "No—though the weather was bad for much of the way. It was Dessy who suffered the most. Magnus was the only one amongst us to be untroubled, but since his last crossing had been under far worse conditions, when he was a boy and had to travel steerage, he thought he was in the lap of luxury."

Charles laughed. "Nothing is more annoying than one who remains disgustingly well when all about him are turning green, and cannot imagine what is the matter with them. But tell me. What do you make of my poor country so far? I am curious for your reactions."

She shrugged. "It is very beautiful. Even I can see that. I care less for London, for it is filthy and noisy. Magnus, who had never before been here either, claims he doesn't understand how anyone ever gets a wink of sleep, for it is like having an army camped beneath one's window. The traffic never seems to stop, and just as one has finally dropped into an exhausted sleep, it all begins all over again."

"Yes, so it seemed to me when I returned after so long a time. But you soon get used to it. But speaking of cities, though I hesitate to broach so painful a topic, how is the rebuilding of Washington coming?"

"Very well. Magnus says you did us a favor, though he was angry enough at the time. The new president's mansion is almost completed, and we are to have real streets in place of the muddy tracks that passed for streets before. Our own house turned out not to have been completely destroyed, though the roof had fallen in and most of the rooms gutted. It should be rebuilt by the time we return."

"I'm glad. I suppose it is true that it's an ill wind. I am looking forward to meeting your father at last, by the way."

She thought they would have little in common and did not relish such a meeting, but she said merely, "And you? Were you in time to take part in the attack on Fort McHenry?"

He grimaced. "I might have known you would not hesitate to go straight to the heart of the matter. Yes, though that, too, I could have well done without. It was a considerable victory for your side, of course. You may have heard that General Ross was killed there. I had little respect for him by that time, but I did not wish him dead."

"Yes, I heard," she said quietly. "And . . . were you present at New Orleans as well?"

"Lord, yes! The entire campaign seemed designed to teach us humility. Pakenham was lost there—Wellington's brother-in-law, you know. I may not have grieved for Ross, but I most sincerely grieved for him, though that battle as well was most vilely mismanaged. We fought it as if we were facing French Regulars, instead of—forgive me!—an army as wily as they were brave, who used our own light tactics most successfully against us. It is little wonder you hold our army in contempt. You'd think we'd have learned something from that earlier war, but it seems we did not. The ultimate irony, of course, was that all those lives on both sides were lost in vain, since the peace treaty had already been signed before it began."

He sounded bitter, which was no doubt understandable. "Were you . . . did you return in time to take part in Waterloo?" she asked, remembering with dread those long months after the news of Napoleon's escape had come and she had not known if he was dead or alive.

He raised a twisted grin. "Yes. The bloodiest battle I—or anyone else for that matter—was ever in and yet I emerged without a scratch from all three. My only wound was suffered under far more ignoble conditions, as you very well know. It is a source of much hilarity among my friends."

She knew him perhaps better than he seemed to realize and guessed by his deliberate lightness how bad they must have been—and how much they chafed at his pride. Her own brief experience of war had forever changed her, and she never looked back on it without a shudder. From all she had heard of New Orleans—not to mention Waterloo—he must bear a charmed life, indeed, as he had once told her. In fact, now that she looked at him more closely, she saw that it had had its inevitable effect on him. He looked slightly older and graver than she remembered, beneath the charming smile.

"And have you sold out now?" she asked quietly. "I notice you are not in uniform."

"Oh, Lord, yes. I sold out at the end of September when I returned. The peacetime military has never appealed to me, you know. In fact, that's what I was doing in America—though I came to regret my bargain, that time. Or at least most of it."

"And Captain Ferriby?" she asked idly, then knew immediately what his answer must be, by the change in his expression.

"He was killed at New Orleans," he said regretfully.

She was surprised at how much the news shook her. "Oh, no! Not that kind young man!" she protested.

He covered her cold hand with his own warm one. I'm sorry. I shouldn't have told you," he said quickly.

She indeed felt cold and had to shake herself to dispel the unwanted memories, then quietly withdrew her hand. "So many deaths. So much horror," she said unwillingly. "And now we sit in a drawing room and make polite conversation to each other. I don't know how you ever get used to it."

"Don't think of it." He hesitated, then said quietly at last, "This is scarcely the place to talk of it, but I meant it when I said I have thought often of you, you know. We . . . parted so hurriedly, I have long regretted all the things I wished to say. But now that you're here, I still seem unable to. And how feeble are mere words! You saved my life, at considerable risk to your own, and I can never hope to repay that debt."

She made a quick movement to stop him. "Don't! We both have reason to be grateful to the other, and so the obligation on both sides is canceled." She ventured to look directly at him and added unwillingly, "You never . . . recovered your lost memory completely?"

"No," he said ruefully. "Though when I first saw you tonight, I had the oddest feeling—almost as if I had been transported back to that dingy little inn. I am assured by the doctors that it is by no means unusual in cases of temporary amnesia, and that the events of that week may never come back to me. Or, on the other hand, they may return without warning, as the bulk of my memory did. In fact, I have racked my brain over and over, and still can remember nothing from the time I was hit until I woke up to find the soldiers there. And though it is clear then and now that you do not wish to be thanked, and seem to feel that what you did was no more than any other woman would do, you are very much mistaken. In fact, I have never known a braver woman, and I will never forget you, Miss Sorcha Mac—"

Then he broke off, and after a moment shrugged wryly. "But I was forgetting. It appears felicitations are in order. You are married now, so I am given to understand."

She jumped and by sheer force of will kept the blush from betraying her again. "What? Oh, yes. I am."

"I hope not to your deadly dull suitor?" he teased.

"No. Geoff and I grew up together."

"Ah. The one who had to play the British army in your games. I remember. Is he . . . with you? I would like to meet him."

"No. He . . . could not get away." She added hurriedly, "And where is your wife, for that matter? Is she here? She must have been more than relieved to have you safely home at last."

He stared at her in astonishment. "My wife?" he repeated. "Good Lord, I am not married. What on earth made you think I was?"

She felt a pounding in her ears, and the room seemed to recede for some reason, and it was her turn to stare at him in growing horror. "W-what did you say?" she faltered. "Of course you are! Y-you told me so yourself."

He shook his head, seemingly amused. "I must have been delirious then, for I am certainly not married."

She was staring at him blankly and could only repeat stupidly, as if her very words would make it so, "But . . . but you must be! I could not have made it up. You even called me by her name once. L-Lisette."

He was frowning slightly by then, but he said, "Ah, now I

begin to understand. I was indeed betrothed to her once, and my mind when I was suffering from amnesia may have been playing tricks on me. But she married another man. In fact, I have reason to believe you have met her. She is Lady Babworth, now a very wealthy and quite happy widow."

She put her teacup down unsteadily, somewhat amazed to discover that her hand shook only a very little. It seemed that fate had indeed marked her out to be the butt of some monstrous jest, and she did not know whether to laugh until the tears streamed down her cheeks, or to give in to despair. Nor did it help that he had not the least memory why his news was so shocking to her, and perhaps never would have.

"Yes, I have indeed met her," she said steadily. "Now, if you will excuse me, I am feeling very tired of a sudden. I think I will retire."

He rose immediately, concern in his face. "I thought you were looking more unwell than you would admit. But we will have plenty of opportunity to talk later."

She thought, but did not say, that they would not if she had anything to do with it. One tête-à-tête had been quite wearing enough, and Magnus or no Magnus, she had the firm intention of returning to London as quickly as possible. She had known it was a mistake to come.

It was all she could do to find her hostess and murmur some vague apology, when what she wanted to do was flee incontinently from the room and keep on going, all the way home to America.

Chapter 20

After she left Charles frowned after her for a moment and did not remain much longer downstairs himself. He went to bed with much to think about and could not be said to have passed a restful night. His sleep was troubled by tumbled dreams of the sort he had not had for months now, not since he had fully recovered from the wound to his head, though when he woke the next morning, he could not recall what they had been or why they had disturbed him so.

In fact, he woke with only two clear convictions. The first was that Sorcha was ill or unhappy for some reason, though he could not guess what reason that might be. And the second was that he had been more thrown than he would have expected by the news that Sorcha was married.

As for the first, perhaps it was no more than being obliged to come to England and leave her new husband behind, though that was not a reason he much cared for. Or perhaps she had met with considerable unkindness since she had arrived—as he had reason to know she had. Lady Babworth's words now conveyed much more meaning to him than they had earlier, and if it was indeed Sorcha they had been talking about, as seemed clear, much might be explained. Lisette and her crowd would be very inclined to meet her with considerable suspicion and resentment; and knowing Sorcha as he did, it was unlikely that she would keep her volatile temper in check, despite the diplomatic nature of her father's mission. Far more likely was that she met such open attacks directly, refusing to be bullied; and since Magnus's mission in England seemed to be to improve relations between the two former enemies, not add to the bitterness, that might indeed be making her unhappy.

It was possible, but he was not sure he was wholly satisfied with that answer. But there could be no doubt about the second. He had thought of her often in the intervening months, and always with pleasure. But he had not known until the moment he had seen her again that his feelings went beyond a natural gratitude and a somewhat grudging admiration. Certainly, he had imagined many times meeting her again, and wondered how she was doing and what mischief she was presently getting into. But somehow he had never imagined her married to another man.

Nor was there any denying that the news had come as a considerable shock to him, and not a pleasant one. It was absurd, for they had spent less than a week together, after all, a good part of which he didn't even remember. It was therefore doubly ridiculous to feel now, as he undoubtedly did feel, that he had received a blow from which he would not easily recover.

That he was in love with her he had not for one moment suspected. He could not help wondering if this emotion that seemed to have emerged out of nowhere at the sight of her had its roots in something that had happened in that mysterious week they spent together. But try as he might, he could not pierce the gloom or remember more than bits and snatches.

He found himself fingering the scar above his temple, as he had done several times already, and impatiently rose and dressed and went downstairs, determined to get to the bottom of at least one of the mysteries.

But Lord Castlereagh's butler, a stately individual of unshakable mein, unwittingly delivered yet another blow. When asked if Mrs. Warburton had come downstairs yet, he replied indifferently that Mrs. Warburton had left for London early that morning and was not expected to return.

His demeanor exuded disapproval, for such irregular goings-on were not what he approved of, but the only additional information he volunteered to Charles's rather sharp questioning were that no, the senator had not accompanied her, and since the temperature had dropped considerably during the night and snow was expected, he had advised Mrs. Warburton to postpone her journey, but she had been adamant. He dared say that in her own country such behavior was entirely normal; but to have so young a lady jauntering about on her own, without so much as a maid to accompany her, was not, he was thankful to say, how English young ladies conducted themselves.

Charles scarcely heard him. "Never mind that!" he said even more sharply. "Only tell me this! Where in this rabbit warren of a house is the senator's bedchamber located?"

Crombie looked even more disapproving, but gave him explicit directions. Charles thanked him and, regardless of the early hour, went to pay a long-delayed visit on the senator.

He found the room without much trouble and knocked unceremoniously on the door. At long last a very Scottish voice called irritably, "Go away! I don't know who in the divil ye are, but can't a fellow get any peace around here?"

The next moment the door was opened by a dignified and elderly black man, who regarded him impassively. Despite his urgency, Charles was momentarily distracted. He returned the servant's inscrutable inspection with interest, saying abruptly, "Are you Ham? Dessy's husband?"

A slow smile dawned in the black man's eyes, but he said merely, "Ah is. And is you Captain Ashbourne, suh?"

His accent was much stronger than Dessy's, but Charles gave a sudden bark of laughter. "I am. Only it is Major, not Captain. I want a word with your master, and I am beginning to think it is long overdue. Whether or not he wishes to see me, I warn you I am coming in, so you may announce me or not, as you please!"

Without saying another word, the black man turned and announced calmly, "Major Ashbourne to see you, suh. Ah'll be outside if you should need me." And after another interested inspection of Charles, he closed the door quietly behind him and withdrew, leaving Charles alone with Sorcha's father.

Charles turned to inspect him with some interest. Magnus was seated in a wing chair before the fire, smoking a pipe and reading the newspaper, attired in a magnificently barbaric dressing gown and with his wiry ginger hair still tousled, as if he had been running his hands through it. He was looking Charles over with equal interest and at last said irritably, "Come in, lad. Come in! It seems I am to have no peace this morning. So ye will see me this morning whether I will or no, eh? Well, ye have your wish, though what you imagine we have to say to each other I can't imagine. But pour yourself a cup of coffee and sit down! I can't stand hovering!"

Charles remained where he was. "Thank you, sir," he said levelly. "But I have already breakfasted. And it seems to me we have a great deal to say to one another."

Magnus gave an unexpected bark of laughter. "Then pour yourself a glass of brandy. Pour me one too—though in my opinion the finest French brandy is inferior to a good Scots uisquebaugh."

He was still grinning as Charles, after a moment's hesitation, went to do as he was bid. As he accepted his glass, Magnus was still grinning, for some reason, and added, sounding even more Scots than usual, "So ye think we've much to talk of, eh? Well, mayhap ye're right! Here's to ye!" and he swallowed a good portion of the brandy in his glass.

Charles calmly tossed his off and set the glass aside. "Yes, we do," he said grimly. "I am informed Sor—Mrs. Warburton has returned to London unexpectedly. Perhaps you will be so good as to tell me where she has gone, and why she felt it necessary to flee, even in the face of a possible snowstorm?"

Magnus was eyeing him in amusement and did not seem overly concerned. "I like a lad who can handle his drink I must confess!" He chuckled. "Perhaps ye're no' quite as bad as the bulk of your countrymen—though that remains to be seen, o' course! And what's it to you where my daughter's gone?"

Charles vied with himself and took a strong hold on his temper. "It is my concern because I can think of only two reasons why she would leave so precipitately the very next morning after her arrival."

"Oh, ye can, can ye?" demanded Magnus, seeming to be enjoying himself. "It would seem ye know my daughter better than I expected. And what are they if I may make so bold?"

Charles hesitated, frowning again. "The first is that she is ill—and I would not be surprised to hear it, for she is too thin and has lost some of her glow. Has she been ill recently?"

"It was a rough crossing," said Magnus blandly, as Sorcha had done. "And what is the second reason you suspect?"

Charles said even more slowly, but with deliberation, "That she is unhappy, sir. It seems clear you have dragged her here against her will—I mean to England, not this house party, of course. And

I suspect that she has met with considerable unkindness. Is that what is behind this sudden flight?"

Magnus was dismissive. "And what did ye expect—that we would be greeted with open arms, after so much enmity between our two countries for so long? Less than a year ago we were at war with one another—and have many more years of bitterness on both sides to overcome. I tell ye the lass is no' such a fool as to care for that!"

Charles's jaw hardened again. "Or at least it pleases you to think so, sir," he said deliberately. "Never mind. Only tell me where she may be found in London."

Magnus tossed off the rest of his brandy and seemed to be eyeing him as if he were a rare and amusing specimen. "And what do ye intend to do if I tell ye?"

"Find her and make her tell me what is troubling her. It seems clear you are little concerned with your only daughter's health and happiness—but then I have known that fact for some time now."

Magnus, however, refused to take offense, for his grin merely broadened. "Nonsense!" he said calmly. "The lass can take care of herself without any help from you—or me, come to that. But something tells me ye don't like me very much, do ye, lad?"

"No, sir, I do not," returned Charles, not mincing his words. "Whatever I may think of you as a father—and though I am uninclined to approve of many of your methods, I must admit the results have been excellent, for Sorcha is one girl in a million. But you may recall that you left her once before to 'take care of herself,' and I shudder to think what might have happened if I had not happened along."

"Nonsense," said Magnus again, refilling his glass. "She'd have done as well without ye. She'd not thank ye to think her as soft and helpless as most women. I didn't rear her to be missish."

Charles again vied with himself. "That much at least is clear, sir. But has it never occurred to you that, however strong she may be, she is a woman, with all a woman's vulnerabilities? It is even more clear that she adores you—for what reason I am at a loss to understand, for I have yet to see you take even proper care of her. All I know is that you left her to fend for herself during wartime, to satisfy your desire to fight your ancient enemy once again; and then brought her here against her will, when you should have known she would be wretchedly unhappy after all the tales you have filled her head with all her life of British treachery and malice. And now you would seem to have let her go off into a snowstorm, unaccompanied even by a maid, while you sit here calmly before a fire drinking brandy. No, sir, I have no desire to be rude, but I am very far from liking you, or approving at all of your methods of protecting your only daughter!"

Magnus was still grinning. "Well ye are. Bloody rude, in fact!" he roared. "And damned impertinent as well! Have ye forgotten that she is answerable to neither of us any longer? She is a married woman now, and I've no control over what she may choose to do."

Charles's jaw tightened again. "I have not forgotten that, no sir," he said shortly. "Though I question whether you ever had the least control over her actions. And as for her so-called husband, I would give much to know why he is not with her at this moment."

"Nay, Geoff's a good lad," said Magnus carelessly.

"I don't doubt it! Still, I have reason to suspect he is likely to have as little control over her as you have yourself, and the very fact he let her come to England without him supports that supposition."

Magnus again laughed, but made no comment.

Baffled by such callousness in the face of his only daughter's safety and happiness, after a moment Charles straightened from where he had gone to lean against the high mantel and remarked with dangerous restraint, "Very well, sir! It appears we have nothing more to say to each other, except this! Do you intend to go after your daughter, or remain seated at your ease while God knows what may be happening to her?"

"Go after her?" repeated Magnus in apparent astonishment. "Are ye daft, lad? Why should I do any such tomfool thing? Besides, it'll no' do to offend his lordship, when I've only just arrived. I've no intention of going trailing out in bad weather just because my daughter took a silly notion in her head to return to London."

Charles had to resist a very real desire to jerk Magnus up by the throat and plant a facer in that bland, smiling countenance. Instead, he turned without another word and snapped, "Very well, then, sir! You will not object, I take it, if I do. And I should perhaps warn you that I intend to whether you object or no."

Magnus merely settled himself more comfortably before the fire and picked up his newspaper again. "I'm no' responsible for whatever daft thing ye may take it into your head to do, lad," was all he said. "Don't slam the door behind you, for I've been disturbed enough already this morning."

Charles resisted the temptation to ignore this last command and closed the door behind him with exaggerated care, seething.

He found Ham still hovering in the hall. The elderly black man regarded him with interest, but made no comment. It was Charles who demanded abruptly, "Where is the senator staying in London?"

Ham did not hesitate. "Berkeley Square, suh. You goin' after Miz Sorcha?"

"I am. You may tell me, since her father seems not to know or care! Has she been well and happy? I know she is given to impetuous actions, but what on earth made her flee this house in so precipitate a manner, especially in the face of a snowstorm?"

Ham shrugged. "There weren't never any predictin' with Miz Sorcha. Powerful hot at hand she is, and the senator, though a fine man in his way, ain't never broke her to bridle, so to speak. Many's the time Dessy's warned him to do so, but he wouldn't never listen to her, and it ain't no use to repine over what's too late to be fixed."

"The senator can go to the devil!" snapped Charles, then strode off without another word.

He stayed only to change clothes and leave instructions with his valet, much to that stalwart's astonishment. But since he had been his batman for many years, and was used to unusual orders, he made no demur, but merely agreed with a wooden expression to pack up Charles's clothes and make his apologies to his host, but first and most important to send word to the stables that Charles would be wanting his curricle immediately.

He did opine mildly, as Charles roughly stripped off his coat and breeches and changed them for buckskins and topboots, and a drab, many-caped driving coat, "Word is in the hall that it's comin' on to some terrible weather, sir. P'raps you should put off your trip for a day or two."

"No, I am going immediately. You know I won't melt for a little snow," said Charles impatiently.

Turby merely grinned, clearly remembering several occasions in Spain and Portugal when they had endured more than a mild snowstorm and said no more.

Charles was on his way downstairs, impatient to be off, when he had the misfortune to run into Lady Babworth. He checked, cursing his timing, then came on downstairs.

She eyed his coat in some surprise. "Charles, darling! Are you going out? It has already begun to snow, and besides, I have been looking for you. Come into the library, where we may have some privacy. It seems I never get a chance to be alone with you lately."

Charles heard only one part of her speech. "Hell and blast!" he said, looking outside. In a traveling coach it was at least four hours to London, though he could make it faster in his curricle. If it had already begun to snow, the journey was likely to take even longer for both of them—if they made it at all.

He would not have hesitated to sidestep the beautiful Lady Babworth, doubly impatient to be off, had she not halted him and wound her arms about his neck invitingly. "Charles! Did you hear what I said? You can go out another time. Come into the library, for I have a great deal I want to say to you, and you must admit you have been oddly elusive ever since you returned."

He looked down into her beautiful, restless face and wondered what he had ever seen to admire in her. It did not seem to occur to her that she could not just whistle him back after all this time, as she had doubtless done so many. He slowly unwound her arms and said in amusement, "You seem to have forgotten, my dear Lisette, that it was you who broke our engagement to marry another man."

She pouted prettily. "Yes, but what else did you expect, darling? It is your own fault, for you were away, and seemed to care for nothing but your wretched career, and even refused to marry me when I begged you and warned you how it would be if you left. What did you expect me to do? Live like a nun and wait until you condescended to return to collect me again like an unwanted parcel? Always assuming that you did return, of course, and were not killed in some dreadful battle." Some spark of remembered resentment crept into her tone. "And I was right. Even after the war in Europe was over, and that dreadful Napoleon defeated, you still didn't come home, but went off to America instead. You cared for your stupid war far more than you ever did me, and it's time you admitted it and stopped blaming me."

He remembered his own thoughts on the subject, so long ago in America, and had to admit that she was by and large right.

"But all that is in the past," she added, turning away to admire herself in a mirror in the hall, patting her golden curls into place with a complacent gesture. "I am a wealthy widow now, which suits me very well, as a matter of fact, and the best part is that it is not too late for us after all, darling."

He turned to look at her reflection in the huge gilded mirror also, looking at her as if for the first time. She had reason for complacency, for he had indeed allowed himself to drift back into something of the old relationship with her since his return. She was still very beautiful, after all, and could be enormously fascinating, and he had found himself thinking more than once that he would eventually marry her, even with the memory of her betrayal and marriage to another man still between them.

Now he asked curiously, "Isn't it? I wonder. Don't forget that I am exactly the same man you jilted almost four years ago."

She again wound her arms around his neck and gazed up at him with her fascinating smile. "Don't be cruel, darling. Anyway, you're mistaken. I find you infinitely more fascinating, if you must know. Then you merely adored me like a dozen others. Oh, I don't say I wasn't in love with you. You were very handsome, after all, and amazingly good fun. But you had this dreadful obsession about honor and duty, and it made you more than a little tiresome, I must confess. But now the war's over, and you are even more attractive than you were when you left. And perhaps I've grown up a little as well. All I know is that I'm willing to forget the past and start anew. We were meant for each other, and everyone seems to realize it but you. Or are you still bent on punishing me for rejecting you? Because if so, I can assure you I have been punished enough. You can't imagine what marriage with Babworth was like! I was relieved when he died so conveniently and left the way open for you again. For you must know I have always loved you." She lifted her face invitingly to him, her eyes half closing, still supremely confident he would come to heel the moment she called.

He ignored the open invitation to kiss her. "I sometimes wonder if either of us were ever in love," he remarked thoughtfully. "And I would seem to have changed less than you think. After all, I still am only a younger son, and my fortune is hardly large enough to tempt you. Besides, I loathe the sort of life you live and always have. It would seem your instincts were more reliable than either of us realized at the time when you jilted me, my dear. I would have made you the worst possible husband. I fear you would soon have been as unhappy with me as you were with your elderly lord."

Her eyes opened quickly, the faintly languorous invitation in them disappearing with a revealing rapidity. She was indeed shrewder than he had suspected, for she said accusingly, "It is that American girl, isn't it? You're in love with her. I saw you sitting with her so rapt in conversation last evening and guessed she must be the one you were telling us about earlier. Anyway, you could never resist a chance to be chivalrous, could you, darling? It almost makes me laugh, for surely you have not forgotten she is married to another man? Poor Charles! It seems you are fated to be forever in love with another man's wife. First me, now her!"

He stared down blindly at her for a moment, seeing a very different face and realizing without surprise that what she said was true. He was in love with Sorcha. Had probably been in love with her almost from the beginning, and only his loss of memory and the immense gulf that lay between them had allowed him to ignore all the signs. Now they would be denied no longer, and it was just too ironic, as Lisette said, that he discovered the truth only after she was married to another man. But he put Lisette from him for the last time, smiling faintly. "If we are to be brutally honest, darling, your current interest in me lies solely in my no longer being a lapdog to be whistled to heel whenever you wish. I am a challenge to you, and that has piqued your interest. Once I was under your spell again, like all your other admirers, you would soon have grown bored with me. Now I must go. Pray make my excuses to Lord Castelreagh. I am returning to London, and I doubt I shall be back."

She stood looking after him for a moment or two, amazement and a gathering fury on her beautiful face. Then she shrugged a slender shoulder and went on up the stairs. Charles laughed, feeling absurdly lighthearted for some absurd reason, and strode out to wait for his curricle to be brought round.

Chapter 21

Charles reached London in the late afternoon. The snow had fallen almost steadily, making driving both treacherous and in an open curricle far from pleasant, and by the time he arrived he was cold, wet, tired, and inclined to question his sanity. The urgency that had made him set out in hot pursuit of Sorcha now seemed, in retrospect, a fit of momentary madness, and it was only the remnants of that earlier compulsion that had kept him going, and made him drive now straight to Berkeley Square instead of to his own lodgings. At least he had seen no sign of Sorcha's coach upon the road, which reassured him that she had not been stranded somewhere, and was likely to have reached home safely.

The door was opened by an English footman, who looked with understandable disapproval at his extremely wet greatcoat and hat and declared firmly that Mrs. Warburton was not at home to visitors.

Charles eyed him, having no doubt that he could get by him if it should become necessary. He might by then have lost a good deal of his earlier urgency, but he had no intention of being turned away after coming all that way without at least seeing Sorcha.

Luckily, he was spared the necessity of starting a brawl upon her doorstep, for at that moment Dessy appeared questioningly in the hall.

Her face lit up with unmistakable pleasure at sight of him, and she exclaimed in her soft accent, "Why, Captain Ashbourne! It sure is a pleasure to see you—and lookin' much better than the last time, I'm happy to say." She herself looked much the same as ever. "Goodness! You're the second one to arrive in the last half hour chilled to the bone! Come in by the fire, do."

"It doesn't signify," Charles said a little impatiently, quickly stripping off his wet outer garments and relinquishing them to the disapproving footman. "Sorcha—Mrs. Warburton did arrive safely then? Thank God for that at least. Inform her that I would like just five minutes of her time."

Dessy looked speculatively at him for a moment; then with the air of one coming to a difficult decision, nodded, and without another word turned to lead the way up the stairs. "Neither of you would seem to have changed," she said over her shoulder in amusement. "Settin' out in a snowstorm, the pair o' you! I'm well aware that chile sometimes has less than common sense, but I had expected better of you, Captain," she scolded.

She led him to a door on the first floor and opened it, saying by way of announcement, "Captain Ashbourne, chile," and stepped aside to let him enter.

Charles took an impetuous step into the room and then stopped dead, stunned at the sight that greeted him there. Sorcha stood before a warm fire, still in her traveling dress, and holding an infant with telltale red curls in her arms.

It would have been difficult to tell which of them was the more startled. Sorcha stood there, seemingly as transfixed as he was, the infant, who looked to be of some six months of age, held tightly in her arms. She had thrown off her hat, and it lay carelessly on a chair beside the fire, along with her pelisse, as if she had come there first before even putting off her outer garments. The room itself was in considerable shadow, and only the fire at her back gave much light, but it made a silhouette of her figure and turned her hair to a flaming halo. The picture she made, standing there with the baby that could only be hers, could not have been more beautiful—or more unexpectedly maternal.

Charles's first reaction was one of supreme and unmerited bitterness, for even knowing she had married had not prepared him for the fact she might already have a child. He felt absurdly betrayed, and a fool as well, and just as he was about to apologize and try to extricate himself with as much dignity as remained to him, something about her pose and the firelight at her back in the darkened room struck an unexpected chord in his memory.

In an instant he knew he had seen her like that before, though he couldn't remember when or where. She had not had a fire at her back then, but the blazing sun, and even as he stared, the extraordinary feeling he had experienced the night before at first sight of her once more swept over him. At the same time he felt a stab of blinding pain in his temple that was so acute he felt weak and dizzy, and instinctively put up a hand to his head, almost expecting to find fresh blood on his fingers. His senses whirled, and though he had a moment before felt distinctly chilled, he was now flushed with heat.

There was no blood, of course, or trace of the old wound, save for a shallow scar that ran above his ear, which his hair conveniently covered. Still the pain persisted, accompanied by a blinding headache more crippling than any he had suffered in the months after being wounded. Moreover, strange half pictures formed themselves before his dazzled eyes, at first disjointed and making no sense, but then with increasing clarity. Flashes of images intermingled with swirling black, and once more he felt himself to be transported from a comfortable house in London back to a primitive little inn in America.

Sorcha watched him helplessly, her heart beating wildly in her breast. She knew as soon as he lowered his hand and looked up again that what she had feared would happen ever since she had first seen him the night before—and what had prompted her wild flight to London—had indeed happened, and he had recovered his memory at last. She was even partially braced to hear him say hoarsely, in a voice she had never heard him use before, "Is the child mine?"

She hesitated, but though she was undoubtedly tempted to lie, she knew that there had been far too many lies between them already. It was her lies that had set up the present ridiculous situation in the first place. So she said starkly, "Yes."

He closed his eyes briefly, looking almost as unnaturally pale in the firelight as he had while lying wounded so many months before. At last he demanded even more harshly, and with none of his notable charm in evidence, "Tell me the truth! Did I . . . rape you?"

She swayed a little, knowing it would be some small scrap of comfort to her to let him believe that. But she scorned so despicable an impulse. Instead, seeing Dessy standing silently in the doorway, she said abruptly, "Here. Take him, Dessy. I . . . I will be up later to put him to bed."

When Dessy had come to silently take the baby from her and closed the door behind her, he said still in that strained voice, "It is . . . a boy? I have a son?"

"Yes." She added even more baldly, "As for the . . . other, no you did not rape me."

Some at least of the strain left his face. "Thank God for that, at least! Why didn't you tell me, you little fool?"

Some tinge of emotion shook her then, though she felt as cold within as she did without. "*Tell you?* When you remembered nothing of the . . . time we spent together, and I had no idea where you were or if you were even still alive? Keep in mind as well that I believed you already married."

"No wonder you were so shocked last night when you learned the truth. So believing me dead or married, you married your childhood friend instead?"

She lifted her chin. "Yes," she said and left it at that.

"Does he know the truth?" he demanded harshly.

That touched her again, briefly. "What do you take me for?"

He laughed, and it was not a pleasant sound. "I suppose I should be obliged to him, then—though I must confess that at the moment gratitude is not my most pressing emotion! Does Magnus know as well?"

"No. No one knows except Dessy. You needn't worry," she added wearily. "We . . . put it about that Geoff and I had been secretly married in the week before he was called up. No one . . . knows, or need ever know. Nor do I expect anything of you if that is what you fear. In fact, I never meant you to find out."

He laughed again. "I thank you! It obviously did not occur to you that I might have been in the least bit interested to learn I had a son? And while we are on the subject, does the so-obliging Geoff know that in all likelihood you are married to me, not him?"

That stopped her in her tracks, as he had been stopped earlier. She had prayed and hoped that she might be spared that, at least, and that he had no recollection of that sordid little ceremony. But she saw that nothing was to be spared her. She had to moisten her lips twice before she could speak, and then her voice was barely above a whisper. "It's not true. It . . . can't have been legal. And even if it were, no one knows of it . . . need ever know of it. Please. *Please*. I told you I expected nothing of you. I knew I should never have come here, but I am going back to America almost immediately. It has all been settled, and there is nothing you can do now. In fact, the only thing you can do, for all our sakes, is to go away and forget those few days again. I only wish I could!"

Then she made herself stop and take a deep breath in an effort to regain control. "I'm sorry. Nothing can be gained by losing our heads. I hoped you would never know, but now that you do, I can only beg you to forget it. You are in no way to blame. It was all the result of my own folly, from beginning to end, and the absurd tangle of lies I told," she finished bitterly. "You have nothing for which to reproach yourself."

Frowning, he now said heavily, "I still am not sure I remember the whole. Am I crazy, or did you deliberately let me believe we were married?"

She blushed hotly. "Yes. I deserve every name you can think of to call me. When I realized you had lost your memory, it seemed easier—*easier!* Oh my God!—to let you believe we were married. All I can say in my defense, is that I lived in constant fear that your memory would return and you would blurt out the truth before one of the Tigwoods. It was obvious from the first that your amnesia was only temporary, and it seemed to me, in my inexcusable folly, that so long as you believed you were American and . . . my husband, you would be safer. I can laugh at that misguided notion now, for you once called me naive, and it seems you were right. Nor does it at all help that at the time I did what I thought best. It was, of course, bound from the beginning to end in disaster. The fault was mine—all mine. You have every right to blame me."

His face had softened still more. He made a movement as if he would have touched her, but when she shrank from him said merely in an unexpectedly quiet voice, "Far from blaming you, I undoubtedly owe my life to you and your quick wits. In fact, I have nothing but gratitude and admiration for what you did. I have not forgotten, if you have, that you found yourself with all of us to protect, and a wounded enemy soldier on your hands who had lost his memory. Given what did happen, I am perfectly willing to believe that had you not maintained the charade the whole time, I might have been captured or even killed." Then he grimaced. "Though it was, as you say, undoubtedly playing with fire."

"It was madness," she said harshly, not willing to accept his easy, face-saving forgiveness. "I assure you I was aware of it at the time, but once the first lie had been told, it became increasingly impossible to extricate myself. The only thing I can say in my defense is that I never intended it to go on for more than a day or two. But if it is any consolation to you, I have had ample time to discover that you were right, all those things you said about me then. I would never have believed I could be such a fool!"

She had turned her back to him and was staring down into the fire, lacking the energy after a sleepless night and the day's fears to cope with any of it. She wished he would simply go, and quickly, and that she need never see him again. She should indeed have known not to come to England and risk stirring it all up again.

Instead of going, however, after a long moment he said quietly, "At least I begin to see why you looked thin and pale. My poor girl, I only wish I had known. I would seem to have brought you nothing but grief, so perhaps it is no wonder you . . . feel the way you do. Do you . . . hate me very much?"

His gentleness almost was her undoing where his anger had not been. "No. I . . . don't hate you," she said wearily.

"I suspect that is more generous than I deserve. So what happens now? Am I supposed to go away and forget that I have a son I did not know existed, and in return for saving my life left you very much worse off than when I met you?"

She lifted her head at that. "Yes. You owe me nothing," she repeated. "The . . . child is legally another man's, and he will . . . he will never reveal the truth. It would have been far better if you had never known as I said."

"Perhaps you may think so, but I am far from agreeing," he commented rather sardonically. "And I fear you have overlooked two important factors, my dear."

That brought her around slowly, against her will. "What are they?"

"That I fell in love with you in those few days in America, and am in love with you still," he remarked calmly, as if he were saying nothing in any way out of the ordinary. "And that I have no intention of walking out of here and leaving my wife—and my son—to another man."

She could only stare at him, at first not believing that she could have heard right. "What?" she demanded. "Are you *mad*?" Then, bitterly, "But what else did I expect you to say? You are, after all, a gentleman. But your honor has now been satisfied. I don't expect you to make an "honest" woman of me."

Unbelievably, he actually laughed. "I fear I am not so generous! In case you are not aware of it, you have haunted me for months, my dear Sorcha—and at the most damnable moments. Despite the . . . er . . . inconvenient gaps in my memory, I have not been able to get your face out of my head. It was not until yesterday, when I saw you again at last, that I began to understand why. I must have fallen in love with you long before we were thrust together in that ridiculous inn, and only the loss of all memory of that time kept me from realizing it. Do you really think I am about to walk tamely away after discovering you again, and learning I have a son as well? If you do, you don't know me very well, my dear, which is something I have every intention of correcting."

She had wordlessly backed before him, still not believing him. "No!" she cried almost violently. "I don't know whether you only say that because you are feeling guilty—or responsible, but I have said I expect nothing from you, except to be left alone. It is too late now. It has all been settled long ago."

"It seems clear you would like me to believe so. But you are mistaken, my dear. Especially if you wish me to believe you feel nothing for me in return."

"Yes! I mean, *no*! I don't. I keep telling you it is too late."

"Little liar." Without warning he took hold of the fine gold chain she wore around her neck that he had noticed the night before. She flinched almost violently from him, but he calmly took the chain in his fingers and pulled it up so that he could see what hung at the end of it, out of sight beneath her clothes.

It was a heavy gold signet ring he had reason to know well. He smiled crookedly at the sight of it and said, "I thought I had lost it somehow in the battle. Now tell me again that you don't feel something for me, for I must warn you now I won't believe you!"

Her face twitched, and she kept it averted from him, though she was held prisoner by the thin gold chain still in his hand. But she said in a low, defiant voice, "You always were incredibly conceited! But you are mistaken. I . . . don't . . . love—"

He gave her no chance to finish. Again without warning he had pulled her violently into his arms and was kissing her in a way she had remembered far too well through too many nights, and had thought never to feel again. For a moment longer she succeeded in holding out against him, struggling to be free. "No! I can't—!" Then she shuddered and abandoned the unequal struggle and was kissing him feverishly back, her arms winding tightly around his neck as if she would never let him go.

With a groan he gathered her even closer, saying huskily, "Oh, God. How could I have forgotten the feel and taste of you, when you go to my head like the headiest brandy. Sorcha. *My darling . . . !* My *wife!*"

Chapter 22

But that pulled her back to some semblance of sanity at last, however too late, and she tore herself away and again put the length
of the room between them. *"Don't!"* She was panting a little and
added with deliberate cruelty, "Haven't you forgotten something?
My . . . my husband?"

He actually smiled. He was a little breathless as well, and a
flame in his eyes as he looked at her threatened her self-control
all over again. "Ah, yes, your husband. I own he is a trifle inconvenient, though in point of fact I suspect it will turn out that I am
in fact your husband, not he. I suppose I must be grateful to him
for stepping in when I could not—though I must confess I'm
deucedly jealous of him as well. He was there to help you when I
should have been, and has been a father to my son, and though I
shall never forgive him for that, I do sympathize with him. Is he
very much in love with you?"

She lifted her head proudly. "Yes."

"And you wish me to believe that you are in love with him?"
His voice, after her foolish betrayal of the last few minutes, was
politely skeptical.

But that was a mistake she was not about to make again.
"Yes!" She said it deliberately.

"Little liar," he said again, caressingly. When she flushed up,
he added, "You may love him—like a brother, perhaps. After all,

I understand you grew up with him. But if you had truly been in
love with him, you would have married him long before I appeared on the scene, and not merely for the protection of his
name. And," he added shrewdly, watching her, "I know you perhaps better than you wish to believe. If he had been deeply in love
with you, I don't think you would have consented to wed him, no
matter how desperate you might have been. You are too honor-
able, and that stiff-necked pride of yours would most certainly
have gotten in your way."

Her eyes flew to his in surprise, unwillingly acknowledging the
truth of his words, though the stiff-necked pride he spoke of kept
her rigidly silent. He regarded her and added still more unexpectedly, "Of course, you may also have married him for your father's
sake. I imagine Magnus may prove to be an even bigger obstacle
in my path than your poor Geoff."

She jumped and cursed the revealing gesture. "Don't be ridiculous. What has Magnus to do with anything?"

"More than you wish to admit, I suspect," he said ruefully. "It
must merely have added to the damnable fix you were already in
to be faced with the formidable task of telling him that you were
pregnant by one of his lifelong enemies, especially when you believed that I was for all intents and purposes out of the picture.
But I am very much back in the picture now, as you see, and however much you may love your father and wish to avoid wounding
him, I refuse to allow his prejudices to color the rest of my life.
Or my son's, for that matter."

"Prejudices!" She almost laughed. "You don't even begin to
understand the meaning of the word! He hates all English, and the
redcoats even worse, and you are both. He has no use for the aris-
tocracy, and you are the son and brother to a duke. What exactly
is it you are proposing, anyway? That I should divorce Geoff to
marry a man my father despises, when the scandal may very well
ruin his political career, and ask him to accept that his grandson,
whom he adores, is half English? And all this so that you may
claim a son you didn't even know existed an hour ago?"

"Do you fear that he will disown you?" he inquired curiously.

"I don't know. He is even more stubborn and full of pride than
I am. Where do you think I got it from? But so long as you . . .
were out of the picture, as you say, I chose not to confront the
issue. Worse, I very much fear it will break his heart. And nothing
you have said has come close to changing my mind. I made the

only decision I thought I could make at the time, and I intend to stick to it."

"I suspect you are underestimating him," he said even more unexpectedly. "In fact, unless I miss my guess, my love, your father knows already."

That brought her eyes to his again, in shock. "*Magnus?* He can't!" she exclaimed involuntarily. Then, with more confidence, "Nonsense. He suspects nothing, and I have no intention that he ever should."

"Well, I will own that it must come as a shock to him that you may be married to one of the despised English, but I would wager a great deal on his knowing already. My poor deluded darling, why else do you think he came all this way, and dragged you as well, to a country he allegedly hates? Even before I knew the truth I was astonished that he had consented to accept a mission here—or was offered one, for that matter, for forgive me, but he must be the least diplomatic person alive, as are you. And when I talked with him this morning, he was certainly behaving most oddly, nor did he do anything to prevent my coming after you, despite his alleged hatred for all British soldiers. I would indeed guess he knows and is far less shocked than you imagine."

She stared at him for a moment in horror, and then exclaimed as a great deal suddenly began to make sense to her, "*Dessy!* Oh, I swear I will murder her! She was pledged to secrecy, but she could never resist his wiles. Yes, and now I come to think of it, she must indeed be hand in glove with him, for she let you in here, when she must have known—"

She broke off belatedly, but he finished obligingly for her, "That I was the last person you wanted to see. But don't blame her too much," he added sympathetically. "I know I shall be eternally grateful to her for standing my friend." He took in her fulminating eyes and laughed, which annoyed her still more.

"I should have known! She ever had a ridiculous soft spot where you were concerned! And this is not a laughing matter!" she said furiously.

"It is not a tragedy, either, my poor little love. You are my wife in fact, even if it should turn out not to be legal as well. I may have missed being there when you needed me—for which I will never cease blaming myself!—and I may have missed my son's birth and the first few months of his life, but I am damn well not going to miss the rest of it. That would be reason enough even if I were not . . . deeply in love with you. Add to all that the fact that I have found you again when I least expected it, and I have every reason to feel as if I am walking on air."

"You talk as if we had only to snap our fingers and make everything right," she cried contemptuously. "I tell you it is impossible. I wish to heaven I had never come to this wretched country and you had never learned the truth!"

He seemed to sober a little at her vehemence, but said as if he was humoring a child, smiling down at her in a way that tested her hard won resolution to the utmost, if he but knew it. "I know you to have more courage than that, sweetheart. You are tired and out of sorts and clearly not yourself, but it is not like you to see shadows behind every tree. I grant it will not be easy, but it is certainly not impossible. Let us take your objections, one by one, and I think you will see that with a little ingenuity they can all be overcome. What are they?"

She was wholly baffled by his annoying cheerfulness in what she saw as the face of disaster and said, deliberately, "Well, it must daunt even you a little to remember that I already possess a husband, for one!"

He grinned. "Yes, I have acknowledged that is a slight problem. But divorce is not unheard of, even in your country. And it may well turn out that whatever ceremony you went through with him was bigamous, which poses an even greater problem to my way of thinking. If you are worried about the scandal, there may be some shocked whispers for a while, but you will never convince me you care very much for that, and nor do I. And if you are worried about your old friend Geoff, I somehow don't believe he would stand in the way of your happiness, however little you may be brought to admit the truth, at least to me. He has stood very much your friend, and unless you are a far better actress than I have given you credit for being, he must have guessed the truth long ago."

She turned away, not caring to discuss that issue. She said instead, challengingly, "Surely even you cannot manage to ignore the fact that we are enemies and have scarcely a thought in common, besides."

"Yes, I thought it would not be long before we were back to that," he murmured provocatively. "But you may have noticed our countries are now at peace with each other. As for not sharing a thought in common, you always were mistaken on that score—I suspect willfully. I hesitate to provoke you any further, but I am vain enough to believe you were not . . . wholly indifferent to me, even as I tumbled headlong in love with you, against all common sense or reason, from the first moment you embroiled me in that ridiculous adventure of yours. It seems love acknowledges no political boundaries."

She blushed, but said furiously, "I see! I am undoubtedly supposed to consider the world well lost for love. But I'm afraid that happens only in fairy tales. The truth is you belong here, and I am as alien and out of place here as you were in America. You must have seen that for yourself last night! To make matters worse, you are a nobleman, and I despise all titles. I could clearly never live here—or raise my son in such a country—and you could never live in mine! Love may ignore political boundaries, but we are not so fortunate. It was clearly impossible from the beginning. Do you think I didn't consider all this long ago?"

"I think you considered it, yes, but I suspect you were scarcely in a state to be rational on the subject," he said soothingly. "Nor are you now if you don't mind my saying so. Yes, I know that angers you, but little though you may believe it, I care not a hang for my title, and as you already know, seldom use it. As for my belonging here, I had already decided since returning that I have been away too long and changed too much to ever fit in completely anymore, if I ever did, which I am beginning to doubt. Why else do you think I joined the army, you little fool? In fact, I think America will suit me very well—and I am perfectly willing to have my son brought up with the most rabid of democratic principles and despising all wealth and inherited titles, if that is what is worrying you. Having the mother and grandfather he does, I would expect nothing else, whichever country he resided in. I daresay he will grow up to be president one day."

"No!" she said stubbornly, desperately clinging to the painful decision she had made so long ago, and refusing to be swayed by his words—much as she might like to. "I tell you I considered everything carefully and made the only decision that was possible. It is far too late to change anything now!"

"My poor darling," he said gently. "You were caught up in a war, with no one to confide in and the author of all your troubles unreachable and perhaps even dead. No, forgive me, but I don't think your decision was made in the most rational or calm of environments." He smiled down lovingly at her and added, enraging her even more, "Besides, it is not like you to lose your nerve. I don't say it will be easy, but you have raised no objection, you know, that can't be disposed of."

She laughed bitterly at that. "You call divorce and abandoning your home and family easily disposed of objections? But then, I had somehow forgotten how annoyingly confident and optimistic you were, even in the midst of complete chaos."

He grinned. "One of the best maxims in any battle—or life, for that matter—is to get over the ground as lightly as possible, and I have always tried to live by it." Then he took another look at her, and before she could prevent him, took her face between his hands, saying with a consummate gentleness that once before had been her undoing, "But I don't make light of it, I assure you, love. I will always blame myself for leaving you to shoulder such a burden alone. My poor darling, was it very bad?"

"No!" she said defiantly, refusing to accept his pity.

"I think it was," he contradicted her. "To find yourself pregnant by an enemy soldier you expected never to see again must have daunted even you, though it is clear you faced it with resolution and the same stubborn courage I had already seen in you. You are the most beautiful and intelligent and gallantly brave woman I have ever known, and it is no wonder that even with my loss of memory I still could not get you out of my mind. I have fallen deeply and inexorably in love with you, little though you may wish to believe it, and I will compound your contempt of me by confessing I am coxcomb enough to think you love me, too. But whatever happens between us, I wish you to know that I will never do anything to hurt you again. You have my promise on that."

She could no longer meet his eyes, which were uncomfortably penetrating, and so turned her face, like a coward, into his shoulder. He took that as an invitation—as perhaps it was, and gathered her close and held her as he had once before. Weakly she clung to him, despite her awareness that she was once again playing with disaster, while the slow, bitter tears of a year's pain and struggle ran silently down her face. She would not let herself believe the vision of the future that he painted for her, dazzling though it might be, and much as she might long to. That way lay disaster, for she knew he was merely being chivalrous, and that she could not trust a word he said. She had not, until she had seen him in his own milieu last night, realized how completely he belonged in this world she could never be a part of. And he, equally, had no place in hers. It was a stalemate, and it was futile to wish it might somehow, miraculously be different. She had been through it all and invariably ended up at the same place.

But as if reading her thoughts, he said into her hair, "And there is one other thing I think you are forgetting, my love—my son."

When she stiffened, he refused to let her go, but added dryly, "Did it never occur to you that he might deserve to know the truth?"

"I . . . would have told him when he was old enough to understand," she said unwillingly into his shoulder.

He chuckled and dropped a swift kiss onto her hair, which she weakly allowed, too spent to object. "I suppose I must be grateful to you for any small favors. But I think I prefer to tell him myself. As I intend to be a part of his life from now on."

He could not know, of course, how much she wanted to believe him. But she dared not, for far more than her own happiness rested upon her shoulders, little though he may choose to believe it. She could not afford to risk the hard won peace that had taken her so long to achieve, however irresistible a temptation it was to just close her eyes and shift all the burdens and decisions onto his shoulders, which she had discovered to her cost before were temptingly broad and comfortable.

The door opening perhaps thankfully put an end to so dangerous a moment. She jumped and tried to draw away, but he would not let her go. It was thus to the spectacle of his daughter being held tight in his enemy's arms that Magnus entered the room, still in his hat and greatcoat, both of which were liberally sprinkled with snow.

"Well!" he roared, taking in the unwelcome sight. "And what in the fiend's name is this?"

"M-Magnus!" she managed in shock, again trying to pull away. "It . . . it's not what it seems."

But whatever she had expected in the way of explosions did not happen. He eyed them for a moment or two, his expression unreadable, and then remarked surprisingly, "I'll say this for ye, lad, ye don't waste much time! It seems I was wrong to believe all English are cold fish, for ye've gotten further with this stubborn lass of mine than I'd have given ye credit for—and in a remarkably short space of time, too. But then," he added dryly with unmistakable meaning, "it seems ye got around her long ago, so I suppose I should no' be so surprised."

"M-Magnus!" said Sorcha again and renewed her struggle to be free, her cheeks flushing hotly with shame.

"Stay right where you are," said Charles firmly in her ear. "I warned you that your father was shrewder than you gave him credit for, my love." He raised his voice and added to Magnus, showing no whit of embarrassment or surprise, "In fact, I don't doubt you engineered the whole from the beginning, didn't you, sir? It puzzled me why you would accept an invitation to such a house party, given your views—unless, of course, you knew all along that I was to be there. I am far from approving of all of your methods, as I have made no secret from you, but in this case it seems I am considerably in your debt."

"Aye, lad, that you are," said Magnus with a twinkle.

Sorcha could scarcely believe her ears. She gave up the un-equal struggle to free herself and demanded in outrage, "Magnus! Is it true? You can't have known!"

Magnus's grin grew. "I'm no' such a fool as ye obviously think me, lass. Of course I knew. In the end it seemed I must take a hand, for little though I ever thought to see the day I'd accept a bloody Englishman as a son-in-law, I don't appear to have much choice in the matter. Don't get me wrong, lass. I'm still far from approving your choice, and it's only the thought of my grandson that at all reconciles me to the fact. And little though I expected it, it seems he has not turned out so badly, despite being half-Sassenach. Nay, lass, don't look so astonished," he added gruffly. "Did ye really think I wouldn't guess the truth, despite that ridiculous farrago of nonsense ye regaled me with? Or that I could turn my back on you, no matter whom you married? I may be a stubborn Scot, but I'm no' a complete fool. And it's been clear to me for too long that ye were deeply unhappy."

She was still staggered. "You knew all along?" she demanded incredulously.

"Nay, no' all along, but I soon enough got the story out of Dessy."

"I trust you have looked into the matter thoroughly, sir," inter-rupted Charles firmly. "Is our marriage legal, as I suppose?"

Magnus nodded in reluctant amusement. "Aye, that it is—though it's clear ye'd no' be long denied even if it weren't, lad! I'll own that originally I hoped to prove it wasn't, but I am becoming momentarily more resigned to the fact. Which is just as well, I suspect. Tigwood is a rogue and a villain, and I've little patience with his peculiar brand of religion, but there seems little doubt he is fully authorized to perform marriages."

"Did he try to blackmail you, sir?" asked Charles curiously.

"Aye, that he did, but you may imagine I soon sent him off with a flea in his ear. He'll no' trouble ye any longer."

"And did Dessy suspect as well that the marriage was legal?"

"Aye, well, poor Dessy has had a difficult time over the whole. On the one hand she'd pledged not to reveal the truth, but on the other she could see that this foolish lass of mine was plainly unhappy. She also knew that you were not married, lad, for it seemed you had earlier told her so. Incidentally, I gather that was a bad moment for the lass last night, when she learned the truth, and explains this craven flight, when I had thought better of her. Dessy's one as usually keeps her own counsel, but we are old friends, and it seems she ultimately has more faith in me than my own daughter would seem to."

But Sorcha heard only one part of that and repeated in astonishment, "*Dessy* knew that he was not married? But she never breathed a word to me."

"Aye, she wouldn't. But this complicated scheme has not been all my doing, I assure you. It seems she took a powerful and unexpected liking to this captain of yours, and I respect her judgment even more than I do yours, lass."

"Then do I take it I have your blessing, sir?" asked Charles in amusement.

"Aye, ye have it—not that, by the looks of it, ye've much use for it. Ye're an impertinent young jackanapes, daring to tell me where I've gone wrong with my daughter, but it seems I have little choice in the matter," he added dryly, since his daughter still stood within the circle of Charles's arms.

That belatedly roused Sorcha at least somewhat out of her present state of shock. "It seems you both have worked it out most satisfactorily," she said scathingly, again trying to pull herself out of his arms. "But I won't be pushed like this, even by Magnus. Or hold a shotgun to any man's head. Do you think I don't know you could say little else, once you learned the truth?" she demanded of Charles bitterly. "Don't forget, I know your absurd sense of chivalry of old. But it is impossible. Too . . . too much lies between us."

Charles exchanged an amused look with his father-in-law over her head. It was Magnus who said regretfully, "Happen I have indulged the lass too much, lad. She's ever one to be thinkin' she's the only one who knows best. But still, there's much in what she said. Well, lad? Can ye live in America—for no daughter of mine will ever live here, that I am adamant about. And recall before ye answer that in America a man is judged on his wits and his courage, no' his blue blood, and that fancy title o' yours won't have all the natives knuckling under and tugging at their forelocks in exaggerated respect, as they doubtless do here. Ye'll have to prove yourself if ye're to succeed there, lad."

Charles's arms tightened still more possessively about Sorcha, and despite her father's presence he dropped another quick kiss on her hair. "You both underestimate me, sir. I know from experience that my blood is no different from anyone else's, and I have spent my entire adult life in the army where a man is judged solely on his worth, don't forget. I suspect America will suit me very well, for I liked it from the beginning."

Magnus chuckled. "Aye, I suspect ye're right, lad. Besides, Lord Castlereagh has been telling me of all the plans he has for yer future in politics here. He tells me ye have wits and integrity, two things that are too often lacking in politicians, on either side of the Atlantic! He will be disappointed to learn he's to lose ye. But it seems that his loss will be our gain, and mayhap ye'll do even better in American politics. Once ye've proved yerself, that is."

Charles laughed. "One step at a time, sir. Besides, will you be able to adjust to my being an Englishman and an aristocrat?"

"With difficulty, lad. With difficulty. But we'll soon knock some sense into ye, never fear."

"And I will in turn do my best to overlook my father-in-law's being a brash Scotsman who thinks he knows right on every topic." Then he sobered and added ruefully, "But there is one slight hitch still remaining, sir, much as I hate to mention it. The . . . er . . . husband in residence, so to speak."

Magnus grinned and glanced at his daughter. "For things to have advanced so far, I thought sure she must already have told ye, lad. You are even bolder than I'd thought!"

As Charles looked in sudden surprise between the two of them, Magnus added in amusement, "Well, lass, will ye tell him, or shall I?"

Sorcha colored and acknowledged that it was indeed time, whatever the outcome. "I will," she said slowly. "Geoff . . . was killed at Bladensburg."

Charles frowned quickly. "At Bladensburg? I'm sorry, but—" Then as the significance of that fact hit him, his arms tightened still more about her, and he repeated in a very different voice, "At *Bladensburg?* But that means—you were never—? You little *wretch!* How dare you put me through such an ordeal! Letting me suffer perfect torments of useless jealousy when you knew all the time that you were never married to him at all—however bigamously."

She shook her head, some of the old mischief stealing back into her eyes and voice. "No. I knew he would not mind my . . . appropriating his name. And it seemed far better than confessing the extent of my folly to Magnus." Then she sobered a little. "Poor Geoff. I did love him, you know. But as a brother, as you said."

But Charles's arms had tightened around her almost to the point of suffocation. "You . . . devil!" he said and would have kissed her there and then, despite the presence of Magnus in the room, as well as a deeply interested Dessy and Ham, who were by then standing beaming in the open doorway.

Sorcha forestalled him only with difficulty, half laughing and half crying, and knowing that she had been most shamefully stampeded by both of them. She would take care it did not happen too often, but for once she was glad to be most ruthlessly overborne. "Charles, Charles!" she cried breathlessly, at the same time putting her free arm tightly around his neck, as if to palliate the rebuke. "Have you run mad? Or have you forgotten that I am a proper married woman now, and a mother besides? *Charles!*" she cried, truly scandalized. "Put me down! You can't kiss me now in front of everyone! Don't you know all English are supposed to be dreadfully proper and staid and keep their feelings decently hidden?"

For he had swung her up wholly in his arms, the ardent light no longer to be denied. "I intend to kiss you as often as I can, and in front of them all, so you may as well get used to it. Sir," he added to Magnus, not taking his eyes off a blushing Sorcha, "do I have your permission to withdraw with my wife?"

"Aye," said Magnus, grinning. "Not that ye need my permission, lad. If I were ye, I'd carry her up to her bedchamber at once.

As ye pointed out to me so impertinently not so long ago, she has no' been at all well, and I doubt but that she needs her rest."

"I intend to, sir." Then he sobered slightly, adding, "And then I must become acquainted with my son. What is his name, by the way?" he inquired softly of Sorcha. "I forgot to ask."

Sorcha's arms were tight around his neck and her face very close to his own, and she had eyes only for him. "Geoffrey Magnus Charles Warburton," she said with a shade of defiance.

His arms tightened, but he laughed. "Poor little mite! He may come to hate us all one day for sticking him with such a string of names. But I intend to add one more to that list if you don't mind. Geoffrey Magnus Charles Warburton *Ashbourne*!" he said and carried his wife triumphantly out of the room.